Books by Tom Hoffman

The Eleventh Ring

The Thirteenth Monk

The Seventh Medallion

Orville Mouse and the Puzzle
of the Clockwork Glowbirds

Orville Mouse and the Puzzle
of the Shattered Abacus

An Orville Wellington Mouse Adventure

ORVILLE MOUSE

and the Puzzle of the
Shattered Abacus

by Tom Hoffman

With lots of love for
Molly, Alex, Sophie, and Oliver

A very special thanks to my
wonderful editors
Beth, Sophie, Oliver,
Alex, and Amanda
for their invaluable assistance
and excellent advice.

Table of Contents

"We meet ourselves time and time again in a thousand disguises on the path of life."

–Carl Jung

"Through all the tumult and the strife
I hear the music ringing;
It finds an echo in my soul—
How can I keep from singing?"

—Author unknown, 1868

An Orville Wellington Mouse Adventure

ORVILLE MOUSE

and the Puzzle of the Shattered Abacus

Chapter 1

On Three

"Eight minutes and twenty seconds, right on time."

"What's right on time?"

Orville Wellington Mouse leaned back against a gnarled tree trunk, studying his paw curiously as the warm east Symocan jungle sun glinted off his honey-toned fur.

"The sunlight is right on time. It takes eight minutes and twenty seconds for light from the sun to reach the Earth. And here it is, bouncing off my fur, right on schedule, not a second late."

"We don't have time for this. Let's go."

"Sophia, you really should learn to relax. Life isn't a race, you know, we're here to enjoy the adventure, enjoy the magic found in the day to day miracles of life, like golden sunlight reflecting off our fur."

"You're not fooling me, I know exactly what you're doing."

"Isn't the view spectacular? Such a delightful medley of greens in the jungle foliage, and the fragrances drifting up from those glorious tropical

3

blossoms... intoxicating is the word I would use. I never imagined the east Symocan jungle being so beautiful. I really could sit here forever."

"Enough. We need to get moving. I want to reach the summit before sunset."

"Don't be in such a hurry. How about a nice relaxing lunch? I'll shape some tasty cheese sandwiches, a pitcher of chilled lemonade, and a tin of Proto's famous little frosted cakes. You can't tell me you're not famished after all that hiking."

"Orville, we have to go, and we have to go now."

Orville gave a groan and rose to his feet, slinging his pack to his shoulder. He didn't like this dream at all and he had no idea why he was having it. Nothing about it made sense.

Sophia pointed to a rocky path leading through a dense tangle of vegetation. "If we take that trail we won't have to fight our way through all the vines and thorny undergrowth. It should cut at least an hour off our climbing time."

Orville studied the brilliant blue sky. "The clouds are stunning. So round and puffy and solid, almost like you could walk on them. Wouldn't that be fun, jumping around on a cloud? That one looks like a mouse dancing to a catchy tune. What do you think the big tall cloud looks like?"

"Stop. You need to stop."

"All right, you win. Let's just get this over with."

"That's the spirit. I'll race you to the top. Last one up is a big purple monkey butt!"

A look of terror flashed across Orville's face. "GIANT CARNIVOROUS CENTIPEDE!"

Sophia popped up a powerful protective energy field

around her, commonly referred to by shapers as a sphere of defense. She whirled around to face the deadly slithering beast. Much to her surprise there was not a single carnivorous centipede in sight. A light of realization flashed in her eyes and she whipped back around, catching sight of Orville as he scrambled madly up the trail.

"That's cheating! You're going to pay dearly for your immature and unscrupulous behavior!" Sophia raced up the rugged rocky path after him.

Less than an hour later the pair of adventurers crested the summit. Orville looked down at the lush jungle foliage far below them. "I feel kind of sick."

Sophia rubbed his shoulder. "It will be all right, monkey butt."

"Do you think it will hurt?"

"It's a dream, it's not going to hurt."

Orville peered over the rim of the volcano, gazing with consternation into the glowing, burbling lava, the air shimmering and undulating around him. He could feel his legs shaking. "It looks really, really hot down there. I mean really hot."

"Of course it looks hot. The temperature of molten lava is at least a thousand degrees, probably closer to twelve hundred. Ready? On three?"

"I guess so. Why do we have to do this?"

"I don't know, we just have to. It's your dream, not mine." Sophia reached over and took Orville's paw, grasping it tightly. "Okay, here we go. One, two, THREE!"

Orville Mouse and his best friend in the world, the brilliant and often bossy Sophia Mouse, leaped from the rim of the volcano, plummeting toward the violently *burbling swells of glowing magma.*

Orville watched in utter and complete terror as the incandescent pool of fiery lava shot up toward him. He had time for one horrified shriek before plunging into the seething volcanic nightmare.

Chapter 2

Payday

"Thank goodness that dream is over. So scary. Why in the world would I dream about jumping into a volcano? I wonder what time it is?" Orville poked an arm out from under his cozy nest of blankets, feeling around for his pocket watch. "I hope I have time for a little more–"

Orville froze. "What in the world?" He yanked his paw back under the sheets. His arm was covered with snow.

"Oh no, what did I do now?" He threw off the covers, staring blankly at the six inch layer of fluffy white snow lying atop his bedside table.

Leaping out of bed he grabbed a wooden bucket from the corner of his room and swept the baffling precipitation into it, drying everything as best he could with a large towel.

Orville flopped back down on his bed, staring at the ceiling. "This makes no sense, none at all. Why would I dream about jumping into a pool of molten lava and then wake up to find a pile of snow on my table? I must have shaped the snow in my sleep, but why? Maybe I was so afraid of jumping into the hot lava that I shaped something really cold. That sort of makes sense. I'll ask Sophia, she'll probably know."

Orville hopped out of bed, casting aside all thoughts of his scary volcanic dream. He had far more important things on his mind.

"Today's the big day! My first payday with the new raise." He rubbed his paws together with a gleeful laugh. "This will be the most silvers I've ever had at one time. Even after I get Mum's birthday present I'll have plenty of silvers left over to buy whatever I want. I can't wait to tell Sophia about Mum's present."

Orville threw his clothes on and dashed down the stairs. Proto, the ten foot tall silver Rabbiton he and Sophia had befriended while solving *The Puzzle of the Clockwork Glowbirds*, stood at the stove stirring a steaming pot of oatmeal.

"Morning, Proto! That's a lovely apron you're wearing."

"I borrowed it from Mum. It's quite functional."

"Umm... it might be just a bit flowery. What's for breakfast? Where's Mum?"

"Snapberry muffins are in the oven, warm oatmeal with brown sugar and cinnamon is almost done, and there's a pitcher of freshly squeezed orange juice on the table."

"Sounds delicious. Mum went to work already?"

"Quite correct, she had to run some errands so she left early. I hope I didn't disturb your sleep with all my racket."

"What racket? I didn't hear anything."

"Ahh, then you may forget I even mentioned it."

"Now I'm curious. What were you doing last night that made such a racket?"

8

Proto hesitated, clearing his throat. "It's possible something may have jumped through an interdimensional photonic simulation barrier I accidentally left open in my room, but I believe I caught them all and sent them back through. Would you care for a warm snapberry muffin?"

Orville tried not to sound terrified. "Caught them all? It doesn't really sound like a very good idea to open one of those barrier things in your room. What kind of creatures came through? Were they scary?"

Proto was considering his answer when there was a loud knock on the front door. "I'll dash and get that while you start your breakfast." Proto scurried out of the kitchen with a nervous glance at Orville. A moment later he swung open the front door.

"Hi, Proto, is Orville ready? I'm walking to work with him."

"A fine good morning, Sophia. I have warm snapberry muffins fresh from the oven if you'd care for one."

"I already had breakfast, thanks." Sophia stepped through the living room into the kitchen. "Hi, Orville. Ready to go?"

"Almost. Today's my first payday with the big raise. I can't wait."

"What are you going to do with all the silvers?"

"I'm going to get a really special birthday present for Mum with some of them. She's going to love it. I can't wait to tell you about it. Hey, I almost forgot, I had a scary dream last night that you and I jumped into a big volcano full of molten lava. Isn't that weird?"

Orville waited for Sophia to laugh, but instead witnessed a complex expression crossing her face.

When Orville analyzed it he could see concern, fear, doubt, a touch of excitement and a snippet of eager anticipation. "Why do you have that weird look?"

"I had a scary dream last night too. I'll tell you about it later, I'm still trying to understand its deeper meaning. It's significant that we both had scary dreams on the same night. I'm sensing an important new chain of events is beginning, and I think it's going to be a scary one."

Orville's eyes widened. "Scary? We might really have to jump into a volcano?"

"We should go. We'll talk about it on the way to the Book Emporium. You can ask Master Marloh about our dreams. He might know if they're connected to another chain of events. Has he said anything more about your papa still being alive?"

Orville looked down into his bowl of oatmeal. "No, he said he can't tell me anything right now because he's afraid I'll go searching for Papa, and he doesn't think I'm ready for something as dangerous as that. He said he sent out a search party of Metaphysical Adventurers from the Dragonfly Squadron, whatever that is. He wouldn't even tell me what kind of mission Papa was on."

Sophia gave Orville a warm and comforting smile. "I know it's really frustrating, but he's probably right. Think how awful it would be if something happened to you. Think how your mum would feel if you and your papa were both missing."

"I guess you're right. I just wish there was something I could do."

"How about we walk to the Book Emporium and you can fill your pockets with silvers?"

Orville grinned. "I like the sound of that." He slipped on his coat and the two best friends headed out the front door. "Bye, Proto! Don't let any carnivorous centipedes into my room!"

Sophia gave Orville a curious glance, then said, "What are you getting your mum?"

"I'm so excited about it, I'm going to get her something they just put in the display window at Sinker's Hardware. Mum will be the first mouse on our street to own one, maybe even the first mouse in Muridaan Falls. I'm going to get her a brand new Excelsior duplonium powered electric bread slicer."

Sophia stared at Orville with unblinking eyes.

"What? Isn't that the best present you could imagine?"

Sophia gave an enigmatic smile. "Do you know what I would do if you got me a shiny new Excelsior duplonium powered electric bread slicer for my birthday?"

Orville panicked, suddenly afraid Sophia was going to kiss him. Maybe on the lips. Probably just on the cheek though. He decided he wouldn't try to stop her if she did. He casually turned his cheek toward Sophia and waited.

Unfortunately for Orville the expected kiss never materialized. What arrived in its place was a severe and rather painful punch to Orville's left arm delivered with some exuberance by Sophia.

"OOWWW! What was that for? Why did you punch my arm?"

"It's called behavioral conditioning."

"What? What are you talking about? Why did you punch my arm?"

"I learned about behavioral conditioning in my science classes on Quintari. When a stimulus is delivered immediately after a mouse exhibits a particular behavior, the probability of that behavior occurring in the future will be altered, depending on the nature of the stimulus, whether it's positive or negative."

"I don't have the slightest idea what you're talking about."

"In this case, I delivered a severe punch to your arm, a negative stimulus, right after you told me you were buying your mum a duplonium powered electric bread slicer for her birthday. Let me ask you this, at this moment do you feel like telling me again that you're getting your mum a duplonium powered bread slicer?"

Orville took a step back, fear growing in his eyes. "No, I don't think I will ever say those words again."

"Excellent. Your behavioral patterns have been altered by negative conditioning, also known as negative reinforcement. Negative reinforcement works quite well, but only for a short period of time. The behavior soon returns, stronger than it was before. The most effective and long lasting form of reinforcement is positive reinforcement. Now, think of a gift your mum would really like for her birthday. Don't think about what you would like, but only something you're certain your mum would truly love."

"You might be onto something. Mum isn't as crazy as I am about new technology, so maybe a duplonium bread slicer isn't the best gift. What about jewelry? Something like a beautiful necklace? I know she loves jewelry as long as it's not gaudy or flashy. I could get her a beautiful necklace."

Sophia leaned forward and kissed Orville on the cheek, put her arms around him and gave him a warm hug. "You are so sweet and so thoughtful, Orville Wellington Mouse. Your Mum would love a new necklace." Sophia stepped away from him and smiled as brightly as she could.

"Umm... well... thanks." Orville rubbed his paw over the spot where Sophia had kissed him. "I... umm..." He gave her a toothy grin.

Sophia's eyes narrowed. "That kiss was a scientific demonstration and nothing more. I'm teaching you about behavioral conditioning and also making certain you don't buy your mum a duplonium bread slicer for her birthday."

"I liked the positive reinforcement a lot more than the punch on my arm."

Sophia gave Orville a severe look. "Here we are. I'll stop by at lunchtime and we can get a necklace for your mum. They have lovely jewelry at Miraculum's Fine Antiques, and their prices are quite reasonable."

Orville waved good-bye to Sophia and stepped into the Book Emporium, his paw still on his cheek. "Good morning, Master Marloh."

Master Marloh was standing behind the long wooden counter sorting through the previous day's receipts. He looked up with a smile. "Good morning, Orville. Ready for payday?"

"Yes, I'm going to get my mum a necklace for her birthday."

"That sounds wonderful. I'm sure she'll love whatever you get."

"Has there been any news about Papa?"

The smile faded from Master Marloh's face.

"Nothing yet, I'm afraid. Finding him is not going to be as simple as I had hoped. The Dragonfly Squadron is attempting to track his movements, but it appears he may have covered a lot more territory than we had originally thought. I promise I will let you know the moment I hear anything. In the meantime, six crates of new books just arrived and we need to price them and get them on the shelves. That should take you most of the day."

"Okay, I'll start on that. I'm going with Sophia to pick out Mum's birthday present at lunchtime, if that's okay."

"Take as long as you want and get a nice necklace for her. It's most admirable of you to spend your hard earned silvers on her birthday gift."

"Could I ask you about a scary dream I had?"

Master Marloh took off his glasses and looked directly at Orville. "What kind of scary dream?"

"Well, it's kind of weird, but I dreamed that Sophia and I had to jump into a volcano filled with molten lava."

"You were fully awake inside the dream?"

"Yes, I knew I was in a dream but we still had to jump into the volcano."

"Hmmm." Master Marloh pursed his lips, deep in thought.

"Is it bad?"

"There are two possible meanings for your dream. The first is that the dream is literal, and at some point in the future you and Sophia will actually jump into a volcano. This seems highly unlikely, in my estimation. The second possible meaning is that the volcano is symbolic of the fires of life, events which are difficult

14

to endure and often life altering. The disappearance of your papa was one such event. It completely changed your life.

"The fires of life can be most distressing, yet they are capable of changing our lives in the very best of ways if we face them head on. You were forced to become responsible at a much younger age than most mice, and you responded with unyielding vigor and perseverance. As a direct result of your efforts you have become a proficient shaper and a valued member of the Metaphysical Adventurers. You and Sophia prevented Symoca from being drawn into a terrible war, along the way proving Draken Mouse was behind the murder of Sophia's Papa, Rowland Mouse. I hate to say it, but if your papa had been here he never would have allowed you to become involved in such perilous undertakings."

"I was trying to be like him."

Master Marloh gave Orville a gentle smile. "When Eldon comes home he will be very proud of you. Now, off to work with you. It's going to take me some time to count out all those silvers I owe you."

The morning flew by and before he knew it Orville heard Sophia's voice coming from the front of the shop. Moments later she was standing next to him.

"Ready to go pick out a necklace?"

"I have to get my silvers from Master Marloh."

The two best friends hurried to the front of the shop. Master Marloh looked up from the counter. "Ah, there you are. I have your silvers all counted out. You're a good worker and you deserve every one of them."

Orville grinned at the sight of the stacked silver coins. "Thanks, Master Marloh!" He scooped them up and dropped them into his coat pocket.

Sophia put her paw on Orville's shoulder and laughed, "Let's go, Master Richmouse."

Chapter 3

The Necklace

It took less than ten minutes for Sophia and Orville to reach the antique shop. Orville gazed up at the gray weathered sign swaying back and forth in the gentle breeze.

MIRACULUM'S FINE ANTIQUES

He dashed up the rickety steps and entered the shop, stopping for a moment to breathe in the air. "Mmm, I love that smell." He closed his eyes for a moment. "There's something about this shop I really like. It's cluttered and comfy and feels magical."

"There's no such thing as magic, there's only science that we don't understand. I've told you that about a thousand times. No magic."

"I know there's no such thing as magic. I didn't say the store *is* magical, I said it *feels* magical. There's a difference."

"You're right. I have a good feeling about the shop too."

The two friends strolled through the store, browsing the wide assortment of curious antiquities. Sophia pointed to an old tarnished oil lantern. "My great grandmum used to have one just like that. I remember her showing me how to light it when I was a little mouseling. She told me if I rubbed it three times my wishes would come true. I think she really believed it. Oh, look at all those books, they're so old. I bet they'd be fun to read."

"There's the jewelry section over there. Let's go see what they have, I don't want to be late back to work. I hope they have a nice one." Orville stepped over to a large glass display case filled with rings, bracelets, brooches, and necklaces.

"They have a lot of jewelry here. You should be able to find one she'll really like."

Orville glanced up to see an elderly mouse shuffling toward the display case.

"Good afternoon, my young friends. Is there anything I might be able to help you find?"

"I'm looking for a necklace for my mum's birthday."

"Ah, excellent, you've come to the right shop. We have quite a collection of lovely old necklaces in a variety of styles and price ranges. May I inquire as to how much you were thinking of spending?"

Orville glanced over at Sophia. "I hadn't thought too much about that, but I guess about ten silvers?"

"Perfect, all the necklaces in this case are ten silvers or less. There are some rather lovely ones, as you can readily see."

"Yes, they're very nice. Sparkly." Orville glanced over at Sophia, who was studying a necklace in the next display case. Even from this distance Orville could see

18

it was exquisite, with an ornate silver chain and three mounted stones. The two smaller gems were a pale iridescent green, the large central stone a brilliant translucent blue. Orville felt strangely drawn to it. He stepped over next to Sophia and eyed the necklace. "There's something about that necklace."

"I know, I can't stop looking at it. I'm getting a very peculiar feeling."

Orville looked at the price tag. It was thirty-six silvers, far more than he'd planned on spending. Master Marloh had given him thirty-eight silvers, which meant he would only have two silvers left if he bought it. Orville whispered to Sophia, "It's really expensive. Maybe I could shape one just like it."

Sophia looked up in surprise. "Did you just say what I think you said?"

"I know the Shapers Guild says we can't use shaping for personal gain, but it wouldn't really be for my own personal gain. I'd be giving it to someone as a gift. Everyone always says it's better to give than to receive."

"I guess you forgot you'd also be saving yourself thirty-six silvers. That sounds a lot like personal gain to me."

"If you think about it I'd just be making my Mum a lovely birthday present. When I was a mouseling I used to make all her birthday presents and she loved them."

Sophia rolled her eyes. "Really? Your mum loved those presents because you put a lot of effort into making them, you didn't just flick your wrist and shape them. Besides, you could be interfering with this new chain of events in ways you don't understand."

"I didn't think of that. There could be something

really special about this necklace in particular." That was the moment Orville heard the voice. His eyes blinked. The voice always surprised him even though he had heard it many times before. Sophia had explained to him it was his inner voice, coming from a deeper part of him that existed outside of space and time. It was a part of him possessing a far greater understanding of the universe and the events he was currently experiencing in his life.

"This is the necklace you must give to your mum. There is no other."

Orville could scarcely breathe. He instantly knew that buying this particular necklace would change his life, and the change would involve walking of his own free will into the ferocious fires of life. He managed to regain his composure, leaning over and whispering to Sophia, "We have to get this one. My inner voice said I had to."

Sophia nodded. "There is no other."

Orville looked up at the elderly mouse who was absently cleaning his small round glasses with a soft cloth.

"Sir, I'd like to get this necklace for my mum."

The old mouse put his glasses on and stepped over to the display case. He looked at the necklace, then looked up at Orville with some surprise. "Oh my, I'm afraid that's a rather precious one. It's quite costly as you can see. Are you certain that's the one you wish to purchase? We have a good many others at lesser cost."

Orville reached into his pocket and pulled out all his silvers, stacking them carefully on the glass display case. He picked up two silvers and put them back in his pocket. "I'm certain. This is the one I want."

20

The shopkeeper nodded, carefully removing the necklace from the case. "It's exquisite. I will put it in a velvet presentation box for you. Your mum is lucky to have such a generous and thoughtful son."

Sophia was studying Orville's face. It was time to tell him about her dream. She was certain now that a significant chain of events was under way. She knew the necklace Orville was buying would play a vital role in whatever came next, but she was at a loss as to what that role might be.

Orville stepped out of the shop sporting a cheery smile. He gingerly opened the velvet case and held it out for Sophia to see. She studied the necklace carefully, touching her paw to the gleaming blue stone. "It's truly beautiful. Your mum is going to love it. I only wish I knew why it was so special, why our inner voices said there was no other."

Orville shook his head. "I don't know. The Thirteenth Monk told me we have to let events run their course and eventually we'll understand the deeper meaning. Until then we have to trust the wisdom and truth of our inner voice."

"I want to tell you about the dream I had on the same night you had your volcano dream."

"You said it was scary?"

"Very scary. I dreamed I was in a deep physics class at the Symocan Institute, a class I've never even heard of. The instructor was lecturing to us on the nature of temporal dimensional variabilities but I couldn't understand what he was saying. Right in the middle of a sentence he just stopped talking. He stopped talking and he stopped moving. He was motionless, a living statue. I turned to one of the other students and saw everyone else in the classroom had stopped moving too. I was scared, and I mean really scared. Way more than if it had happened when I was awake. A horrible, shapeless fear filled me, and I couldn't stop thinking about you and your mum. I had to find you. Without even thinking I blinked back to Muridaan Falls in three jumps. There wasn't a mouse in sight and the village was deathly quiet. It was so spooky, there was no wind, no rustling leaves, even the clouds were still. The horrible fear was growing worse with every step I took, but I managed to reach your front door. I knocked, but no one answered so I ran inside and called to you but heard only a dreadful empty silence. Even the big clock in your living room had stopped ticking. I found your mum standing next to the kitchen table, frozen like the mice at school. I ran upstairs to your room, flung the door open and saw us."

"Saw us?"

"You were at your desk showing a funny drawing to Proto, and I was sitting on your bed writing in a notebook. We were living statues. It was so strange to see myself. I screamed but nothing came out. My legs were shaking so badly I fell to my knees and started crying. I've never cried so hard, I couldn't stop. When I woke up my pillow was soaked. I'd been sobbing in my sleep."

Orville let out a long low breath. "Creekers. What do you think it means?"

"I've been thinking about it a lot. Master Marloh told you the volcano dream probably meant you would have to walk into the fires of life, and I had a dream everyone in Symoca was frozen like statues. I'm sure those two things are connected, since we had our dreams on the same night."

Orville grabbed Sophia's arm. "Remember how I stopped time the night we exposed Draken Mouse as a murderer? What you described is exactly what it looked like. I even remember thinking that everyone in the room looked like a living statue."

Sophia's voice was barely a whisper. "Something is trying to stop time in Symoca."

Chapter 4

The Rolling Puzzle

Sophia, Orville, and his mum were seated at the dining room table when Proto marched in with the birthday cake. Orville's jaw dropped at the sight of the exquisitely decorated three-tiered cake with its warm flickering candles. "Whoa! Did you make that, Proto?"

"It's stunning!"

Orville's Mum gasped. "Good heavens, Proto, you didn't need to go to so much trouble!"

Proto beamed with delight. "I'm so pleased you all like the cake. I'm rather proud of it, and I assure you it's just as tasty as the little frosted cakes you are all so fond of."

Orville laughed, "We're not the only ones who like them. Those sticky green ball creatures on Periculum went wild over those tasty cakes."

Proto chuckled, setting his magnificent culinary creation on the table. After a moderately lovely rendition of the Symocan Song of Birthdays, Orville's mum blew out the candles.

Sophia turned to Orville with a grin. "Did you have something for your mum?"

Orville reached inside his coat and pulled out a

beautifully wrapped package. "This is for the best mum in all of Symoca. Happy birthday, Mum."

Sophia rubbed her paws together. This was going to be so much better than an Excelsior duplonium powered electric bread slicer.

Orville's mum could barely speak when she opened the velvet case. She looked at Orville, then at the necklace, then at Sophia, and then back at Orville. "Oh, this is too much. You really, really shouldn't have. It's so beautiful! I think it's the most beautiful thing I own." She kissed Orville on the cheek and gave him a long hug. "I couldn't ask for a more wonderful son. I will treasure this forever."

Proto clapped his hands. "Who's ready for cake?"

Two hours later Sophia had blinked back to school, Orville's Mum had retired for the night, and Orville was sitting on his bedroom floor, leaning back against his bed.

"Mum really loved the necklace. Thank goodness Sophia convinced me to get that instead of the bread slicer. I wish Papa could have been here. He would have been proud of me."

A deep sadness washed through Orville. Maybe they'd never find him. Maybe he wasn't alive. Maybe the Metaphysical Adventurers ring they found didn't mean anything. He could have lost his ring because something bad happened. Master Marloh said Orville's papa was one of the best shapers he knew. There was only one thing Orville could think of that would keep his papa from coming home.

Orville slowly rose to his feet and opened his top dresser drawer, feeling around in the back corner for the blue marble his papa had given him. He remembered how Papa had winked when he said the marble was magic. It was the last thing Papa had given him. If the marble was magic, that was the reason why. He slumped back down on the floor, gripping the marble in his paw, his eyes burning. How could he be so happy and so sad on the same day? With a long sigh he set the marble down on the floor in front of him. It was strange how a tiny object could hold such power over his feelings. He watched the marble slowly roll across the sloped floor to the other side of the room. It was rolling away from him like his papa had. Tears welled up in Orville's eyes. He was about to cry when he realized something was very, very wrong.

"Huh?" Orville jumped up and ran across the room. He grabbed the marble and dashed back to his bed. Setting the marble down on the floor he watched as it rolled across the room and bumped into the wall. He did it again. And again. And again.

Orville stared blankly at the marble in his paw. Their house was old, and over the years the shifting ground had tilted the foundation. That explained their sloping floors, but what it didn't explain was why the blue marble was rolling up the slope and not down the slope.

Orville had a difficult time falling asleep that night. He couldn't stop thinking about the marble and what could possibly cause it to roll uphill. It was clearly breaking the laws of physical motion and yet he had seen it with his own eyes. It reminded him of the clockwork glowbirds. It couldn't be happening, and yet it was. Finally he drifted off to sleep. When he woke up the next morning his bedside table was covered with snow.

This time Orville converted the snow to a field of

energy called a thought cloud, threw his clothes on, grabbed the blue marble and dashed downstairs. Proto had a delicious breakfast waiting for him.

"Good morning, Orville, I do hope you had a lovely sleep. I'm pleased to inform you I remembered to deactivate the interdimensional photonic simulation barrier, so you'll find no unwanted visitors slithering about the house today. I hope you didn't mention anything about our little mishap to Mum."

"*Our* little mishap? Wait, you said the creatures were slithering?"

"Ahh, the muffins are done, and your oatmeal will be ready in less than a minute. Doesn't it smell tasty?"

Proto was a master of avoidance.

An hour later Orville was hunched over a cart in the Book Emporium, marking prices in the new books and placing them on the shelves. He spotted two of the strangers meandering through the bookshelves, drifting toward the rear of the store. Several minutes later they had surreptitiously slipped behind the blue door.

When he started working at the Book Emporium these strangers had been an unsolved puzzle. Now he knew they were members of the Shapers Guild visiting the Shapers Guild Library, the largest and most complete collection of shaping books in all of Symoca. Orville also knew when Master Marloh opened the blue door using the paw bearing his Metaphysical Adventurers ring the door opened to an ancient spiral stone stairway leading down to the Metaphysical Adventurers headquarters. The headquarters was a vast underground complex containing many thousands of technologically advanced devices brought back from other worlds by MA members.

Orville was prying open a crate of new books when he was startled by a voice behind him.

"Ready for lunch? I shaped each of us a sandwich. I thought we could eat in the meadow behind the old barn where we keep *The Glowbird*."

Sophia was referring to the flying machine which resembled an enormous glowbird, a craft built by Mirus Mouse, the inventor fondly referred to as the Mad Mouse of Muridaan by the Metaphysical Adventurers. They often relied on his legendary ingenuity to create unique vehicles and devices for use on their missions. Sophia and Orville had flown *The Glowbird* deep into Pavorak Gorge when they were tracking the mysterious glowbirds. It was also where they discovered Proto the Rabbiton living in a huge stone cube abandoned many centuries ago by the Elders.

Orville glanced around the shop, whispering to Sophia, "I have something to show you. Watch this." Orville took the blue marble out of his pocket and set it down on the wooden floor. Sophia watched as the marble rolled down the sloped floor.

"What? Why are you rolling that marble?"

"It's supposed to roll up the slope, not down."

Sophia stared at Orville. "Are you trying to be funny?"

"No, I'm not joking. When I rolled this marble in my room, it rolled up the sloped floor, not down."

"You're certain?"

"Yes, I'm certain. I tried it five times in a row, and each time it rolled uphill."

"Let me see it." Sophia took the blue marble from Orville's paw. "This is the marble your papa gave you before he disappeared?"

"Yes. Wait, do you think it might have something to do with why he's missing?"

"I don't know." Sophia scrutinized the marble. "It doesn't look like anything special, just blue glass with some little white lines in it. There's nothing to suggest why it would roll uphill." Sophia closed her eyes. Orville could almost hear her brilliant mind working. Seconds later she opened her eyes and gave the marble back to Orville.

Orville looked at her questioningly. "What do you think?"

"Here's what I think. If the marble rolls uphill at your house but not uphill here, there must be a force present in your home which is acting on it, a force which is not present in the Book Emporium. This mystery force is either attracting or repelling the marble, and is more powerful than gravity, the force which causes objects to roll downhill. We need to go to your house and identify the force responsible for the strange behavior of your papa's marble."

"Why would there be some weird force at my house making the marble roll uphill?"

"How would I know? That's what we have to find out. Let's go eat lunch and I'll stop by your house after work. I have to blink back to school, but I'll meet you after dinner."

Chapter 5

Blue Molasses

Sophia appeared on Orville's front doorstep precisely at six o'clock. The front door swung open before her third knock had ended.

"My mum had to work late today so we'll have plenty of time to investigate the blue marble."

"Show me where it rolled uphill."

Sophia followed Orville as he dashed up to his room. He sat on the floor next to his bed and put the marble down in front of him. "Watch what it does." The marble rolled across the room to the opposite wall.

Sophia's eyes followed the small blue sphere. When it hit the wall she reached into her pocket and pulled out a brass cube with a bright yellow circle on one side. She set it on the floor and waited. There was a small beep and she scrunched down to examine it. "You were right. My leveling cube says your floor has a three degree upward slope. The marble is definitely rolling up the slope, not down. We need to figure out why. Let's think about this logically. Your bed is on the outside wall. I don't see anything under your bed, so if a force is pushing the marble, it would have to come from outside your house, which seems unlikely. That means a force inside your house is attracting the marble. It's not an electromagnetic force because the marble is made of glass, not metal, so it has to be another form of energy. What's on the other side of your bedroom wall?"

"My mum's room."

"Okay, let's try something." Sophia picked up the marble and stepped out into the hallway. She set it on the floor, watching as it rolled up the sloping hall, veering to the right. The marble stopped in front of the bedroom door. "Something in your mum's room is attracting it."

Orville looked dubious but opened the bedroom door. The marble rolled briskly across the room, stopping at the base of his mum's dresser. Sophia got down on her knees and examined the marble closely, being careful not to touch it. "The marble is quivering, vibrating. Whatever is attracting it is very close."

Orville grabbed Sophia's arm. "I know what it is. I know exactly what it is!" He stepped over to the dresser and pulled open the top drawer. Reaching in, he withdrew the velvet box containing his mum's birthday necklace. He stepped into the hallway, his gaze on the marble as it trailed behind him.

Sophia's eyes were wide. "This is incredible, but I don't understand the forces at work here. Why would the marble be attracted to your mum's necklace?"

Orville shook his head. "I don't know." He removed the necklace from its velvet case and set it gingerly on the floor.

The marble sped across the floor, halted six inches

from the necklace and began to emit an eerie glow. Sophia gasped, pointing her paw at the necklace. The beautiful translucent blue stone was melting, becoming a viscous fluid.

"It looks like blue molasses. What's it doing?"

Orville watched in astonishment as the blue liquid ran across the floor toward the glowing marble. The liquid flowed over it and was absorbed into it, the marble growing to twice its original size.

Sophia and Orville stared in silence at the now motionless marble, trying to fathom what they had just seen. It seemed impossible, and yet they had both witnessed it.

"The stone is gone from Mum's necklace! What am I going to tell her?"

Sophia picked up the necklace and held it in front of her. She flicked her paw and with a flash of light a blue gem appeared in the silver mounting. "This new stone looks exactly like the original one. Put the necklace back in your mum's dresser and let's figure out what just happened."

Orville returned the necklace and they hurried downstairs. Sophia flopped down on the sofa and held up the blue marble with one paw, studying it closely. "It looks identical, except it's larger now. It's the same sky blue color with some barely visible white wiggly lines inside it."

"And now that it's merged with the gem from the necklace it doesn't roll uphill."

"This is a good puzzle. Let's try to figure it out. Your papa gave you this marble and told you it was magic. He may have known something about the marble that he wasn't telling you, but it's also possible he thought it was simply a glass marble and was being silly when he told you it was magic. Either way, we know it's not an ordinary marble. We also know the necklace that your inner voice told you to buy contained a gem made of the same material as the blue marble. For some reason they were attracted to each other and when they were close enough they merged."

"It could be important that the stone from the necklace is the one that turned to liquid and joined the marble, and not the other way around."

"That's a good thought. A very good thought, as a matter of fact. The marble your papa gave you is the driving force behind this strange event. Now, how does all this help us?"

Orville frowned. "It doesn't help us at all, really. It's still a complete mystery and we have no idea what's happening. Do you think Master Marloh might know something about it? We could show him the blue marble and see if he can identify it."

"Good idea. I'll do some research in the school library and you show the marble to Master Marloh. Even if he doesn't know what it is, he might know a Metaphysical Adventurer who could help us find out."

Orville nodded. "I'm getting a strong feeling about this. If we follow the trail of the blue marble it will lead us to whatever is trying to stop time in Symoca."

"I know it will. That's how the universe works."

Orville woke up in the middle of the night with the sudden insight that Proto might be able to identify the marble. The following morning he grabbed the blue marble and ran downstairs.

"Hey, Proto, you know a lot about geology and stones and gems, right?"

"I have read quite a number of books on those subjects. Why do you ask?"

"I'm trying to identify this stone." He held the marble out for Proto to see.

Proto took the marble from Orville's paw and held it up to the window, letting the morning sunlight pass through it. "Quite lovely. I will use my full spectrum magnosensor to examine it more closely." Proto's eyes glowed with a brilliant orange light as he studied the marble, turning it slowly in his hand. "Very peculiar."

"What's peculiar? What do you see?"

"What is peculiar is that I have no idea what I'm looking at. The marble is not glass and is not a naturally forming stone or crystal. I'm afraid I am unable to identify this. It is almost certainly a synthetic material, but what it might be I cannot say."

"Thanks, that actually helps a lot to know it's synthetic. I'm going to show it to Master Marloh and see if he knows what it is."

"Whatever it is, it's quite stunning. It reminds me of the blue gem in the necklace you gave Mum for her birthday."

Orville nodded, but said nothing.

Proto turned back to the stove. "Ahhh, the snapberry flapcakes are done. Have a seat, they're best when they're nice and warm."

Chapter 6

The Dragonfly

Orville arrived at the Book Emporium to find Master Marloh unlocking the front door.

"Good morning, Orville. You're here earlier than usual."

"I had something I wanted to ask you before any customers arrived."

"That sounds serious. What did you want to talk about?"

Orville held out the blue marble for Master Marloh to see. "I'm trying to find out what this is made of. Proto thinks it's a synthetic material but he's never seen anything like it before."

"Interesting. How did you come to possess such an object?"

Orville told Master Marloh everything, including Sophia's dream about time stopping in Symoca, and that Papa had given him the marble. Master Marloh's eyes had widened slightly when Orville told him how the stone from his mum's necklace had liquefied and merged with the marble.

"You're certain your inner voice told you to buy that particular necklace?"

"More than certain. Sophia felt it just as strongly as I did."

Master Marloh absently rolled the blue marble around in his paw, lost in thought. Finally Orville said, "What do you think?"

"Sorry, you've given me a great deal of information to process. Something is most certainly afoot here. Your search for the true origin of this marble must continue. If you would be so kind to keep an eye on the shop, I will take the marble down to the Metaphysical Adventurers headquarters. If no one is able to identify it, you and Sophia will have to visit a very reclusive mouse who most certainly will be able to tell you what it is. Unfortunately, he resides in a rather inaccessible area and your trip will require a certain amount of preparation."

Master Marloh looked as though someone had just told him a humorous anecdote. Orville's eyes narrowed. Things that amused Master Marloh never seemed to amuse Orville.

Half an hour later Master Marloh returned from the Metaphysical Adventurers headquarters far below the shop. There were customers in the store so Master Marloh spoke in a hushed voice. "No luck, I'm afraid. They all agree with Proto that it's a synthetic material, but were at a loss to explain how it could transform into a liquid and then back to a solid again. Whatever the substance is, it's many, many times harder than glass or stone or crystal, maybe even harder than Morsennium, the material used by the Anarkkians to build their interstellar ships."

"So we have to visit this reclusive friend of yours?"

Master Marloh gave Orville the amused look again.

36

"Yes, I'm afraid so, but first you'll need to pay a visit to Mirus Mouse. Tell him you need to visit Ollo the Rock Mouse."

Orville tried to sound enthused. "We'll talk to Mirus. You think this Ollo the Rock Mouse fellow can identify the marble?"

"I will tell you this much, if Ollo the Rock Mouse doesn't know what it is, then no one on this planet will know. I'll send a thought cloud to Sophia and tell her to meet you at Mirus' complex tomorrow morning. I'll also let the dean of her school know she'll be gone for a day or two."

"A day or two? How far away does Ollo the Rock Mouse live?"

"Oh, I think it's about five hundred miles or so southwest of Muridaan Falls. Finding his house will be a little bit tricky, I'm afraid. Mirus will give you a map showing the general location of his hideaway."

Orville was quite certain Master Marloh was not telling him everything he knew about Ollo the Rock Mouse.

Now that Orville's mum knew he was a member of the Metaphysical Adventurers and a proficient shaper, it was a far simpler task to go adventuring with Sophia. His mum was familiar with the routine, having seen Orville's papa Eldon go out on hundreds of missions. Orville told his mum he and Sophia would be gone for two days, assuring her it was not a dangerous trip, they were just going to visit a Metaphysical Adventurer named Ollo the Rock Mouse.

Orville's Mum furrowed her eyebrows. "Ollo the Rock Mouse... now why does that name sound so familiar? You know, I think your papa may have gone to see him once." A light blinked on in her eyes. "Oh! Ollo the Rock Mouse!" She gave a silly grin.

"What? Why is everyone laughing about this mouse? He's a geologist or something, I think. He knows all about rocks and gems."

Orville's Mum smiled and said, "Have a safe trip, sweetie. Say hello to Sophia for me."

Orville shrugged and gave his mum a hug. He'd find out soon enough about Ollo the Rock Mouse. Slinging his pack onto his shoulder he headed for the front door. Less than an hour later he stood at the gates of Mirus Mouse's sprawling twenty acre complex. He eyed the rows of long buildings and enormous barns, containing a multitude of vehicles built by Mirus over the years. Orville remembered when Mirus had taught him how to fly *The Glowbird*. There was no doubt Mirus was a brilliant and innovative inventor, but he was also a smidgeon on the eccentric side. Maybe a lot more than a smidgeon. Orville grinned to himself, abruptly realizing it was the same silly grin his mum had given when she mentioned Ollo the Rock Mouse.

Orville swung the gate open and strolled into the complex. His ears perked up at the sound of voices emerging from a low green building. When he reached the structure he peered in through an open door and gave a squeak of fright, skittering backwards. A thirty foot long green iridescent dragonfly was perched in the middle of the cavernous room, its wings moving lazily up and down. A raucous laugh resembling the cry of the wild Kukululu bird echoed through the building. Orville recognized the laugh and poked his head back through the doorway.

"What's the matter, never seen a Dragonfly before?

Get in here and I'll show you how to fly her. It's as easy as walking!" Mirus Mouse stepped out from behind the Dragonfly and let loose another screechy bird laugh.

"Hello, Mirus. I wasn't exactly scared of the Dragonfly. I thought I heard Sophia so I went to check."

Sophia popped out from behind the huge green insect and waved. "What do you think? Mirus invented Dragonflies. It's amazing, it has two duplonium motors and flies way faster than *The Glowbird*. It's what the Dragonfly Squadron uses. He said I could name this one *The Dragonfly*."

Mirus slapped his leg and cried out, "Flies faster than *The Glowbird*? That's nothing! It can take off straight up into the air and hovers like a real dragonfly! You could land her on top of a pin if you wanted to. This one's an early version of the Dragonfly Squadron ships. Hop in and I'll show you how she works. You'd better be a fast learner, because you leave in a half hour for Ollo the Rock Mouse's secret hideout."

Orville stepped across the room, his eyes sweeping the gigantic mechanical insect. "This thing really flies?"

Mirus Mouse gave a great screech. "Great heavens, mouse, of course she flies! Hop in and I'll show you how."

Orville looked hesitant, but climbed into the cockpit next to Sophia. Mirus Mouse clambered into the seat behind them. "She'll carry four mice easy as pie, she's three times faster than *The Glowbird* and even easier to fly. Hey, that rhymes! All right, my young friends, fly her just like *The Glowbird* but you don't need to get her up to forty miles an hour before you lift off. Both front seats have controls, just like you're used to. Push the left stick forward and her wings start flapping, the farther you push it the faster they flap. Push it more than halfway forward and she'll go straight up like a red rocket on Symoca Day. Left stick left, she rotates left, left stick right, she rotates right. Got it? Push the right stick and she'll fly forward, pull it back and she'll fly backwards. You heard me right, she'll fly backwards, I said! Push it left, she flies left, push it right, she flies right. Got it? Ready to go?"

Orville gave a squeak. "No, wait! What? She'll fly backwards? Could you say all that again but not so fast?"

Mirus gave Orville a slap on his back and hopped out of *The Dragonfly*. "I'll open the doors and you fly her out. No time like the present to learn how to fly this bug!" He dashed across the room and swung open the two enormous barn doors.

"Sophia, what do we do? Does he really want us to fly it?"

"It looks easy. I'll do it." Sophia slipped on a pair of flying goggles, handing a second pair to Orville. "Put these on. If you turn the little dial on the left they'll magnify your vision, and if you push the silver tab on the right side you can see in the dark. Mirus invented them."

"You can see in the dark? That's amazing. Wait, we don't even know where Ollo the Rock Mouse lives."

"There's a map in that little compartment. Mirus marked the location. We just follow the compass heading south southwest for four hundred and seventy-two miles."

"You're sure you can fly this?"

"How hard can it be? We flew *The Glowbird* just fine."

"Well, it's not quite the same, but if you think you can do it..."

Sophia gave Orville a smug look and pushed the left stick forward. *The Dragonfly* blasted straight up toward the ceiling. Orville screamed, "Look out! We're going to hit the roof!"

Sophia pulled back on the stick and the ship dropped like a stone. Orville screeched again. "Too much! Too much! We're falling!"

"Quit being a nervous ninny! I'm just testing the controls. Okay, here we go!" *The Dragonfly* was hovering ten feet above the floor when Sophia pushed the right stick forward. The ship responded smoothly, zipping out through the open barn doors.

Mirus hollered, "What are you waiting for? Get flying, you two!"

Sophia jammed the right stick forward. The craft shot across the grassy field, pressing Orville back against his seat. "I think we're going way too—"

"Hold on to your hat! Here we go!" *The Dragonfly* was ripping across the open field ten feet above the grass at over seventy miles an hour when Sophia pushed the left and right sticks forward as far as they would go. They shot up into the air, screaming through the brilliant blue sky at over a hundred and sixty miles an hour.

Sophia shrieked, "Woo hoo! This is amazing!" She glanced over at Orville and grinned. He was hunched over, both paws covering his eyes.

41

Chapter 7

The Iron Door

"I wasn't scared, I had something in my eye because we were flying so fast."

Sophia snorted. "You had goggles on."

"Well, there must have been dust in the goggles that got into my eyes. I'm fine now, so maybe we should just stop talking about it. I'm starting to get a good feel for how the ship flies. How fast am I going?"

"Twenty-five miles an hour. We should get there in time for your mum's next birthday."

Orville rolled his eyes. "I'm going to try something." He gingerly pulled the right stick back until *The Dragonfly* came to a halt, hovering almost a thousand feet above the ground. "This is amazing! Look at the view from here. I'm going to see if she really flies backwards."

Orville pulled back on the right stick and sure enough, the craft darted backwards. "Whoa! This is incredible! Here we go! It's the dread Captain Orville at the controls, so hold onto your adventuring hat!"

Sophia looked at Orville and grinned. There was no

one else in the world she would rather go adventuring with, even if he did fly like her grandmum.

Orville pushed the right stick forward and the ship zipped ahead, the wind whistling through the cockpit. "How fast are we going now?"

"Thirty-five miles an hour, dread Captain Orville."

Orville frowned, then jammed the right stick forward. Soon they were flashing through the clouds at one hundred and ten miles an hour. Orville shrieked, "Captain Orville to the rescue!"

Sophia burst out laughing and slapped Orville on the shoulder. "Now that's what I call flying!"

Two hours later Orville had grown accustomed to the nimble Dragonfly and was finally relaxing. The two adventurers were cruising along at one hundred and thirty miles an hour.

Orville glanced at the compass and adjusted their course. "This is incredible. We're probably the fastest two mice in history."

"The Elders had interstellar ships that traveled many thousands of miles a second. Blinker ships like the one we found on the mesa in Periculum could fly over fifteen hundred miles an hour in the Earth's atmosphere."

"The Elders were rabbits, not mice. Even if we're not the fastest two mice in history, today we're the fastest two mice in the world."

Sophia snorted.

"How far have we come?"

"I've been monitoring our speed and time and I'd say roughly three hundred and sixty miles, so we should reach Ollo the Rock Mouse's home in under an hour."

"Does the map show exactly where he lives? Master

Marloh said we might have trouble finding his house. He seemed to think it was kind of amusing."

"It looks as though he lives in a canyon about the same size as Pavorak Gorge. It shouldn't be too hard to spot a house in a big gorge like that. Besides, with *The Dragonfly* we can hover and look around till we see it."

"I didn't think of that. Mirus said the only way to reach Ollo's house was with *The Dragonfly*. Maybe that's what he meant."

"Look at the fields of wildflowers down there! Drop down and let's fly right over them. They're glorious, so many different colors – blues and yellows and violets and pinks. So pretty!"

"As per your command, Master Captain Sophia!" Orville pulled back on the left stick and the ship descended smoothly. Soon they were racing along twenty feet above vibrant swaths of brilliant wildflowers.

"Look at them all! Magnificent!"

"I'll slow down and maybe we can smell them."

"Watch where you're flying, I don't want to crash into a tree or something."

"Are you questioning the piloting skills of Captain Orville Mouse, the greatest–"

Orville never finished that particular sentence. He never finished it because he was blinded by the sun reflecting off a gleaming object five hundred feet ahead of them. When Orville finally realized what the object was, they were only two hundred feet away from it.

"SPIDER! GIANT ANARKKIAN ATTACK SPIDER!" Orville pushed both sticks forward as hard as he could and just as Mirus Mouse had promised, the ship shot up into the sky like a red rocket on Symoca

Day.

Sophia cried out, "Faster! The spider has force beams! Get us out of here!"

The ship was screaming upward at over one hundred and seventy miles an hour, but unfortunately for Orville and Sophia, the brilliant red force beam which blasted out of the spider's crimson glowing eyes was traveling at one hundred and eighty-six thousand miles per second, the speed of light. It was no contest, the powerful beam instantly obliterating the left front wing of *The Dragonfly*. The ship veered wildly, plunging toward the ground. The good news was this unexpected detour proved to be quite fortuitous, their sudden erratic flight path causing the spider's second force beam to flash harmlessly past them. The bad news was they were plunging toward the ground, the ship spiraling wildly out of control.

Sophia instinctively popped up a sphere of defense around them while Orville jammed the left stick forward and used the right stick to counteract the missing left wing. The ship shuddered wildly, but the spinning stopped. "Push your left stick forward!"

Sophia slammed her silver control stick forward and *The Dragonfly* groaned as it fought against the tremendous forces being thrust upon the three remaining wings and the ship's fragile fuselage. Orville felt himself losing consciousness as the ship began pulling out of its dive less than a hundred feet above the ground. He managed a glance at the speed indicator, trying to focus on the wavering dial. They were traveling over two hundred miles an hour.

"Hold on!" Time seemed to slow down. Sophia slumped over in her seat. Orville's vision was blurring badly as he watched the field of beautiful flowers rushing up toward him. The last thing he noticed was how pretty the flowers looked in the afternoon sunlight.

When he opened his eyes the first thing Orville saw was Sophia's face. "Orville, wake up! Wake up! Are you all right?"

The second thing he saw was their shattered canopy covered with wildflowers. "Where are we? Those flowers are pretty. Is this a dream?"

"Orville, we crashed, but you pulled the ship out of its dive just in time. It looks like we bounced across the meadow but the ship held together. My sphere of defense must have helped."

Orville was trying to focus. "I remember now. The spider! Where is it?"

"I don't see it. It could be miles behind us. I don't know how far we flew before we hit the ground."

Orville sat up. "It's a miracle we're alive."

"We should check the ship. Maybe it's not too badly damaged and still flies."

Orville clambered out of the craft, jumping into a swath of spectacular yellow wildflowers. He walked around *The Dragonfly*, examining it closely. "It doesn't look too bad. The landing struts are all twisted, and the bottom of the ship is scraped badly, but structurally it looks okay. The canopy is shattered but we have our goggles."

"Do you think it will fly with only three wings?"

"Let's find out." Orville hopped back into the ship and started the duplonium motors.

"Motors sound all right. I'll try the wings."

Orville pushed the left stick gently forward and the ship jerked violently, but seconds later the wings were

46

humming smoothly. "The wings must have gotten jammed in the crash and that's why the duplonium motors stopped. Lucky for us. It's running fine now. I'm going to try to take us up."

"You might want to hurry."

"Why?"

Sophia pointed into the distance at a great silver spider meandering in their direction.

"Not again!" Orville held the right stick all the way over and pushed the left stick forward. *The Dragonfly* shot up into the air. "It works! Push your right stick all the way to the right and hold it there while we're flying."

"Better get moving, I think the spider just spotted us."

"I'm going up!" Orville slammed the left stick forward and the ship blasted straight up into the clear blue sky at one hundred and twenty miles an hour, pushing the two adventures down into their seats.

"That should do it! We're at five thousand feet, the spider's force beams can't hit us up here." Orville finally managed a grin. "Just another day in the life of a daring Metaphysical Adventurer!"

Sophia plucked a few wildflowers from the shattered canopy. "Mmmm, these smell wonderful. We'll have to come back when there's not quite so many attack spiders in bloom."

Orville laughed, looking back at the gargantuan eight legged sparkling silver predator far behind them. "Better luck next time, spider!"

Sophia and Orville flew on toward Ollo the Rock Mouse's secret hideout. "It's not too hard flying with three wings, as long as you're holding the right stick over."

Sophia nodded, her eyes on Orville. "That was scary. We could have been killed. It really was Captain Orville to the rescue." Sophia leaned over and kissed Orville on the cheek. "That's for saving the day."

Orville had a very silly grin plastered across his face for the next twenty miles and kept glancing over at Sophia.

"Quit grinning like a ninny, all I did was kiss your cheek."

"I don't know what you're talking about. I was just thinking of a joke Proto told me yesterday. That's why I was smiling."

"There's the canyon! Eyes open, we don't want to run into another spider."

"How much farther to Ollo the Rock Mouse?"

"Fly into the canyon and head north for about five miles. We should see a rocky spire that Mirus circled on the map."

Orville pushed the left stick forward and the ship's altitude increased by five hundred feet. "I'm going to try out these goggles." Orville twisted the small dial on the side of the brass goggles and gazed down the length of the great canyon. "Whoa! This is amazing, it's way better than my sea captain telescope at home. More powerful. I see the spire. We just follow the gorge and we'll be there."

Orville pulled back on the left stick and pushed the right stick forward, their ship descending into the great canyon. He slowed down to get a better view of their surroundings.

Sophia pointed to the walls of the gorge. "It's a lot like Pavorak Gorge but the layers of rock that run along the canyon walls are much brighter, especially the red layers."

The Dragonfly shot forward, the towering sides of the canyon flashing past them in a colorful display. Ten minutes later Sophia called out, "There's the rocky spire. It looks almost like a cloudscraper on Quintari."

"Where is Ollo the Rock Mouse's house?"

"One mile past the spire. Slow us down to thirty miles an hour."

"Okay, we're at thirty. Keep your eyes open. Master Marloh said it would be hard to find."

Two minutes later Orville brought the ship to a standstill, hovering at five hundred feet. The two adventurers peered over the side of the ship, studying the canyon floor for any sign of a dwelling.

"I don't see anything. It looks like the rest of the gorge, barren rocky terrain."

"Mirus's map definitely says this is the location, one mile past the spire. We must be missing something."

Orville dropped down a hundred feet and slowly rotated the ship while they scanned the canyon. "Do you think he might live in a cave or something? Mirus called it Ollo's secret hideout. Look for anything that seems out of place."

Sophia pointed to a section of canyon wall. "Look at that ledge, there's a dark shape in the shadows behind it. It might be something."

Orville eased *The Dragonfly* over to the other side of the canyon and dropped down fifty feet until they were hovering only twenty feet from the ledge.

"That's it! Back behind that big boulder, there's a door built into the rock face. It has to be Ollo's house, what else could it be?"

"Now I know why Mirus had us take *The Dragonfly*. We have to land on that ledge. There's room, but it's going to be tricky."

Sophia laughed. "Nothing Captain Orville Mouse can't handle!"

"I hope you're right."

Orville barely touched the sticks, easing the ship six feet higher and nudging it forward. The only sounds were the north wind whistling through the gorge and the steady hum of *The Dragonfly's* three wings.

Sophia called out, "That's it! Set her down!"

Orville pulled the left stick gently back and brought *The Dragonfly* down onto the narrow ledge. He shut off both duplonium motors and leaned back in his seat. "Whew! We never could have done that with *The Glowbird*."

Sophia hopped out of the cockpit onto the ledge. "Smooth landing, Captain. The ledge is only twenty feet across at the widest point."

Orville climbed out, keeping a safe distance from the edge of the cliff and its four hundred foot drop to the canyon floor. He stepped behind a large jagged boulder, eyeing the door to Ollo the Rock Mouse's home. "Creekers, that door is ten feet tall, six feet wide, and made of solid iron reinforced with strips of Morsennium."

Sophia studied the immense door. "I don't see a bell. I'm getting a feeling Ollo is not fond of visitors."

Orville grinned. "Remember how we got into Norrich Bunker on Periculum?"

"I don't think that's likely to work twice."

"No harm in trying. "Orville stepped up to the door and knocked. "Ouch! That hurts my knuckles." He picked up a rock and hit the door three times. "That should get his attention."

They waited patiently for several minutes but there was no response. Orville sat down and leaned back against the door. "You know, I'm thinking Ollo the Rock Mouse might be even more eccentric than Mirus."

"Why would a mouse who lives in a cave five hundred miles from the middle of nowhere be eccentric?"

"Ha! I can't imagine."

"Try knocking again."

Orville grabbed the rock and hit the heavy door three times. "Maybe he has a hearing problem."

Sophia was about to reply when she heard the sound of metal squeaking. She looked up in time to see a hinged slot at the top of the door closing, a folded piece of paper falling toward Orville. The paper fluttered down to the ground next to him. He unfolded the note and read it aloud to Sophia.

KNOCK TWICE IF YOU ARE SELLING SHOES.
KNOCK ONCE IF YOU ARE NOT.

"What does that mean?"

Sophia was as baffled by the note as Orville. Orville shrugged, then hit the door once with the rock. There was no response.

Three minutes later a second note emerged from the slot. Orville picked it up and read it.

KNOCK TWICE IF YOU ARE SELLING
EXCELSIOR ELECTRO-VACUUMATORS.
KNOCK ONCE IF YOU ARE NOT.

Orville hit the door once with the big rock. "What is wrong with this mouse? Do you think he can really help us? He seems pretty far off the road, if you know what I mean."

"I don't think Master Marloh would have sent us here if he couldn't help us."

Another note drifted down.

KNOCK TWICE IF YOU ARE TRYING TO
PERSUADE ME TO VOTE FOR A
PARTICULAR ELECTED OFFICIAL.
KNOCK ONCE IF YOU ARE NOT.

Orville smacked the door once.

KNOCK TWICE IF YOU ARE SELLING
MAGAZINE SUBSCRIPTIONS.
KNOCK ONCE IF YOU ARE NOT.

Orville hit the door again.

KNOCK TWICE IF YOU WANT ME
TO JOIN AN ORDER OF MONKS
WHO WEAR PURPLE ROBES.
KNOCK ONCE IF YOU DO NOT.

Orville hit the door.

Sophia was leaning back against the rocky wall, her eyes closed, her head nodding.

"This mouse is undeniably loopy."

"Really? What makes you think that?"

KNOCK TWICE IF YOU WANT ME TO
ATTEND A MEETING OF ANY KIND.
KNOCK ONCE IF YOU DO NOT.

Clunk!

KNOCK TWICE IF YOU ARE A
METAPHYSICAL ADVENTURER AND
MASTER MARLOH SENT YOU HERE
TO IDENTIFY A STONE.
KNOCK ONCE IF YOU ARE NOT.

"Now we're getting somewhere. I think this might
be the end of it!" Orville gave the door two sound
whacks with the stone.

KNOCK TWICE IF THE STONE IS RED.
KNOCK ONCE IF IT IS NOT.

Orville put both paws over his eyes. "This mouse is
going to drive me nummers in the head!"

Clonk!

KNOCK TWICE IF THE STONE IS BLUE.
KNOCK ONCE IF IT IS NOT.

"Oh, great heavens, this might be it!" Orville hit the
door twice with the rock.

There were no more notes, only the sound of the
lonely north wind whistling through the great canyon.

Sophia was sound asleep and Orville was drifting off
when the great iron door squealed open. They both

jumped to their feet.

A voice from behind the door shrieked, "Hurry up! Get in here! Hurry!"

The two adventurers dashed through the doorway into Ollo the Rock Mouse's secret hideout.

Chapter 8

Ollo the Rock Mouse

Orville and Sophia stared with intense curiosity at the mouse who stood facing them. He was shorter than Sophia and wore a blue and white striped vest, green pants covered with white stars, and a large pair of black goggles with an odd assortment of magnifying lenses welded to the frame. The cave interior was fifty feet across in both directions, had twenty foot tall ceilings, and much to Sophia's surprise was tastefully furnished. On the far wall Orville spotted seven wooden doors, each one a different color.

Sophia gave her warmest smile. "Hello, Ollo, it's so lovely to meet you. Master Marloh had nothing but glowing things to say about you."

Ollo gave Sophia a dark look and held out his paw.

Orville stared at the open paw. "Oh, the stone! You want to see the stone." He reached into his pocket and pulled out the blue marble, placing it in Ollo's open paw.

Ollo said nothing, but held the marble up and gazed at it, rotating it slowly. He flipped down one of the large magnifying lenses and a small bright light blinked on. "Hmmp." He examined the stone closely.

Orville said, "What do you think?"

Ollo glared at Orville.

"Sorry, I didn't mean to interrupt you."

"Follow Ollo. Follow Ollo." Orville glanced over at Sophia but said nothing. He was trying not to laugh.

Ollo walked across the room to the blue door and swung it open. Sophia and Orville followed him down a long winding stone tunnel which led into an enormous room with forty foot tall ceilings. Hundreds of floor to ceiling shelves lined the walls. Each shelf contained thousands of small square compartments, and resting in each compartment was a blue stone. Sophia quickly calculated that the room held roughly four hundred thousand individual blue stones.

The two adventurers waited silently as Ollo the Rock Mouse scanned the vast wall of stones. Finally he gave a short laugh and set the marble down on the floor. It rolled across the smooth stone to the left side of the room, stopping at the base of the shelves. Ollo rolled an enormous ladder down the wall and scampered up to the ninth level of shelves. He plucked a stone from one of the little wooden compartments and with another humorless laugh slid down the ladder, picked up the blue marble and scurried back over to Sophia and Orville.

Ollo set the marble and the blue stone from the shelf on the floor and hunched down, his eyes bright and focused. He gave a loud guffaw as the stone from the shelf liquefied and flowed across the floor to the marble. The melted stone was absorbed by the marble, which now had a diameter of almost three inches.

56

Ollo picked up the marble and tossed it to Orville. "Don't want it, not a stone." He rose to his feet, put his paw over his eyes and tilted his head down.

Orville looked at Sophia questioningly. She raised both her eyebrows and shrugged.

Thirty seconds later Ollo the Rock Mouse raised his head. "The sample was purchased nine years ago from Myrmac the Brave in Tatuid Village at the base of Mount Ianua for the sum of thirty-six silvers on an extremely humid summer day at three fourteen in the afternoon. Ollo was wearing green striped shirt, purple pants, white stars."

Orville gulped. His Mum's necklace had cost thirty-six silvers, the same as the blue stone. "Thank you so much, Ollo. You have a marvelous memory. Is there any chance you might be able to give us the location of Mount Ianua? We're trying to find the original source of the marble."

"Deep in the east Symocan jungle is where you'll find Mount Ianua."

"One last question, and then I promise we'll leave. Is there anything distinctive about the mountain which might help us locate it?"

"Not a mountain, a volcano."

Orville made a small whimpering noise. Sophia grabbed him a split second before he fainted.

Ollo watched without expression as Sophia dragged Orville back to the huge iron door. He pulled a long silver lever and the massive door groaned open. "Out! Hurry! Get him out!"

Sophia pulled Orville onto the ledge and the door squealed shut behind them. Orville groaned, opening his eyes. "What time is it? Am I late?"

Sophia grinned and patted the top of his head. "It's time to head back to Muridaan Falls, my brave Captain Orville."

"Wait, did Ollo say something about a volcano or did I just dream that?"

"Mount Ianua is a volcano."

"Oh, no."

"Relax, we're not going to jump into Mount Ianua. We will decide what we're going to do, and one thing we're not going to do is jump into a volcano."

"But I had that dream."

"I dreamed I was a bird once. Does that mean I'm going to turn into a bird?"

"I guess not."

"Hop into *The Dragonfly* and let's go home. Keep the ship at five thousand feet so we don't get hit by a spider. If we lose another wing we'll be walking home."

Four hours later Sophia called out, "I see Muridaan Falls!" Orville guided the ship around the outskirts of the village to Mirus Mouse's complex and they touched down in front of the long green shed that housed *The Dragonfly*.

Mirus stepped out of a nearby building, waving to them with both arms. "You made it safely back, I see! You found Ollo the Rock Mouse? That's one loopy mouse, I will tell you that much." Mirus threw his head back and gave a great squawking bird laugh, but stopped short, his eyes focusing sharply on the ship. He gave a shrill piercing screech. "What happened to my ship?? Where's the wing? You're missing a wing! The landing struts! What did you do? You smashed my canopy to pieces!!"

Sophia looked as apologetic as she possibly could. "I'm so sorry, Mirus, we were hit by a dreadful force beam from an Anarkkian attack spider who just came out of nowhere and we crashed in a meadow. We're lucky to be alive. The spider's force beam destroyed the wing, that's why we crashed. It was all your wonderful flight training that saved us."

"Anarkkian spider? What?? What's wrong with you, mouse? Why didn't you use the scramble beam? Have you been eating fermented snapberries?"

"What's a scramble beam?"

Mirus looked as though he might explode. "What's a scramble beam?! I told you five times! The scramble beam is in the port side storage compartment. Take it out, point it at the spider, push the red tab and badingo, the spider wanders away into the sunset. It scrambles his sensors, that's why they call it a scramble beam! How many times do I have to tell you these things?"

"Oh dear, I don't really recall you mentioning anything like that to us. Maybe I misunderstood what you said. Or maybe I just forgot."

"Why didn't you fix the wing?? I told you five times about the two spare wings rolled up in the tail of the ship! I showed you how to fix them! A first year mouseling could do it!"

Orville gave Sophia a nervous glance. "I'm so sorry, Mirus, I guess we forgot you told us about the spare wings and how to replace them. Sorry."

Sophia nodded. "We just forgot everything. We did find out where the blue marble came from though."

"Of course you did! Ollo the Rock Mouse is as loopy as a Mintarian Flatbird eating fermented brimbleberries, but he knows everything there is to know about rocks. Where is it from?"

"From deep in the east Symocan jungle. He purchased it in Tatuid Village near the base of Mount Ianua."

"The volcano? Are you talking about the volcano?"

Orville grimaced. "Yes, the volcano."

Ollo furrowed his eyebrows. "Interesting, most interesting indeed."

Orville gulped. "Why is it interesting?"

"Why wouldn't it be interesting, mouse?"

Orville stared blankly at Mirus.

Sophia raised her paw. "Umm... Mirus, would you mind dreadfully if Orville and I took *The Dragonfly* to Mount Ianua? We need to track down the source of the blue stone."

"What? Of course you can! What's wrong with you, mouse?? Come back tomorrow and *The Dragonfly* will be as good as new. I'll show you how to replace a wing and how to use a scramble beam. How hard is it? Easy as pie, that's what I would tell you."

Chapter 9

Up and Away

"I would really feel much better if you took Proto along with you."

"It's not going to be dangerous, Mum. Master Marloh knows exactly where we're going. We're taking *The Dragonfly* to Tatuid Village, asking Myrmac the Brave where he got the blue stone, and then flying straight home."

"You sound just like your papa, always trying to convince me his adventures were perfectly safe, a lovely stroll through a field of pretty wildflowers on a warm summer's day."

"Well, I don't think it's going to be dangerous, but I guess it wouldn't hurt to take Proto. *The Dragonfly* can carry four mice so there's plenty of room."

"Thank you, I feel much better already."

Proto stepped out from the doorway. "Did I hear someone say adventure? Do you think there will be terrible ferocious snapping creatures like the ones we–"

Orville held up his paw for Proto to stop. "Mum doesn't want to hear about our boring adventures. I'm sad to say we won't be encountering any such creatures on this trip. It's going to be quite uneventful, probably very tedious."

Orville's Mum put her paw on Proto's arm. "You'll watch out for Orville and Sophia and keep them safe?"

"Of course, Mum, I promise. It will be Proto to the rescue, as always. I remember on our last adventure we confronted a ferocious autonomous A6 warrior who was trying–"

"PROTO! We have to go! We're meeting Sophia at Mirus' complex and he's going to teach us how to use a scramble beam and replace a wing on *The Dragonfly*."

A light seemed to blink on in Proto's eyes. "Oh, I see what you're doing. We don't want Mum to worry about us, do we?"

"Quite right, we don't want Mum to worry about us."

"I'll be right back. I just have to grab a few things from my room." Proto dashed down the hallway and up the stairs.

Orville's Mum gave him a long hug. "Have a safe adventure, sweetie. You'll keep an eye out for Sophia?"

"I will." Orville didn't mention it was usually Sophia who did the rescuing.

Proto reappeared wearing an enormous canvas backpack. "Just a few odds and ends which might come in handy on our very uneventful and extremely safe adventure with no chance of meeting any ferocious creatures." He gave Orville a painfully obvious wink.

"Let's go. Bye, Mum, we should be back in a week or so. Don't worry if we're a little bit late."

Orville and Proto headed out the door and down the front steps. An hour later they strolled through the gates of Mirus' complex.

"*The Dragonfly* is in that long green building."

"Do you think Mum believed me when I said the trip would be extremely safe and uneventful? I didn't want to worry her by mentioning all the terrifying creatures we'll probably encounter."

Orville nodded. "I think she believed you. Thanks for not mentioning the dreadful creatures. I know she was pleased you agreed to go with us, especially after I told her how many times you've come to our aid."

Proto beamed. "I'm more than happy to rescue my two best friends in the world."

"We're lucky to have you for our friend. Hey, there's Sophia and Mirus!"

Sophia waved. "Hi, Orville! Hi, Proto! Mirus showed me how to replace a damaged wing on *The Dragonfly*. It's really simple and we have two extra wings rolled up inside the tail of the ship. Oh, and he showed me how to use a scramble beam. It's easier than walking!"

Mirus gave a great screechy laugh.

The three adventurers stepped into the Dragonfly hangar. Proto gasped when he saw *The Dragonfly*. "Oh, my, what a lovely little flying machine. In all my years I've never seen one like this. How thrilling! I do hope we don't get attacked by a Gnorli bird, I'm afraid they would make short work of this delicate little craft."

Sophia smiled. "I think we'll be fine. Fortunately for us, Gnorli birds are only found on Periculum. Besides, the Gnorli bird we met there seemed like rather a pleasant fellow, even if he did have a dreadful memory."

Mirus clapped his paws together. "If you asked me what I'm hearing I'd tell you I'm hearing too many flapping jaws and not enough flapping wings! Jump into *The Dragonfly* and let's get this bug into the sky!"

Orville laughed. "I'm with you, Mirus. Proto, you sit in the back and Sophia and I will sit up front. I'll teach you how to fly the ship once we're airborne. It's easier than pie, that's what I would tell you!"

Mirus gave another squawking bird laugh and slapped Orville on the back. "You sound just like me, mouse! All right, let's hit the clouds!"

The three adventurers climbed into *The Dragonfly* as Mirus swung open the barn doors. Orville started the two duplonium motors, then inched the left stick forward. The gleaming transparent wings became a blur and the ship rose several feet above the barn floor.

Sophia grinned. "All set, Captain Orville! Let's take her up into the blue!"

Orville nodded and pushed the right stick forward. *The Dragonfly* darted out of the barn and across the grassy field. Orville shoved the left stick forward and the craft shot up into the sky at one hundred and thirty miles an hour.

Sophia raised both arms above her head. "Whoo hoo! How do you like *The Dragonfly*, Proto?"

"Quite marvelous, Sophia, but it might be wise to ascertain the craft's maximum velocity and maneuvering speed. You never know when we might have to evade some dreadful flying creature with a fondness for tasty mice."

"Hopefully we won't run into anything like that." Sophia flipped open the storage compartment and pulled out a map. "Mirus marked the location of Mount Ianua with a red circle. We head east southeast for about seven hundred and fifty miles. It's going to take us a while, even cruising as fast as we are. We can set down at noon and have a nice lunch."

Proto leaned forward between Orville and Sophia. "No need to worry about shaping lunch. I have prepared a lovely noonday repast for you and Orville, and I'm certain you'll find the fare quite to your liking. I've included sandwiches, four tasty cakes, four oatmeal cookies, a small box of lemon and orange cream chocolates, and chilled lemonade."

Orville grinned. "You're the best! Thanks! Say, do you have any stories you could tell us to help pass the time? You know how much Sophia loves to hear your stories. The longer the better, right, Sophia?"

Sophia kicked Orville's leg sharply. "That's so thoughtful of you, but I'm quite tired. I was up with the sun this morning so I think I'll take a short nap."

Proto leaned forward again. "A nap is an excellent idea. Perhaps this will help." He reached into his backpack and pulled out a large fluffy pillow.

Sophia took the pillow and laughed. "You really are amazing! Is there anything you don't have in that pack?"

Proto thought for a moment. "Well, now that you mention it, I didn't bring insect repellant. I decided it would be ineffective against the monstrous and terrifying venomous insects we'll have to contend with."

Orville glanced over at Sophia, who raised both eyebrows in mock horror. Orville realized at that moment there was nowhere else in the world he would rather be, and no one else in the world he would rather be with.

Chapter 10

Two Bees or
Not Two Bees

Sophia was still sleeping when Orville spotted the lovely meadow passing below them. He pulled back on the right stick and *The Dragonfly* slowed to a hover. Orville twisted the dial on his flight goggles and peered over the side of the ship, his vision magnified six times by Mirus' invention. "Beautiful! Look at all those flowers. Sophia will love this, it's the perfect spot for a yummy picnic lunch."

Proto nodded. "Quite pastoral indeed. I only hope there's nothing dreadful lurking in the trees, some menacing creature waiting to pounce on their unsuspecting prey."

"Proto, Proto, Proto. Sometimes a beautiful meadow is just a beautiful meadow with no terrifying creatures lurking about waiting to devour us. I'm taking us down." Orville pulled the left stick back and the humming of the wings diminished, the craft slowly descending. A minute later *The Dragonfly* touched down in a spectacular field of violet, blue, and gold wildflowers.

Orville shook Sophia's arm. "Wake up, sleepy bones! Time for lunch!"

Sophia opened her eyes and looked around. "What is this place? It's beautiful!"

The three adventurers hopped out of the ship and looked around at the lush sparkling sunlit meadow.

"Over there, next to that shade tree, the perfect spot for our picnic!"

Sophia and Orville strolled to the center of the meadow and flopped down in the soft grass beneath the tree. Proto was rummaging around in his pack. "Ah, here they are." He pulled out a checkered picnic blanket, two porcelain plates, a pink cardboard box, and a set of silverware, setting them down in front of Orville and Sophia.

"We get a picnic blanket and plates? You're amazing, Proto." Orville flipped open the pink box, eyeing the contents. "Yum! This looks delicious! Would you care for a tasty sandwich, Captain Sophia?"

"I would indeed, I'm famished. What a lovely day it is. This might be the most relaxing adventure we've ever had." Sophia leaned back against the tree with a long sigh.

Twenty minutes later Orville had eaten two sandwiches, two oatmeal cookies, three tasty little cakes and six lemon cream chocolates. "Mmm, so delicious. That was the best lunch I–" He stopped in mid sentence, gazing across the meadow. "What is that? It kind of looks like two fat birds, but they're flying oddly, almost like humming birds. It must be some kind of oversized hummingbird that lives around here. Maybe they caught the scent of those tasty little cakes. Remember how much the green sticky ball creatures on

Periculum liked them?"

Proto nodded, his eyes on the birds across the meadow. "There are more of them now. At least a dozen just flew out from the trees. I hate to alarm you, but they could be a mutant species of carnivorous bird, you know."

Orville laughed. "I'll solve this puzzle." He dashed over to *The Dragonfly* and grabbed his flying goggles from the cockpit, slipped them on and twisted the small dial on the left side. Orville studied the plump birds for a moment, then ripped his goggles off and shrieked, "Into the ship! We have to leave right now!!"

Sophia jumped up and dashed toward *The Dragonfly*. "What are they?"

"Huge bees! At least a foot long, maybe two, and the trees are packed with them. There must be a gigantic hive over there. Hurry, Proto! We have to go!"

Proto ran toward the ship, calling out, "I'm afraid it's far worse than that! Bees are one of the few predators dragonflies have. If there's a hive of them they'll swarm our ship and tear it to pieces."

Orville leaped into the cockpit and fired up the duplonium motors.

Sophia cried out, "Sphere of defense! They're heading this way!" She sprang into the craft followed by Proto. "Take us up! We have to outrun them!"

Orville jammed both sticks forward. The wings blurred and they shot up into the air. Sophia popped up a powerful sphere of defense around the cockpit, glancing behind them. Her eyes grew wide. "Orville, there's at least a hundred bees chasing us!"

A dozen of the huge bees slammed into Sophia's sphere of defense only to be knocked senseless, tumbling through the air to the meadow below. The rest of the swarm was closing in rapidly on *The Dragonfly*. Proto cried out, "They're landing on the ship! They'll tear the wings apart!"

Twenty of the huge bees were now clinging to the tail of the craft, the duplonium motors straining with the additional weight.

Orville hollered, "Hold on, I'm taking us straight down!" He pulled the left stick back and slammed the other stick as far to the right as it would go. *The Dragonfly* made a snap barrel roll and shot down toward the ground at over a hundred and seventy miles an hour. Sophia cried out, "We're going to crash!"

When the ship was fifty feet above the ground Orville shoved both sticks forward, back, then forward, flipping *The Dragonfly* and sending it straight up into the sky. Orville's vision went dark. He realized he was blacking out from the enormous forces of their sudden turn. Right before he lost consciousness he glanced at the ship's tail. His maneuver had thrown all the bees off the ship.

When Orville woke up he gave a shout. "What? Where are the bees?!"

Sophia grabbed his arm. "They're gone. Proto took the controls when you blacked out. You knocked the bees off the ship and most of them were disoriented. Proto managed to outfly the few that weren't. We're up to five thousand feet, well above where bees can go."

Orville leaned back against the seat. "That was terrifying."

Proto nodded. "Quite dreadful, but I'm afraid those bees were just the beginning. Who knows what other ferocious creatures are lying in wait for us deep in the mysterious and forbidding Symocan jungle."

Orville suddenly slapped his paw against his forehead. "Oh, no!"

Sophia's eyes darted wildly around the sky scanning for bees. "What is it?"

"We left the tasty little cakes and a box of orange cream chocolates back in the meadow!"

Sophia stared blankly at Orville. "I'm starting to think there is something very wrong with you. We just escaped from a huge swarm of deadly giant bees and you're worried about tasty little cakes you left in the meadow?"

"What? All that excitement made me hungry."

Proto leaned forward between the seats. "Nothing to worry about, I have two more boxes of tasty little cakes tucked away in my pack."

"Perfect! I couldn't BEE happier. Get it? I couldn't BEE happier?"

Sophia groaned. "I get it." She glanced back at him, then stopped, a smile creeping across her face. She leaned over and kissed him on the cheek. "Thanks for saving us from the giant bees, Captain Orville. You really are the best pilot I know."

Chapter 11

The Newspaper

The adventurers flew onward, high above the sprawling primordial forests of central Symoca. Sophia gazed over the side of the ship, watching as the emerald green carpet of trees gradually diminished, eventually replaced by desolate and starkly mountainous terrain. Orville was forced to take *The Dragonfly* up to twelve thousand feet to traverse the rugged peaks. Sophia blinked a sphere of defense around the cockpit to protect them from the thin frigid air at that altitude, then flicked her paw again and shaped warm winter coats for her and Orville.

"Thanks, I was about to turn into a block of ice. Another half hour and we'll be over the range and heading back down to warmer temperatures."

Sophia leaned back in her seat and closed her eyes. "Let's set up camp at the base of the mountain range. We can have a relaxing dinner and get some rest before we head for Mount Ianua."

"Is something wrong? You're sounding a little weird."

"I don't think our trip is going to be quite as uneventful as you promised your mum. My inner voice told me events are going to become chaotic and unpredictable. It also said no matter how bleak the situation seems we must make no effort to alter the chain of events."

Orville frowned. "I'm not sure I like the sound of that. We do need a break, though. We can rest and gather our thoughts. We'll spend the night and leave in the morning for Tatuid Village."

Proto leaned forward, poking his head between the two front seats. "Sophia, just out of curiosity, did your inner voice happen to give you any specific details regarding the nature of these upcoming chaotic events?"

"If you're asking about those fearsome beasts you're so fond of, I can't say. All I know is we will be facing a series of unforeseen obstacles. Orville calls them the fires of life, difficult events which are capable of changing us profoundly."

"Well, whatever happens, I will be right beside you and Orville, ready to pluck you safely from the jaws of whatever dastardly creatures we encounter. Once again it will be Proto to the rescue!"

"Thanks, Proto. It was our lucky day when Orville and I found you in Pavorak Gorge."

Orville called out, "We've crossed the range, I'm taking her down!"

As *The Dragonfly* was descending Sophia and Orville removed their winter gear and converted it back to thought clouds. "Whew, it's warm on this side of the mountains." Orville spotted a wide rocky shelf with a spectacular view of the sprawling jungle below and brought the ship gently down. He switched off the two duplonium motors and studied their surroundings. "Any giant bees?"

Sophia grinned, hopping out of the ship. "Don't BEE such a nervous ninny."

"Stop stealing my jokes."

"I have no idea what you're talking about, Orville Wellington Mouse. Besides, why would I –" Sophia stopped, her eyes fixed on the horizon. "Look! Way over there!"

Orville felt a shiver pass through him. "Is that..."

"It's Mount Ianua. That's where we have to go."

"I wish I hadn't had that dream about us jumping into a volcano."

"We're not going to jump into a volcano. Stop and think. There's absolutely no reason why we would ever do that. Ever. It was just a symbolic dream you had about us leaping of our own accord into the fires of life."

"I guess. You did say we would lose control over what happens to us though."

"I don't think we will be losing that much control. In your dream it was our choice to leap into the volcano. We made a conscious decision to do it. That's simply not going to happen. You shape tents and sleeping bags and I'll shape us a roaring campfire."

Proto rubbed his large silver hands together. "I have everything I need in my pack to prepare a lovely dinner for my two best friends. For dessert I have a large box of tasty little cakes and several dozen of Orville's favorite oatmeal cookies."

By the time dinner was over the sun had set and a brilliant yellow moon was drifting through the sky over

Mount Ianua. The three adventurers leaned back, taking in the glorious lunar display in the east Symocan night sky.

Orville gave a sigh. "Mount Ianua looks so small and so peaceful, and that moon is lovely. It's hard to imagine it will be as perilous as your inner voice says."

"The most beautiful things can be the most dangerous. A glimmering snow covered forest in the middle of winter can be quite deadly to a mouse without his winter gear."

"You're right. Maybe I'm just trying to convince myself it won't be so bad."

"We'll get through it. Best friends can get through anything together."

Proto laughed, putting his great silver hand on Orville's shoulder. "Especially if your best friend is a ten foot tall indestructible Rabbiton who will dash in at the last moment and save the day."

Orville grinned. "You're both right. I don't think there's anything the three of us can't handle. Let's get some sleep so we're well rested for whatever tomorrow sends our way."

Proto stood up and flicked on his enhanced optical night vision. "While you two are sleeping like little mouselings I shall be scouring the landscape for any dreadful nocturnal creatures who might leap down from above in search of a plump and tasty bedtime snack."

Orville crawled into his sleeping bag with a groan. "Thanks, Proto."

The night passed without incident, and it was a rather disappointed Proto who gently shook Orville's shoulder the next morning. "Rise and shine, adventurers! Next stop is Mount Ianua. Who knows what we'll find in that dark and forbidding land. It is a jungle, so keep your eyes open for giant carnivorous centipedes."

"You keep forgetting those giant centipedes only live on Periculum. There's not enough oxygen in the atmosphere for them to live on Earth. We don't have to worry about them here."

Sophia popped up from her sleeping bag. "Good morning, everyone! Ready to get a good close look at Mount Ianua, Orville? You might want to wear a light shirt and a pair of shorts. It's going to get quite warm, especially when you're swimming in thousand degree molten lava." She let out a great guffaw.

Proto gave a loud staccato laugh. "Ha ha ha ha! Excellent joke, Sophia. I will have to remember that one."

Orville frowned. "How can you two even joke about something like that?"

"Oh, relax, we'll be fine. Mmm... what's that delicious aroma? Do I smell snapberry flapcakes?"

After a tasty breakfast they converted their camping gear into thought clouds and jumped into *The Dragonfly*. "Ready to take this bug up, Captain Orville?"

Orville attempted a cheery grin. "Ready to go, Captain Sophia. Next stop is the very peaceful and friendly village of Tatuid, nestled snugly at the base of lovely Mount Ianua, the happy little volcano that mice never, ever jump into."

Sophia snorted.

Orville flipped on both duplonium motors and pushed the left stick forward. *The Dragonfly* rose up into the brilliant blue sky. "Hold on to your adventuring hats!" He shoved the right stick forward and the craft shot toward Mount Ianua.

With the foothills of the mountain range behind them, Orville descended to a few hundred feet above the dense jungle. "I can't believe we're really here. When I was growing up I heard so many stories about the jungles of east Symoca. Most of them were tales made up to scare little mouselings though. I never met anyone who had actually been here."

Sophia nodded. "It really is amazing, so lush and so beautiful and covered with bright yellow and red tropical blossoms. It's not dark and spooky like the jungles of Periculum."

Orville pointed to the volcano. "We're getting closer. It won't take us long to get there at this speed."

Sophia nodded, her eyes on the rapidly approaching volcano. "Fly over the top so we can look inside the crater and see if it looks like your dream."

Orville was not completely enthralled with Sophia's suggestion, but he pushed the left stick forward and they soared upward. Several minutes later they were at an altitude of nine thousand feet, approaching the peak of the volcano. When they were directly over it Orville pulled back on the right stick and brought *The Dragonfly* to a hover. With some trepidation he peered down into the volcano. Orville groaned, "It's exactly the same. Just like my dream. A big round orange lake of bubbling lava."

Sophia eyed the rippling glowing magma, her eyes narrowing. "Interesting. Let's go, we need to get to Tatuid Village. I'll check the location." She reached into the small storage compartment and pulled out the map Mirus had given her. "Tatuid Village is about two miles southwest of the volcano."

Orville nodded, his eyes on the round compass between him and Sophia. "Southwest it is." The ship made a sharp banking turn and shot forward. Several minutes later Orville called out, "I see a village. It must be Tatuid. I'm going to land a good distance away. I don't want to scare the villagers by landing a giant dragonfly in the middle of their town." The ship sped on for another few minutes until Orville brought it down in a small clearing. He kept the wings humming as he scanned their surroundings. "It looks safe enough. I don't see anything scary. What do you think?"

"I think this is exactly where we're supposed to be. Everything that has happened since you saw your papa's blue marble rolling uphill has been leading us to this very spot."

"I hope you're right." Orville switched off the motors and hopped out of the craft. "Everyone keep your eyes open. We have no idea what kind of creatures inhabit this jungle."

Proto chortled, rubbing his silver hands together. "Oh, my, this is quite thrilling! Far more exciting than watching over glowbirds in the Cube."

Sophia climbed out of *The Dragonfly* and pointed to a well traveled jungle trail. "That's heading in the right direction. Let's take that."

Orville nodded and they trekked off toward Tatuid Village. "Eyes open, stay alert. Be ready to blink up a sphere of defense."

They had traveled no more than a half mile when Sophia froze. She had spotted something heading toward them. "What is that? What is it holding?"

Powerful spheres of defense shot up around Orville

and Sophia. Orville squinted, trying to get a better look at the approaching creature. Proto flipped on his enhanced magnovision and scanned the mysterious jungle denizen. "It appears to be some sort of multi-legged creature strolling along reading a newspaper."

"What do you mean, reading a newspaper?"

"There's really no other way to say it. The creature is hidden behind a large newspaper."

Sophia and Orville stepped off the trail and waited for the curious pedestrian to pass by. As it strolled alongside them the creature slowed down, eyeing them with mild curiosity. Orville had no idea how it might react to their presence, but to his great relief the creature simply gave a polite nod. Until it noticed Proto.

When its eyes landed on Proto the creature lurched backwards, almost dropping its newspaper. It stared intently at him, slowly stepping away, then glanced at Orville and Sophia. The creature dropped its paper and raced off down the trail.

Orville managed to find his voice. "Did I just see a six foot tall ant reading a newspaper?"

Sophia turned, tracking the extraordinarily large ant as it scurried down the trail. "I think so. We may have just met one of the inhabitants of Tatuid Village."

"Ants? It's a village full of ants? Why didn't someone tell us it was ants? We have to go into a village filled with giant ants? I don't think I can do this. Giant ants??"

"Orville, calm down. Think about it, please. Did the ant try to attack us? Would a deadly predator be strolling along reading a newspaper and nod to us politely?"

Orville furrowed his brow. "I guess not. Now that you mention it he didn't seem especially interested in eating us. He sure had his eye on Proto, though."

Proto threw his shoulders back and stood up straight. "I do have quite a commanding presence, being as tall as I am. Perhaps he thought I was an A6 Autonomous Warrior Rabbiton. It wouldn't be the first time someone has made that mistake. He seemed to be a pleasant enough fellow, quite unlike the creatures on Periculum."

"I guess you're right. He seemed harmless enough. I was just surprised to see an enormous ant."

Sophia let out a gasp, slapping her paw across her mouth.

"What? What is it? What do you see?" Orville scanned the jungle for some unnamed horror.

"You didn't faint! You saw a creature that scared you, but you didn't faint!"

Orville stared at Sophia, a smile creeping across his face. "You're right. I didn't faint. I didn't even think about fainting."

Proto nodded. "I am quite familiar with the process of overcoming personal fears. I recall with great clarity the moment I conquered my fear of Anarkkian scout ships, with their dreadful neuro beams. It came as a complete surprise when I was strolling through Pavorak Gorge and realized I was thinking about the lovely colors of the gorge and not worrying about having my neuronic brain fried by one of those awful ships. I would offer you my deepest congratulations on this momentous personal achievement."

Orville couldn't stop grinning. "Thanks, that means a lot to me."

Sophia patted his shoulder and said, "Let's go, Orville the Brave. Something is trying to stop time, and it's our job to make certain they don't succeed."

Chapter 12

The Great Silver Rabbit

Sophia was the first to spot the red and yellow striped crossing gate blocking the jungle trail. "Look at that gate. This might be the entrance to Tatuid Village."

"There's a big wooden shack next to it, probably for guards. I wonder why we can't just walk into the village?"

Sophia shrugged. "I guess we'll find out soon enough."

The three adventurers strode down the jungle trail toward the checkpoint. Soon they were standing in front of the heavy red and yellow iron gate.

Sophia called out, "Hello? Is anyone here?"

The door of the guard shack squealed open and two large ants clad in bright red uniforms stepped out. They strode briskly over to the gate, stopping in their tracks when their eyes hit Proto. They gave each other significant looks but remained silent. One of the guards carried a voluminous notebook crammed with reams of miscellaneous papers. He frowned, silently flipping through his documents until he found the one he was searching for. He turned to the three adventurers, his eyes occasionally jumping over to Proto.

"Your papers, please." The guard held out one arm.

Orville gave the friendliest smile he could. "Papers? What sort of papers? Newspapers?"

The guard's eyes bulged. "This is neither the time nor the place for levity, sir!"

"Sorry, I wasn't trying to be funny. This is our first visit to Tatuid Village and I don't know anything about your rules and regulations."

The guard relaxed slightly. "You must show me your identification papers. It is imperative that we have the most comprehensive documentation possible for each and every visitor to Tatuid Village. No exceptions." His eyes locked onto Proto. "Almost no exceptions. Your papers?"

Orville reached into his coat pocket and pulled out his wallet, quickly flipping it open. "I have my Easterly School identification card, my library card, my Book Emporium employee card, and membership cards for the Science Club and the History Club at school."

Sophia gave a loud laugh. "You were in the Science Club? Really?"

The guard shrieked, "DO NOT SPEAK UNLESS YOU ARE SPOKEN TO!" He smacked his heavy notebook loudly on the iron gate.

Sophia's jaw dropped. "Oh… sorry." Orville gulped.

The guard extended his arm again. "Papers!" Orville passed the five identification cards to the guard, who scrutinized each one in agonizing detail. He flipped to another page on his notebook, then pulled out a yellow pencil from his uniform pocket. "CLIPBOARD!"

A blue uniformed ant dashed out of the shack carrying a large clipboard which he thrust into Orville's paws. "Your clipboard, sir!"

The guard in the red uniform was studying Orville's cards, a dark frown covering his face. "These identification cards are substandard at best. Under any other circumstances you would be instantly turned away from Tatuid Village." He looked pointedly at Proto, raising one eyebrow. His focus returned to Orville. "You will need to construct organizational stratification flow charts displaying the operating ruling personnel in these five socialization units. Start from the supreme controller and work down, clearly identifying your own position and status both vertically and horizontally within the current ruling hierarchy."

"What?" Orville had absolutely no idea what the guard was asking him to do.

The guard's eyes bulged again as he tried to contain his boiling anger. He spoke very slowly and deliberately, as though Orville was a tiny mouseling. "Draw a chart in which you name all the members of these five groups. List each member's position in the group, from most important to least important. Do not fail to indicate your own position in the current hierarchy. Am I making myself quite clear?"

Orville nodded. He was not going to ask any more questions. He sat down on the ground with his clipboard and began to sketch a chart of the Easterly School administrators, teachers, and all the students he could remember. After a while he began making up names and positions, designating himself as Chief Clockwork Glowbird Flight Instructor for the science club. Sophia flopped down next to him, holding an identical clipboard. "You're lucky, I had nine identification cards, six from Quintari. Why on earth do they need all this information?"

Orville shrugged. "Who knows. I'm just making up names. It's not like they're going to check."

"Good idea."

Proto had been standing idly by, hands clasped behind his back. Neither of the guards had approached him. He cleared his throat, trying to get their attention. Both guards looked up in stunned surprise. One of them spoke rapidly in a high pitched anxious voice, "How may I be of assistance to you, sir?"

"I couldn't help but notice you asked for identification cards from Orville and Sophia, but not from me. I would be more than happy to produce my original manufacturing documentation if you would like, although I was a prototype, not simply a standard production model."

The guard gave a nearly manic laugh. "Oh, good heavens, sir, that will not be necessary at all. No identification is needed, sir. None whatsoever. You are most welcome to enter our humble little village resting peacefully in the shadows of great Mount Ianua. Most welcome indeed, sir. Most welcome."

The second guard stammered, "No identification needed at all, sir. It is a great and memorable honor to welcome you to our humble little village."

Orville nudged Sophia with his elbow. "Why are they being so respectful to Proto but so rude to us?"

Sophia eyed the guards. "There's something strange going on here. It's as if they already know who he is."

Orville glanced down the jungle trail. Three new guards had just arrived and were pointing at Proto, speaking in hushed voices. A fourth guard appeared, this one wearing a purple uniform with a bright yellow stripe on each sleeve. Orville whispered to Sophia, "More guards are showing up and they're all staring at Proto. I think the color of their uniform indicates their rank. Blue is lowest, then red, then–"

"STOP THAT TALKING! THE GREAT SILVER RABBIT HAS BETTER THINGS TO DO THAN STAND AROUND WAITING FOR YOU TO FINISH YOUR VISITOR DOCUMENTATION FORMS!" The guard smacked his notebook on the iron gate.

"I'm sorry, sir. We've both finished our charts."

The guard snatched the clipboards from their paws, giving the charts only a cursory glance. "This will have to do. An antling could have done a better job, but I will NOT be the one held responsible for keeping The Great Silver Rabbit waiting." He turned to the blue guard and bellowed, "You WILL inform the Purple Guardmaster that all appropriate documentation HAS been satisfactorily completed and he may now assist The Great Silver Rabbit!"

A green thought cloud drifted out of Orville's ear over to Sophia. "The Great Silver Rabbit? What are they talking about?"

Sophia sent a blue cloud back to Orville. "I have no idea. They must have mistaken Proto for another Rabbiton, one they're afraid of. This is very curious."

The blue guard dashed down the trail, quickly relaying the red guard's message to the Purple Guardmaster, who in turn raced back toward the crossing gate and stood at full attention directly in front of Proto. His sharp staccato voice pierced the air.

"GREAT SILVER RABBIT, the King of Ants

wishes you to know he is deeply and profoundly honored by your magnificent shining presence. He is awaiting your arrival at the King's Royal Palace in Tatuid Village. Please follow me if it is your will to do so." The Purple Guardmaster gave a long sweeping bow before Proto.

Proto smiled politely. "Oh dear, I'm afraid you must think I'm—" Proto never finished his sentence. He never finished it because he was interrupted by Orville's extremely loud and bombastic voice.

"O GREAT SILVER RABBIT, YOU MUST SPEAK ONLY WITH THE KING OF ANTS AND NO OTHER. IT IS THE LAW!"

Proto and Sophia turned in surprise at Orville's sudden outburst. Sophia blinked, then gave an imperceptible grin. Her voice boomed out, "YOUR LOYAL AND HUMBLE SERVANT ORVILLE MOUSE IS QUITE CORRECT, MOST MAGNIFICENT GREAT SILVER RABBIT. YOU MUST SPEAK WITH NONE OTHER THAN THE KING OF ANTS. IT IS THE LAW AS WRITTEN BY ALL SILVER RABBITS WHO CAME BEFORE YOU!"

Orville snickered.

A light came on in Proto's eyes. He nodded, giving Orville a great wink. With a dramatic wave of his long silver arm he commanded, "GUARD, TAKE ME TO THE KING OF ANTS! I WOULD SPEAK WITH HIM! MAKE ALL HASTE!"

Chapter 13

The Shrieking Terror

Reaching Tatuid Village took longer than the adventurers had anticipated. According to Proto they walked for two hours and six minutes before spotting the main gates of the village. Orville eyed with curiosity the thirty foot tall wooden stockade constructed of massively stout logs which encircled the town. The Purple Guardmaster halted abruptly at the foot of the front gates.

"ON THIS DAY THE BELL OF FATE SHALL BE RUNG THREE TIMES!" The Guardmaster grasped the clapper of an enormous silver bell hanging next to the brightly painted stockade doors. Three loud gongs resonated through the jungle. An ant clad in a bright yellow uniform popped his head up over the top of the stockade and looked down at the visitors. Orville could hear the ant gasp when it spotted Proto.

The Purple Guardmaster cried out, "OPEN WIDE THE GATES OF TATUID, FOR THE GREAT SILVER RABBIT HAS COME TO FULFILL THE GLORIOUS PROPHECY AS SET FORTH BY THE FATHER'S FATHER OF MYRMAC THE BRAVE!"

A feeling of dread rippled through Orville. "Glorious

prophecy? What is that all about?"

Sophia shook her head. "I don't know, but I don't like the sound of it. Wait, isn't Myrmac the Brave the one who sold the blue stone to Ollo the Rock Mouse?"

Orville didn't reply, his attention focused on the stockade wall, his eyes running across the massive wooden construction. He gulped, grabbed Sophia's shoulder and pointed. The front of the stockade was covered with gigantic claw marks. Orville could feel his knees shaking. "Look at the size of those claw marks, at least four feet across. What could possibly have claws that big?"

Proto had also spied the gigantic claw marks. He gave a great gasp, whirling around to face Sophia and Orville. He pointed to the monstrous gouges in the wood with undisguised glee. "How dreadful! What manner of horrific beast could possess such fearsome claws?"

The great gates of Tatuid Village groaned open and the Purple Guardmaster stepped into a rippling sea of ants. A thousand voices sounded. "Where is he? Do you see him? Is it really the Great Silver Rabbit? How big is he? Is he really silver?"

Proto stepped through the gates to a deafening roar. "It's him! It's the Great Silver Rabbit! He has come! He has come to save us all!" Thunderous cries erupted from the great throng of ants. A thousand ecstatic ants whooped, a thousand ecstatic ants hollered, a thousand ecstatic ants stomped their feet with great abandon, a thousand ecstatic ants wept for joy. The Great Silver Rabbit had arrived, and he would save them all.

Orville and Sophia followed behind Proto, staring with wide eyes at the deliriously jubilant crowd. Orville moved closer to Sophia, taking her paw. He was not necessarily happy to be surrounded by a thousand screaming ants, all of them taller than he was.

Orville sent a thought cloud to Sophia. "They think he's here to save them from something. What have we gotten ourselves into?" He turned to Sophia, but she had her paws pressed tightly over her ears and her eyes squeezed shut. He knew immediately what was happening. Sophia was getting a message from her inner voice, but the look on her face told Orville it was not good news. He did not want to know what her inner voice had just told her.

The Purple Guardmaster bellowed to the crowd, "MAKE WAY FOR THE GREAT SILVER RABBIT! MAKE WAY! HE WOULD SPEAK WITH THE KING OF ANTS! MAKE WAY!"

The crowd parted, becoming eerily silent as Proto followed the Guardmaster down the main street of Tatuid Village toward the King's Royal Palace. Orville and Sophia hurried after Proto.

The King's Royal Palace proved to be somewhat less magnificent than Orville had imagined. It was in fact nothing more than a simple log building not much bigger than the Book Emporium. The Guardmaster knocked three times on the front door, then sank to his knees, bowing his head. The door swung open and an ant bedecked in a bright orange uniform motioned for Proto, Orville, and Sophia to enter. The door closed behind them.

The orange ant stared intently at Proto, then motioned for them to follow him. He stepped briskly over to a set of white doors and tapped three times. A muffled voice called out from the other side of the door.

"Enter!"

The orange ant swung the doors open, bowing deeply to the three adventurers. "The King of Ants awaits your most magnificent presence."

Proto stepped through the doorway, followed by Orville and Sophia. The first thing to catch Orville's eye was a large ant in a shimmering white robe, seated comfortably on an enormous green stuffed chair. The second thing Orville noticed was an ant in dark green trousers and a worn leather vest leaning against a wall. This ant was eating a very large cheese sandwich.

The white robed ant rose to his feet and stepped over to Proto, grasping his hand firmly while studying his face. "The Great Silver Rabbit has arrived. I was beginning to wonder if our infamous prophecy was entirely accurate." The ant eating the cheese sandwich gave a loud cough.

"Relax, Myrmac, you know as well as I do your grandfather wasn't the most stable ant in the colony. I'm not saying he was as loopy as a drunken napsnikker, but you know as well as I do his feet were planted firmly in the sky." The white robed ant had not loosened his grip on Proto's hand. "A pleasure to meet you, Great Silver Rabbit. I am the King of Ants, as you may have surmised. You may be seated." The King motioned them toward a row of three ornately carved wooden chairs.

Proto smiled politely. He had never met a king before, but the depth of the Elders' programming was unparalleled, preparing Proto for almost any circumstance. "It is a great and profound honor to meet you, your Highness. Please call me Proto."

The King of Ants shook his head. "I shall do no such

90

thing. From this day forth you will be known only as The Great Silver Rabbit."

"I do beg your pardon, but I'm afraid I simply could not relinquish my name. It was my dear friend Orville who gave me the name Proto when we first–"

The King's eyes bulged out in stunned surprise. "YOU DARE TO DISOBEY A DIRECT ORDER FROM THE KING OF ANTS?!"

Proto had never been spoken to in such a manner, but remained true to his original programming parameters, his reply both polite and cordial. "Oh, dear, I apologize, your Highness. Under other circumstances I would never question the orders of a great and powerful ruler such as yourself."

The King looked puzzled. "Other circumstances?"

"Well, for instance, if I were an ant living in Tatuid Village rather than a Great Silver Rabbit visiting from his distant home of Muridaan Falls to fulfill your great prophecy."

The King of Ants blinked several times, then burst out laughing. "Well said, Proto. I shall treat you and your two friends as the honored guests that you are. Perhaps we might be able to reach a compromise. Would you allow yourself to be called The Great Silver Rabbit for the duration of your visit? The villagers were clearly elated by your arrival, and they would be confused and disheartened if we announced you were not The Great Silver Rabbit."

"A marvelous compromise, your Highness, and one I heartily agree to uphold. I am curious, however, as to why the villagers were so elated by my arrival in Tatuid?"

"Of course you are." The King of Ants gestured to

the ant who was eating the cheese sandwich. "Myrmac will tell you everything you need to know about the prophecy. It was his very eccentric grandfather who revealed it to the village years before Myrmac was born. The villagers have been waiting for the Great Silver Rabbit for over twenty years. The ant who spotted you on the jungle trail has already been rewarded with the Royal Silver Rabbit Prize Package, receiving a purse of twenty silvers, an authentic silver plated rabbit statuette, and a complimentary dinner for two at the King's Tavern, drinks not included."

Myrmac turned to the three adventurers and bowed deeply. "The King is quite correct, as always. It goes without saying your arrival has caused quite a stir in our little village, and I am truly honored to make your acquaintance. I am known throughout the land as Myrmac the Brave."

Sophia sat up straight. "You're Myrmac the Brave? You're the one Ollo the Rock Mouse told us about! You sold him the mysterious blue stone."

Myrmac glanced over at the King of Ants. "Yes, the infamous blue stone. I remember quite well selling it to Ollo for the tidy sum of thirty-six silvers. A shrewder ant than I would have walked away with two or three times that number of silvers. An interesting stone, to be sure. We'll return to that topic later, but first I shall relay to you the essence of my grandfather's prophecy. He was, as the great and noble King of Ants so graciously informed you, edging a little toward the eccentric side. He claimed to possess some form of mysterious inner voice which would tell him things, and it was that inner voice which revealed to him the great prophecy. In short, the voice told him that during the lifetime of his grandson, which of course would be me, a series of events would occur placing our world in the gravest of danger. As ridiculous as it may sound, the chain of events he described would ultimately cause time to stop across our land. All life as we know it would cease to be."

Sophia gasped. "That's what I saw in my dream! Everyone in Muridaan Falls was frozen! Time had stopped. That's why we're here. We are here to prevent this catastrophic event from happening."

Myrmac nodded. "That was his prophecy. There is more to it than that, however. The prophecy contained two parts. The first half states clearly that The Great Silver Rabbit would rid Tatuid Village of the Shrieking Terror, a beast which was unknown to us at that time. It paid its first visit to our village exactly one year ago."

Orville blinked rapidly. "Wait, I'm sorry, did you say... the Shrieking Terror?"

"Quite so. You may have noticed the monstrous claw marks on the outside of the village stockade? All courtesy of that despicable beast."

Proto's ears perked up. "Precisely what manner of beast is this?"

Myrmac shrugged. "I'm afraid no one has ever seen its true form and lived. It appears in the darkest of night, filling the air with unearthly shrieks. It attempts to claw its way through the front gate, but on occasion scrabbles over the top into the village. On those particular nights I'm sad to say it devours six or eight of our loyal citizens."

"Oh dear, it sounds like an absolutely abysmal beast. Do you have any idea at all where it might live?" Orville could tell Proto was making a valiant effort not to grin with delight over the presence of this horrible creature.

"Most certainly. Its sinister lair lies only three miles away in an enormous labyrinth of caves and tunnels at the base of Mount Ianua. We've sent a few of the village guards into the caves on reconnaissance missions, but unfortunately none of them ever returned."

Orville gave a groan. "Caves, why do they always live in caves? I hate caves."

Sophia put her paw on Orville's shoulder. "Remember, we are the ones who sent the Red Mouse to Malgraven Prison. We are the ones who defeated the giant carnivorous centipedes of Periculum. We are the ones who outwitted an Autonomous A6 Warrior Rabbiton in Norrich Bunker."

Orville nodded. "I know you're right, but it's called the Shrieking Terror and it lives in a big creepy cave at the base of a volcano."

"Those are only words, only names. Don't be scared of words."

"Maybe you're right. It's the name that scares me most. Well, plus the fact that it devours six or eight giant ants for dinner."

Proto stood up and rubbed his silver hands together. "I believe we should pay this pesky fellow with the oversized claws a visit. Orville, if you apply your keen sense of logic to this puzzle you will see we are destined to be victorious. The prophecy clearly states we arrive in the village and rid them of the Shrinking Terror. It does not say we arrive in the village and are devoured the next day by the Shrinking Terror."

"It's called the Shrieking Terror, not the Shrinking

Terror."

"Even better. Shall we be on our way?"

Myrmac slapped Proto on the back. "Well said, Great Silver Rabbit. I would highly recommend that you change your name to Proto the Brave. It would suit you well."

Proto beamed with delight. "Do you really think so? Would that be too much? Too boastful? Proto the Brave? I do like the sound of it."

"They've been calling me Myrmac the Brave for years. You get used to it."

"May I ask how you came to be called Myrmac the Brave?"

"We can discuss the second half of the prophecy after you have vanquished the Shrieking Terror. The very best of luck to you, and we'll be anxiously awaiting your safe return. Oh, I almost forgot, here's a little map showing the precise location of the Shrieking Terror's cave. From this point on it's all up to you and your two stalwart adventuring companions."

Fifteen minutes later the three adventurers were striding down a shadowy jungle trail toward Mount Ianua and the clawed horror known as the Shrieking Terror of Tatuid Village.

Chapter 14

The Cave You Fear

Proto was the first to spot the cave. "Over there, through those vines!"

Orville peered through the dense jungle thicket to an ominous black opening at the base of the massive volcano. "It looks really dark inside."

Sophia crept forward. "Keep your eyes open. Defensive spheres up. We have no idea what sort of creature we're facing."

Orville stopped. "Wait a minute, we should have a plan. If we run into some giant clawed scary monstrosity, what are we going to do? We're Metaphysical Adventurers and can't use lethal force, so how are we going to stop it?"

"We'll just have to see what happens. Maybe we can blink big chains around it or something."

"Blink big chains? That doesn't sound like a very–"

"You're being a nervous ninny again. We'll think of something once we know what we're up against. That's what Metaphysical Adventurers do."

"I'm not being a nervous ninny, it just seems

reckless to dash into a giant dark cave without a plan." Orville glared, blinking up a powerful sphere of defense. He hated being a nervous ninny.

Proto stepped in front of Orville. "I am completely indestructible, so I shall enter the cave first." Before Orville or Sophia could reply Proto slipped through the dense stand of vine covered trees and disappeared into the inky black interior.

Orville and Sophia followed Proto into the cave. Orville still had a dark frown on his face. Sophia flicked her paw and a bright glowing sphere floated up to the glistening black tunnel ceiling. "Myrmac the Brave said it was a system of caves, not just one big cave. The tunnels along that far wall must lead to the other caves."

Orville pointed to the largest entrance. "We know the creature is large, too large to fit through the three smaller tunnels. We should take the big one."

Sophia scanned the cave floor. "You're right. There's a trail of scrape marks leading into it." She sniffed the thick acrid air. "What's that smell? It burns my nose. It smells like vinegar, or some kind of acid."

"It's probably from the creature, or something it was eating."

"Ants produce a venomous form of acid. If it's snacking on ants that could explain the smell."

Orville sent a second brilliant sphere of light into the large tunnel. "Proto didn't wait for us. He seems to be in an awfully big hurry to meet this Shrieking Terror."

The two adventurers crept forward through the jagged rocky passage. Sophia pointed to the glinting ebony tunnel walls. "Be careful around the walls, they're made of volcanic glass and are razor sharp.

Keep your sphere of defense up."

"You don't need to remind–" Orville stopped in his tracks. "Did you hear that?"

A shiver ran through Sophia. "I heard it. Now we know why they call it the Shrieking Terror. At least we're heading in the right direction."

"Maybe we could shape something to make it sleep. Some kind of sleeping powder or something?"

"That might work for a while, but what happens when it wakes up? The prophecy says we're supposed to rid the village of the Shrieking Terror, not stand around and watch it take a nap."

"It was just an idea, all right? Maybe Proto will think of something. The prophecy only mentioned the Great Silver Rabbit, not his two brave and stalwart companions."

"That's a good point. That could be why he didn't wait for us."

"This tunnel splits into three more tunnels. If we're not careful we could get lost in here. Who do you think made all these tunnels? The Anarkkians?"

Sophia shook her head. "No one made them, they're natural volcanic formations called lava tubes. We won't get lost. I've been shaping a blue circle on the wall every fifty feet or so."

"Good thinking. It looks like the scrape marks on the floor go into the tunnel on the right. Hey, the shrieking stopped."

"I'm not sure if that's good or bad."

Orville followed the trail of drag marks into the next lava tube. He flicked his wrist and his glowing orb darted forward, illuminating a long curving cylindrical tunnel.

Fifteen minutes later the tunnel split again. Sophia examined the rocky floor for tracks. "The marks go into both tunnels."

Orville thought for a moment. "Both tunnels could lead to the same cave."

"We must be getting close. Dim the orbs so we don't startle whatever this thing is."

Orville's glowing orb rapidly faded to a small point of light. "I'm worried about Proto. I know he's indestructible, but he could have fallen into a crevasse or something. I wish he'd waited for us."

Sophia stopped short, holding up one paw. "Listen!"

"It's shrieking again. I'm starting to feel a little sick. Do you think this dank cave air could be affecting me?"

"I don't think it's the air. I think it's you imagining getting clawed to pieces by the Shrieking Terror. Look on the bright side, you haven't fainted."

"Me faint? If my middle name wasn't Wellington, I would be Orville the Br–" Sophia held up her paw motioning for silence.

She whispered, "The shrieking stopped, but the smell is getting much worse."

Orville curled his nose. "Eeew! That's bad. A certain Shrieking Terror needs to take a long soapy bath. Whew!"

"Okay, stay right behind me." Sophia blinked off her glowing orb and crept forward, cautiously feeling her way along the tunnel wall. Orville put his paw on her shoulder, following behind her. The putrid smell from the Shrieking Terror was dreadful and growing worse with each step they took.

Sophia felt the tunnel wall end and sent a thought cloud to Orville. "We're in the creature's cave. Don't make a sound."

Orville padded silently forward. The beast's cavernous lair was enormous, at least two or three hundred feet across and a hundred feet tall. Orville spotted a dim light coming from behind a large boulder sitting in the center of the cave. He pointed toward the enormous rock and inched forward, sending Sophia a thought cloud. "We can sneak around that big rock. We need to find out what that light is."

Sophia nodded, silently waving him forward. Step by cautious step Orville crept across the cave floor, finally reaching the massive round boulder. He drew close to it and began to feel his way around to the other side. He stopped, his voice low and raspy. "Bad, very bad."

"What's wrong?"

Orville took Sophia's paw and touched it to the rock. Much to Sophia's dismay, rather than pressing against volcanic glass, her paw was pressing against a wall of coarse matted hair. They were not sneaking around a huge boulder, they were sneaking around the Shrieking Terror.

A great shrill voice echoed through the cave. "For goodness sake, stop creeping about and poking at me and come around here where I can see you. Your silver friend and I have been having a perfectly pleasant conversation, so let's not spoil it with all your creeping and poking."

Orville managed to choke out a reply. "S-s-sorry, Shrieking Terror."

The creature gave a moan of exasperation. "What is wrong with those ants? Why would they call me that? Proto, I want you to be brutally honest. Does my

TOM HOFFMAN

singing sound like shrieking to you?"

Orville and Sophia made their way around the Shrieking Terror. Proto was sitting on the floor, his ear lights illuminating what appeared to be the creature's long tapered tail.

Orville whispered to Sophia, "What is it? Is that its tail?"

"Oh, great heavens, what ever happened to manners? *Is that its tail?* How rude can one small mouse be?"

Proto rose to his feet. "I apologize profusely for my two young companions. I am afraid they have never previously set eyes on such a magnificent specimen as yourself, failing to recognize the regal profile of a great and noble giant anteater. Please do forgive their behavior, I assure you there was no malicious intent on their part."

"I suppose so. Very well. Hello, mice, I am a giant anteater. I eat ants. Now, Proto, back to my question, in all honesty, could my singing possibly be misconstrued as shrieking?"

Proto thought for a moment. "I suppose to the untrained ear, to one who is unfamiliar with the delicate nuances and wide tonal variations of classical discordant anteater symphonics, it could resemble shrieking. It is of course simply the ants' glaring lack of musical sensitivities and melodic understanding which would result in such a grievous error of judgment."

"Just as I thought. The brilliance of my highly evolved euphonic prowess soars far above their pedestrian harmonic paradigms."

Proto took a seat in front of the anteater, a look of deep concern on his face. "How is your stomach feeling now?"

"Still quite dreadful, I'm afraid. Some days I can barely make it out of the cave to look for ants. Once I eat a few of them I feel a little better, but then the pain worsens soon after."

Proto nodded. "In your world, were the ants as big as the ones here?"

"Oh, good heavens no. They were very tiny and quite delectable. I could eat thousands of them and never feel the slightest twinge of discomfort. The ants here are so grotesquely large, so crunchy and dreadfully hard to digest."

"Have you tried altering your diet?"

"What do you mean?"

"Well, eating a more balanced diet. You know, fruits and vegetables and that sort of thing. It's most certainly your current vast intake of chitinous exoskeleton which is causing you so much gastrointestinal distress. I believe a rather severe alteration of your diet is in order."

"That's preposterous. I'm an anteater. Ant. Eater. I eat ants. Well, I do on occasion eat a piece of rotten fruit or two. Quite tasty, I will admit."

"There you go, an excellent start. Until you are able to return to your own world I would highly recommend maintaining a strict diet of fruits and vegetables. The surrounding jungle holds an abundance of both. I'm quite certain these dreadful stomach pains and digestive issues will fade away to nothing within a few days of starting this new diet."

"Perhaps you're onto something. I have noticed the pain does subside somewhat when I eat a bit of rotten fruit. You know what? I'll do it. I shall eat nothing but fresh fruits and vegetables."

Sophia and Orville were deeply impressed by Proto's diplomatic skill and his adept handling of the giant anteater. Orville sent a puffy blue thought cloud to Sophia. "Proto's amazing! He rid the village of the Shrieking Terror just by talking to it!"

Sophia returned a cloud. "You mean the Giant Singing Anteater?"

Proto rose to his feet. "It's been lovely talking with you, and I'm certain you'll be right as rain in a few short days. Oh, I nearly forgot, you never did tell me how you found your way into this world."

"Quite a remarkable event, but the technological aspects are well outside my limited scientific acumen. I was climbing the side of a rather steep rocky incline, digging through the snow searching for a tasty, minty variety of red mountain ant when I chanced upon a large round shimmering blue disk. Very peculiar. It resembled a vertical wall of rippling water. Of course I was intrigued, and poked my nose into the water, which as it turned out was not water at all. When I stepped through the disk there was a flash of light and there I was, standing in the middle of this very cave."

"Remarkable. Perhaps we shall discover a means for your safe return home. I will keep my eyes open. You know, it's terribly embarrassing, but I don't know your real name, and I certainly don't wish to refer to you as the Shrieking Terror. What should I call you?"

The great anteater studied Proto's expression, then said, "I am quite moved by your most considerate behavior. I am known among friends as Arthur Anteater, and that is what you may call me from this day on."

"Well, Arthur, it has been a pleasure meeting you,

and if we discover a doorway leading back to your world we will certainly let you know."

Proto turned to Orville and Sophia. "Before we leave, would you be willing to shape our friend Arthur a large platter of tasty fruits and vegetables? It would be a lovely gesture of our newfound friendship."

Twenty minutes later the three adventurers bid their farewells, leaving Arthur the Singing Anteater snacking on an enormous dish of fresh fruits and vegetables.

As they headed down the tunnel the anteater called out, "Thank you, Proto! These bananas are delightful, quite similar in taste and texture to fresh ant brains!"

"Ant brains! Gakk! Blekkk!" Orville made a gagging sound and pretended to throw up on Sophia.

Sophia gave him her most withering glare. "There really is something very, very wrong with you."

Chapter 15

The Fine Print

The triumphant return of the three adventurers resulted in the largest, longest, and loudest celebration in the history of Tatuid Village. In the span of one day The Great Silver Rabbit had become a hero of mythic proportions.

Several hours prior to this legendary celebration, Proto had been describing to Myrmac the Brave how he persuaded the Shrieking Terror to alter his diet from ants to a much healthier menu of fresh fruits and vegetables, a diet which would alleviate his gastrointestinal distress.

Myrmac the Brave listened without expression to Proto's story. When Proto was done Myrmac slowly shook his head. "I'm afraid your memory does not serve you well, my tall silver friend. That's not what happened at all. Follow me. Watch and learn from the master, Myrmac the Brave."

Myrmac led Proto out onto a balcony overlooking a throng of several thousand wildly cheering ants. He motioned for Proto to take a seat, then raised his arms dramatically, waiting patiently until the crowd fell silent. He paused for effect, his piercing eyes scanning the sea of ants. He began in a low voice, a voice which grew louder and stronger and more vibrant with each passing second, describing in grim and graphic detail the epic confrontation between the venomous, bloodthirsty Shrieking Terror of Tatuid and the stalwart and loyal Great Silver Rabbit from the distant Kingdom of Muridaan Falls. The fearsome battle had lasted for sixteen furious hours, both opponents desperately trading the most brutally violent assaults imaginable upon each other until the final heart wrenching moment came when the Great Silver Rabbit realized he had been mortally wounded, the end of his life drawing near. As he prepared himself for the final journey to the Great Beyond, the noble Silver Rabbit raised his eyes up to the heavenly blue skies above. There was a blinding flash of golden light and a gleaming silver sword descended out of nothingness into The Great Silver Rabbit's hand. In less than an instant his deathly wounds had healed. He let loose a terrible roar, his eyes blazing with a fearsome new light. With one impossibly powerful stroke of his mystical silver sword he brought to an end the savage reign of the heartless Shrieking Terror of Tatuid.

Two thousand ants thundered their approval, shrieking and stomping and crying out the name of The Great Silver Rabbit, Hero of Tatuid, Destroyer of the Shrieking Terror. Myrmac motioned for Proto to stand and lifted his arms skyward. The sea of screaming, frenetic ants erupted into wild unparalleled celebration. Myrmac leaned over to Proto with a smirk. "That's how it's done, Proto the Brave."

The celebration of the Great Silver Rabbit's miraculous victory lasted for three days. One day later the village slipped back into its normal sleepy routine.

Orville, Sophia and Proto found themselves back in the King's Palace. The King of Ants was relaxing in his large stuffed chair while Myrmac the Brave was consuming another very substantial cheese sandwich. "Mmm... excellent cheese. I do hope you all enjoyed that rather exuberant celebration. The villagers need heroes like you, Proto. The day to day life of an ant in Tatuid Village can be somewhat dreary, to say the least. Ironically, their lives will be drearier than ever now that the Shrieking Terror is dining on fruit salad rather than citizens. It is a certainty, however, that our taverns and homes will be filled with tales of The Great Silver Rabbit's magnificent exploits for many generations to come. You have given them a new model of bravery and loyalty and strength, something far more meaningful than simply ridding the village of the Shrieking Terror."

The King of Ants gave a great yawn. "If you're quite through, Myrmac, could we move along with the prophecy? Let's not drag this out any longer than necessary."

"Your wish is my command, O Great and Noble King of Ants." Myrmac gave a low sweeping bow.

"I believe I'm quite capable of recognizing sarcasm when I see it, Myrmac. The prophecy please?"

Myrmac turned to the three adventurers. "What I have not disclosed to you is my part in the prophecy, or the reason I came to be known as Myrmac the Brave."

The King of Ants rose from his chair. "I've heard this story far too many times. If you need me I shall be in the King's Tavern having lunch."

Myrmac waited until the King had left, then

motioned for them to sit. "The King's departure is quite fortuitous. There are bits and pieces of the prophecy I do not wish him to be entirely familiar with." Myrmac gave them a wink, then slumped down onto the King's stuffed chair.

"The blue stone you spoke of, the stone I sold to Ollo the Rock Mouse. There were two of them, you know. The prophecy stated that once I had the two blue stones in my possession I would sell one to a mouse wearing stars and one to a foreign trader wearing a silver moon, and that is precisely what I did."

Sophia looked at Myrmac curiously. "Ollo the Rock Mouse wears green pants with stars on them. Who was the trader?"

"I have no idea. All I know is he was a traveling dealer of precious gems and stones who was wearing a long cap with a silver crescent moon medallion dangling from the end of it. Odd name... Skizzle, Skeezle, or something like that. Where the second blue stone ended up I have no idea."

Orville rose from his chair. "The trader must have sold the second stone to a jeweler, who made a necklace out of it which eventually found its way to Miraculum's Fine Antiques. That was the necklace I bought for my mum. The marble my Papa gave me led me to the stone in Mum's necklace, which in turn led me to Ollo the Rock Mouse and his blue stone, which led us to Tatuid Village."

Sophia clapped her paws together. "It is miraculous how events have conspired to bring us all together. Wait, you haven't told us where you found the two blue stones." She turned questioningly to Myrmac.

Myrmac gave a long sigh. "I'm afraid you're not

going to be entirely thrilled with the second half of the prophecy, the part I call the fine print."

Orville suddenly felt like he was going to throw up. He knew what was coming next. His voice was barely a whisper. "We have to jump into the volcano."

Myrmac gave a grim smile. "Bingo! Give that mouse a complimentary dinner for two at the King's Tavern, drinks not included."

Sophia shook her head. "I don't understand. That's absurd. Why would we ever do something like that? What would that possibly accomplish?"

Myrmac's eyes darted around the room to make certain no one else had entered the King's quarters. "A very good question indeed, and one that leads me to the story of how I became known as Myrmac the Brave."

Orville's eyes opened wide. "You jumped into the volcano."

Myrmac nodded. "That was why I called it the fine print of the prophecy. I had to leap of my own accord into the crater of Mount Ianua and return with the two blue stones."

Orville shook his head. "That's not possible. No living creature could survive molten lava. Even the most powerful shaped sphere of defense would not protect you."

Myrmac gave a wry smile. "Well, my young friend, things in this world are often not what they appear to be."

Sophia gave a laugh. "It's not an active volcano. The lava tubes we used to reach the Shrieking Terror were ancient, and when we flew *The Dragonfly* over the crater there should have been a powerful updraft caused by the heat rising up from the lava. There was no updraft, no heat. Whatever that orange lake in the crater is, it is not molten lava."

"You, dear Sophia, are a very astute and clever mouse. It's not lava, it's a doorway to another world, a world where I found the two blue stones. A most perilous world, and one which you must enter of your own accord. I will confess to you that I did not purposefully leap into the volcano. I was most certainly not Myrmac the Brave when I climbed up to the crater's rim. Several times I worked up enough courage to almost jump, but could not complete the task. It seemed pointless to throw my life away on the word of an eccentric old ant, even if he was my own grandfather."

"What happened?"

Myrmac shrugged. "I was leaning over the rim searching for a safe way to climb down into the crater when a rock dislodged and I tumbled over the edge, falling through the orange lake into the next world. That's how I became Myrmac the Brave."

Proto said, "What did the prophecy say about this other world? What are we supposed to do there? What are we looking for?"

Myrmac gave a long sigh. "I wish I had an answer for you. The prophecy says only that the Great Silver Rabbit and his two companions will leap into the crater and never be heard from again. It does go on to say three black circles shall pass through our skies, but I am unable to explain the significance of that cryptic message, or even if it has anything to do with the three of you. All I can say is, whatever you find or do in the other world will disrupt the disastrous chain of events which is catapulting our planet toward the end of time."

The next morning found Orville and Sophia hiking

up the steep slopes of Mount Ianua toward the crater's rim.

Orville stopped to tighten his bootlace. "Myrmac is certain Proto was going to the rim?"

"He saw him heading up the trail an hour after dinner. He was definitely going to the crater and he said something to Myrmac about a promise he had made to your mum."

"He promised Mum he'd look out for us, keep us safe. He must have jumped already. I guess he wanted to make sure there weren't any terrifying creatures waiting for us on the other side. It's strange how he can be kinder and more thoughtful than a lot of mice I know."

"That's how the Elders programmed him. It's really no different from you being taught by your parents to be kind and respectful to other mice. You're taking rather a long time to tie your boot."

"I'm not trying to slow us down. It's not as scary as it was in my dream because I know it's not a real volcano. It will be kind of fun to see this other world where Myrmac found the blue stones. Maybe we'll find more of them."

"Or maybe the volcano is real and Myrmac just made up that whole story so he can get rid of us and take all the credit for saving the village from the Shrieking Terror."

Orville's eyes blinked rapidly as he processed Sophia's statement. "What? Do you think that's possible? We might be jumping into a real volcano?"

Sophia burst out laughing. "Come on, Captain Orville, we have a world to save. I'll race you to the crater!"

Chapter 16

The Other Side

Orville peered over the rim of the volcano at the rippling orange lake below. Sophia slung her pack onto the rocky ledge and flipped it open.

"What are you doing?"

"I want to take a few measurements before we jump. I'm just curious." Sophia pulled a dark green metallic sphere from her pack and tapped two colored tabs on the top. A small yellow light blinked on and the device made a low humming sound.

"What is that thing?"

"It measures gravitational waves."

"Gravity has waves? Like the ocean?"

"I want to make certain this really is a spectral door. They all have essentially the same wave signature. Watch." Sophia inched over to the edge of the rim and pointed the cube's narrow yellow beam down into the crater, tapping twice on each tab. A series of rippling concentric blue circles appeared just above the surface of the lake, the narrow circles on the outer perimeter increasing in width as they flowed inward. A pulsing white light appeared at the center of the blue rings. "It's a spectral door. It's safe for us to jump. All you really have to do is hold your paw over the crater. There's no heat rising up from the orange lake."

"Who put the doorway there?"

Sophia shook her head. "Civilizations come and go and leave remnants of their technology behind, footprints in the sand. It's possible this was used during the Anarkkian wars to transport troops or supplies to and from another world. It also could have been here before the mountain was. An expert in ancient technologies would have to examine it. Papa would have known what it was. He knew all about those things."

"I'm sorry, I didn't mean to remind you of..."

"It's okay. Are you ready?"

"I think so."

Sophia slung her pack onto her shoulder. Orville took her paw in his. "Just like in the dream, but without the crispy toasted mouse part. On three?"

"I'm ready when you are, Captain Orville."

"One, two, THREE!"

The two adventurers leaped off the rim of the volcano, plummeting down toward the burbling orange lake. Orville had the strangest feeling that time was slowing down. The closer they got to the surface of the lake the slower they seemed to be falling.

"Why are we falling so slowly? What's happening?"

"I'm not sure, I've never gone through a doorway like this one before. It might be ancient technology from long before the Anarkkians."

"We're floating toward the center, where that white light was."

"Don't let go of my paw."

"I won't. This isn't like my dream when we fell into the lava."

"Dreams can be a mix of symbolism and reality, a mix of content and form."

"We're almost there. I'm feeling kind of weird. Like I'm stretching out or something. I don't really like it."

"You're feeling the effect of the denser gravitational waves on–"

"AAGGHHH!!" Orville was careening head over heels through a bitterly cold blinding white maelstrom. "Snow! We're in snow!"

Orville rolled to a stop. "SOPHIA! SOPHIA!"

"Over here! It's so cold!"

Orville fought his way up to the surface, poking his head out of the deep snow into the frigid air. He was on a steep mountainous slope, neck deep in soft powdery snow. He flicked his wrist and blinked up two heavy winter coats, tossing one over to Sophia.

"Thanks. Are you all right?"

"This is it! The snow! When I woke up from my volcano dream my bedside table was covered with snow. Now I know why!"

"We need to get off this mountain and find Proto."

Orville looked up at the mountain peak. "Look up there!" Orville pointed to an enormous round blue disk several hundred feet up the slope. He could see the trail they left in the snow when they tumbled out of the gateway.

"The blue disk! The other side of the spectral door is blue, not orange. This is the gateway Arthur Anteater went through. This must be his home world!"

"I'm cold. Is the whole planet this cold?"

"I don't think so. An anteater couldn't survive in a frozen world. Let's go."

Sophia began pushing her way through the deep snow, inching her way forward. "This is too hard. I have a better idea." She flicked her wrist and a long wooden snow sled appeared. "We can ride this all the way down."

"I think the mountain is too steep for–"

"Hop on, nervous ninny! It'll be fun, more fun than blinking down! Pop up a sphere of defense. We'll be fine."

Orville shrieked like a little mouseling for most of their ride down the rugged mountainside. They only rolled the sled once, tumbling wildly through the powdery snow for almost a hundred feet. Sophia couldn't tell from Orville's hollering whether he was terrified or having fun, but when they reached the bottom of the snow line he had an enormous grin on his face.

Sophia studied the flat layer of dark clouds extending out across the horizon. "I don't like the look of these brown clouds. For one thing, I can't see the surface of the planet."

"Can't we just climb down through them?"

"I guess so. They could be toxic though. They don't look like normal clouds. Pop up an airtight sphere of defense while we're descending through them. You'll have to shape fresh air every ten minutes or so."

It took them an hour to descend through the forbidding cloud layer that blanketed the planet. Orville gave a cheer when they finally emerged and had a clear view of the new world. Unfortunately the new world proved to be an endless sea of shattered rubble, the ghastly remains of sprawling gargantuan cities. The land was lifeless, no trees, no plants, no birds, no movement. The words 'silent as a grave' popped into Orville's head. "What happened? What do you think happened here?"

"I think war happened here. This must be one of the planets obliterated by the Anarkkians. They destroyed dozens of worlds, maybe hundreds. I've seen pictures in books and on holodiscs, but I've never been to one. It's horror on a scale beyond imagination."

"How could they do that? All those lives."

Sophia shook her head. "I don't know. Greed and insatiable hunger for power I suppose. Let's look for Proto."

"I have a better idea." Orville raised one paw and a brilliant white light flashed up into the sky. With a thunderous boom that rolled across the landscape, mammoth glowing golden letters appeared below the layer of dark ominous clouds.

PROTO, WE'RE HERE!

Sophia grinned. "He'll have a hard time missing that. Let's head down the mountain. We'll need to be careful. I read once that–" Sophia stopped short, her eyes darting nervously over to Orville.

"You read what? What did you read?"

"Nothing, just to be careful around old ruins for... buildings that might collapse."

"That's it?"

"I told you it was nothing. Let's go. I want to see if Proto found any blue stones."

"I don't see how a decimated planet like this could

have anything to do with stopping time on our world. It doesn't make sense."

"The universe sent us here for a reason and it's our job to figure out what that reason is."

Two hours later the pair of adventurers reached the base of the mountain. The devastation set before them was staggering. "There's nothing left."

Sophia had no words.

"I guess we should look for Proto. He must know we're here by now. We'll have to be careful on these streets, they have giant cracks in them we could fall into. Scary. At least we know there's no weird creatures here."

Sophia nodded but made no reply.

"Let's head over to that dark green building that's still kind of intact. We can climb up on the roof and look for Proto."

"Good idea. We should probably blink up a sphere of defense."

"Why?"

"No reason, just to be on the safe side."

Orville gave Sophia a suspicious glance, popping up a powerful sphere of defense. "There's something you're not telling me."

"Maybe we'll find some old technology we can take back to the Metaphysical Adventurers headquarters. If it's good enough they'll pay you silvers for it. Papa used to make extra money doing that. Mostly he just liked hunting for it."

Sophia and Orville wove their way through the collapsed buildings, carefully avoiding the massive gaping crevasses formed by the monumentally destructive forces which had ravaged the planet. "Look, that low building has one section that's not destroyed. We should look inside. Maybe there's old tech. I could use a few silvers. I have to buy a birthday gift for my best friend. I overheard her telling Mum she wants an Excelsior duplonium powered bread slicer, and those aren't cheap."

Sophia whacked Orville's arm with her fist. "Your negative reinforcement seems to have worn off. Do you still want to get me a bread slicer for my birthday?"

"Owww! Wait, didn't you tell me positive reinforcement works a lot better than negative reinforcement?" Orville raised one eyebrow, giving Sophia a silly grin.

Sophia rolled her eyes. "Ewww. The only thing you're going to get is–"

The blinding vermillion force beam that exploded between the two adventurers sent Sophia flying into a towering wall of concrete and steel. Orville was thrown in the opposite direction, tumbling wildly across the web of cracks and open fissures which once had been a bustling city street. As luck would have it he bounced over a two foot wide gaping fissure, rolling through an open doorway into a crumbling building. With a painful groan he staggered to his feet and hobbled outside, calling for Sophia.

"SOPHIA! WHERE ARE YOU?"

"ORVILLE, DON'T COME DOWN HERE! ATTACK SPIDER!"

She was alive. Orville ducked down behind a huge chunk of shattered concrete, peeking around the side. He spotted a monstrous spider leg protruding from behind a wall of twisted steel. He hadn't realized how big attack spiders really were. A dark thought popped

118

into his head. "Maybe a spider got Proto."

Orville spotted a blue thought cloud floating down the street and drew it to him. "Use thought clouds. It can hear us. They're attracted to movement and sound. We can't destroy it, the only thing we can do is hide from it. I wish Proto was here."

Orville sent a return cloud. "I'm going to distract it by shooting shaped spheres behind it. Try to get down here while I keep it occupied."

"Good plan, it's about a hundred feet behind me now."

Orville raised one paw and a five inch round metal sphere shot out, arcing through the air and landing with an enormous crash fifty feet past the spider. The silver beast sprang out from behind the building and scuttled down to where the iron ball had landed. Even from this distance Orville could see the creature's glowing red eyes. He fired another heavy sphere, this one landing well past the spider and exploding with a brilliant blast of green light. The spider raced toward it, firing its powerful force beams as it ran.

Orville kept an anxious eye on Sophia, watching as she dashed between the piles of rubble, keeping as low as she could. He fired one more sphere at the spider just as Sophia appeared in a flash of light next to him. She flopped down, trying to catch her breath. "Whew! I decided to blink. It still makes me a little nervous, but under the circumstances..."

"You saved our lives. If we hadn't had our defense spheres up the force beam would have killed us both."

Sophia grinned. "Maybe it's not such a bad thing to be a nervous ninny. You were right, there was something I wasn't telling you. The Anarkkians left their autonomous creatures behind when the war ended. And sometimes there are mutated life forms roaming around."

"I don't think we'll have to worry about that on this planet. They didn't leave any life forms to mutate. Let's go."

The two best friends dashed toward the building that still had a rooftop. Orville glanced behind them every few seconds to make certain the spider wasn't following them.

"Almost there." Sophia and Orville raced around the last towering pile of rubble. As it turned out, the only obstacle standing between them and the undamaged building was the thirty foot tall gleaming Anarkkian attack spider directly in front of them, its glowing red eyes pulsating rapidly.

Sophia Mouse was a lot of things, but one thing she was not was a nervous ninny. She had faced perilous circumstances on dozens of missions and never once lost her composure. That being said, the sudden shock of seeing the silver spider in front of her was too much, even for her. For the first time in Sophia's life she could not make herself move. Orville stood frozen next to her, his mouth hanging open, unable to shout a warning, unable to blink out of the way. The gigantic spider took one step toward them, its red eyes flaring brightly as it prepared to blast them into oblivion with its intensely powerful force beams. At this distance, even Sophia's most powerful sphere of defense would prove less than adequate.

The bloodcurdling scream Sophia heard did not come from Orville, and the bloodcurdling scream Orville heard did not come from Sophia. The source of the scream was a shadowy figure who had leaped off a huge pile of rubble onto the spider's back. The eight legged silver monstrosity jerked sideways, trying to dislodge its phantom assailant, but it was too late for the spider. The nimble attacker raised one massive fist and smashed it down on a triangular yellow protrusion directly behind the spider's head. There was a shrill whining noise as the massive beast shuddered and sank to the ground, its eyes fading rapidly from brilliant red to dull black. Their mysterious savior slid down from the immobile spider and revealed himself.

"It's Proto the Brave to the rescue once again!"

Chapter 17

Wild Flowers

"How did you do it? I thought you were terrified of those attack spiders."

"You're quite correct, I was terrified of them, but now I am not. I read that most creatures fear things they don't understand, so over the last few months I've been in my room doing a great deal of research on Anarkkian attack spiders, uncovering their weaknesses and programming parameters. The yellow protrusion on their back is a sort of reset tab in the event their engineered intelligence becomes corrupted or damaged. It takes almost a full day for the creature to rebuild its intelligence and become functional."

"You're saying it's going to wake up?"

"Precisely, but I have a remedy for that." Proto stepped around to the side of the great creature and flipped open a curved panel, revealing a row of five switches. He pulled the first four and with a whirring noise a three foot long cylinder slid out from the spider's torso.

"What is that?"

Proto pointed to a glowing sphere floating inside a transparent cube. "That is a CDETS, sole source of the spider's power. I'll remove it and render him harmless."

Sophia grabbed Proto's arm. "Wait, is there any way to alter the spider's engineered intelligence so it won't harm us? If we could control it we could use it as a vehicle."

"An excellent thought, Sophia. It should only take me an hour or two, given my current research on their programming. We will be able to ride on its back while controlling it with a small electro-responder device. I will begin immediately. Once I have reprogrammed its neuronics you can shape the necessary parts to fabricate the control device."

Orville was grinning. "We get to ride on the back of an Anarkkian Attack Spider. Can you make it shoot those force beams?"

Proto nodded. "I don't see why not. It should be a simple enough procedure."

Sophia frowned. "I don't think we need to be shooting giant force beams."

Orville tried to sound mature and thoughtful. "I'm only suggesting it because it would come in handy if we had to break through piles of rubble or clear big obstacles from our path."

Sophia looked dubious. "Or if you just wanted to blow things up because you thought it would be fun."

"That sounds a little immature, but I guess we could do that if you want to. You know, blow up buildings and stuff." Orville grinned at Proto.

Sophia rolled her eyes. "Fine. I'll set up camp inside this building. We should be safe here. Why don't you scout around and see what you can find. Keep an eye out for those blue stones. And watch out for spiders."

"I won't go far. Don't worry, I'm a nervous ninny."

Orville circled around to the rear of the building, keeping his eyes open for spiders, blue stones, and old tech. The dreary sky had lightened somewhat, making the temperature almost pleasant.

"That's interesting." Orville found what appeared to be the remains of an old vehicle, but it was so badly damaged he couldn't tell how it was powered or even how it moved. As he strolled along he gazed across the devastated city. "I wonder who used to live here? What they looked like. The doorways seem pretty big, so I don't think they were mice. I wonder if–" Orville gave a sudden start, grabbing his coat pocket. The blue marble was tugging, trying to roll.

"There must be a blue stone around here!" Orville withdrew the four inch blue marble from his pocket and set it on the ground. It rolled forward, veering to the left. Orville strolled along behind the meandering marble. Twenty minutes later it was still rolling. "I should probably head back, this is a lot farther than I'd planned on going." He glanced around the sprawling mounds of debris looking for any sign of old tech. He let out a low gasp. "Creekers!"

Orville was facing what was left of an old foundation, but it was not the smashed and shattered concrete wall which had captured his attention. It was what sat in the shadows next to the broken wall. In stark contrast to the overwhelming decimation of this bleak world stood a single purple flower with soft emerald green leaves. Orville gazed at it in wonder. "Such beauty in the midst of horrific devastation." He stepped over to the bright blossom and hunched down beside it. "Hello, lovely little flower. It's quite a surprise to find you here. I can't wait to show you to my best friend

Sophia. She loves flowers, especially bright purple ones like you."

It was with a sense of reverence that Orville brushed one of the delicate green leaves with his paw. He never had a chance. With a loud hiss the flower lashed out, stabbing a long razor sharp thorn into his paw. Whatever the flower injected into him burned like nothing he had ever felt before. He staggered to his feet, grasping his paw.

"AGGHHH! IT HURTS! IT HURTS!! It... unggh... hurts... wait, it's not so bad now. I'm feeling a little better. That wasn't so bad. I'm feeling a lot better. I feel great, better than I've ever felt before. What a lovely little flower this is, it's so beautiful and of all the places to find a happy little purple planty... brave little purply flower, growing in a dark and scary world, you're my best little leafy green friend and I've known you forever. I love this world, it's so beautiful, like my best friend Sophia. She's beautiful too, I should tell her that more often. I'm part of this world now and its where I belong, I'm connected to it. Sophia and I should move here. It's my true home. The brown clouds are so warm and soft and snuggly. I'm part of the clouds, part of all things, connected to the sky, the land, the stars and galaxies, I am unending infinite love flowing across all–" Orville never finished his lovely sentence because he sank to the ground, his face wrapped in a supremely blissful smile. He was the happiest mouse in the entire universe. He closed his eyes with a great joyous sigh.

The purple flower scuttled over next to him. It reached out with one leaf, sharply poking the end of Orville's nose, checking for a response. When there was none the flower made a shrill chirping noise and dashed across the street into a nearby building.

"*Isn't this beautiful, Sophia? All those rolling hills blanketed with vibrant swaths of colorful wildflowers. And those tall trees, so majestic, so graceful.*"

"*Yes, it's a lovely dream. Very nice.*"

"*I wish there was a lake or something.*"

"*There's a lake right over there. As soon as you wished for one it appeared.*"

"*I like this dream. Look how blue the lake is. I don't know which is bluer, the sky or the lake.*"

"*They should be about the same. The blue color of a lake is simply a reflection of the sky above it.*"

"*Why do you always say things like that?*"

"*Like what?*"

"*When I point out how beautiful something is you turn it into a science fair project and explain how it all works. Why can't you just say it's beautiful?*"

"*Orville, the concept of beauty is simply an evolutionary mechanism which allows mice to–*"

"*Stop! You're doing it again! Science is interesting, but there's more to life than just science. We're here to experience this beautiful world, all the wonderful adventures we go on, all the weird creatures we meet. Remember the Gnorli bird? I liked him, he was funny.*"

"*I don't remember him.*"

"*Huh?*"

Sophia burst out laughing. "*Get it? I DON'T REMEMBER him? He had such a dreadful memory? Get it? I don't REMEMBER him?*"

"*That sounds like one of my jokes. Are you stealing my jokes again?*"

"*You're in charge of this dream, not me.*"

"*Hey, are you really Sophia? You're acting kind of*

126

weird."

"Oh, I don't know, would Sophia make a dumb joke like that?"

"You're right, she wouldn't. So you're my own made up dream version of Sophia?"

"Am I? You tell me, Master Smarty Mouse."

"I guess you are, the real Sophia wouldn't be rude like that. I'm creating a Sophia in my dream based on everything I know about her, but since it's my dream she's also like me."

"Let's go look at that lake. A big stone castle just appeared right next to it with a dock and some boats. You could go sailing if you wanted to."

"I don't really like boats. Especially when they sink in a storm."

"You're thinking about your papa. He didn't die in a storm, you know that. Master Marloh is trying to find him."

"If he's alive, why hasn't he come home? He would come home if he could, I know he would. He wouldn't stay away from me and Mum, he would come home."

"Your dream castle is amazing!"

"Whoa, it's way bigger than I thought it would be. It's huge. I'm going to look inside. Maybe it has a spooky dungeon."

"With really creepy, scary stuff in it that will make you faint."

"Now I know you're not the real Sophia. She's way nicer to me than you are."

Orville swung open the massive wooden castle doors and stepped inside. "Those big stairs probably lead down to the dungeon."

Sophia darted down the stairs. "I hope it has really

scary monsters with big gnashing fangs."

"Now you're sounding like Proto." Orville dashed after Sophia, taking the stairs two at a time. When he reached the bottom of the twisting stone staircase Sophia was nowhere to be seen. *"Sophia? Where did you go?"*

"Orville! Where are you? It's dark down here!"

"Why is it so dark? This is scary!"

"Good! I'm trying to wake you up!"

"I don't like this dream anymore. Ow! What is that? Something is biting my leg!"

"You need to wake up, Orville! You really need to wake up!"

"I still want to find the– OW!! Something bit me again!" Orville tried to swat whatever it was that was biting his leg. *"Stop! Stop biting me!"* He felt a set of little teeth sinking into his leg, then two more, then four more, then three on his arms. *"AGGGHH!! They're biting me all over!"*

"WAKE UP, ORVILLE! YOU NEED TO WAKE UP RIGHT NOW!"

Orville opened his dream eyes as wide as he could and slapped his cheeks rapidly with both paws.

When he woke up the first thing Orville noticed was the horde of purple flowers dragging him across the street toward an open doorway. For a moment he thought he was still dreaming. At least a hundred of the flowers had hooked their long curved thorns into his clothes and were pulling him over the rough concrete surface. A dozen flowers were on his legs, trying to bite him. It all came back to him in a flash. He remembered the purple flower that had injected him with its venom.

"AGGHH! Let go of me!" Orville tried to shake the

128

flowers off but he was still groggy from the venom. He managed to knock a dozen of them off with his paw before one of the flowers leaped onto his chest, stabbing him in the shoulder with its long curved thorn, injecting him with a thick green fluid. A minute later Orville was asleep, once again the happiest mouse in the universe.

The next time Orville woke up he remained absolutely motionless, just as Sophia had told him to do in his dream. He waited a full minute, then cracked his eyelids open just enough to see where he was. He was in a large dimly lit room lying on the stone floor. There was a concrete wall with a large jagged hole in it leading into the next room. Shadows were flitting across the walls, shadows from purple flowers darting about making their high pitched chirping noises.

"This is bad. This is really bad. Wait, what am I thinking?" Orville blinked up the most powerful sphere of defense he could muster and staggered to his feet. "Try to jab me now! In my world flowers don't go running around stabbing mice with poison thorns!"

It was total chaos, a thousand madly chirping purple flowers swarming the room within seconds. Scores of them leaped at Orville, only to collide with his powerful sphere of defense and tumble back to the floor. Within half a minute the bottom third of his sphere of defense was smeared with slimy dark green venom from the hundreds of flowers who had tried to inject him. The flowers backed away, but he was still encircled by them, the sound of their hideous chirping almost deafening.

Orville squinted, peering around the darkened room. "I need to find a way out of here. Sophia will be worried sick."

When Orville flicked his wrist and shaped a brilliant sphere of white light, something unexpected happened. The flowers squealed in horror and scampered out of the room. Within three seconds Orville was alone. "Whoa, I guess they don't like bright light. That's good to know." He sent a brilliant orb into the next room then stepped through the gaping hole in the concrete wall.

The first thing he noticed was the skeletons. There were five of them and they had long curved tusks and claws. "Eeew, I wonder if the flowers ate them?" Orville gulped but he didn't faint. That was the very last thing he needed to do. "Wait a minute, I've seen those skeletons before. Now where did I... I know, it was on Periculum on the giant mesa. These are Anarkkians! They must be old, from during the war."

Orville entered the next room, spotting three more skeletons. "This place is too creepy, I need to get out of here."

The sound of Orville's inner voice made him jump. "Every atom, every molecule, and every bouncing marble is exactly where it should be at every moment in time."

When he heard the word 'marble' Orville slapped his paw to his forehead and said several words his mum would most certainly not approve of.

"Oh no, I forgot to pick up the blue marble! It was still rolling when I saw the purple flower. I've lost Papa's marble." Orville sank to his knees. He had ruined everything. Their sole mission was to find the original source of the blue stone and he had lost it. He had lost the last gift his papa ever gave him. He felt sick.

"Every atom, every molecule, and every bouncing marble is exactly where it should be at every moment in time."

Orville sniffed, wiping his eyes. "Why do you keep saying that? I don't understand what it means. Are you saying the blue marble is where it's supposed to be and I am where I'm supposed to be? If every atom and every molecule is where they're supposed to be, you're saying everything is where it's supposed to be. Sophia said the universe sent us here, but it's up to us to discover the reason why. There must be something in this place I'm supposed to find."

Orville sent a half dozen brilliant white lights into the nearby rooms. "That should keep the flowers away." He moved from room to room, painstakingly searching each one for anything which might hold some significance.

When he entered the fifth room his insides turned to ice. His inner voice had spoken again. "You must descend into the darkness." Orville eyed with great trepidation the set of stone stairs against the far wall.

"I don't like the sound of that." Nevertheless, Orville the Brave stepped over to the stairway, the bright orb of light following him. He flicked his wrist and the orb floated down the stairs. Orville followed, his eyes searching for movement. He reached the bottom of the steps and jumped backwards, startled by a sudden flurry of motion. Several dozen purple flowers had dashed out of the room when Orville's orb of light appeared. The room was thirty feet square and contained hundreds of wooden racks filled with small rectangular envelopes. Everything was covered with a thick layer of dust. When he picked up one of the envelopes it disintegrated in his paw. Several dozen tiny spheres fell to the floor. Orville kneeled down and examined them. "Seeds. They look like seeds."

Orville got to his feet and surveyed the room again. "It must have been a seed store, or maybe a garden shop." He spotted another set of stairs leading downward. "Really? More stairs descending into the darkness?"

Once again he made his way down the stairs. Once again he sent his orb of light ahead of him. He heard the scurrying of a hundred purple plants running from his light. This new room was filled with an assortment of unknown mechanical devices and equipment. It reminded him of the Metaphysical Adventurers headquarters, tables and benches filled with glass beakers and spiraling glass tubes. A few of the larger machines were still operational, with small blinking lights on dust covered panels. Orville kept his distance from those machines. He spotted a wide green door at the far end of the room. He knew whatever he was looking for was behind the green door. With a sigh of resignation he approached it, slowly pushing it open. A dozen purple flowers dashed out, some of them brushing up against his sphere of defense. They held their leaves over their faces, shielding themselves from Orville's brilliant sphere of light.

When he entered through the doorway Orville saw two things. One was a glowing green stone the size of an orange, and the other was a skeleton lying on the floor wearing a uniform decorated with medals. He made his way to the curious green glowing stone. It was lying in a small crater, as though it had smashed into the floor at enormous velocity. When he looked up at

132

the ceiling his suspicions were confirmed. There was a hole where the stone had blasted down through the building. He got down on his knees to examine it. There were six small envelopes lying next to the stone, all of them torn open. He gently dusted off one of the ancient seed packets. He could just make out the image of a purple flower on the front of the envelope. He jumped away from the stone. He knew whatever the green stone was, it had been responsible for the creation of the deadly mutated purple flowers.

Next Orville examined the uniformed skeleton. This was no low level ground trooper. The creature was not Anarkkian, as it had no curved tusks or long claws, its head resembling that of a snake. Orville was getting a powerful feeling about the creature.

"I need to check the pockets. There's something in the pockets. Eww, I have to reach into a dead skeleton's pockets." He gingerly pushed his paw into the first pocket. It was empty, as was the next one. The third pocket was not. Orville pulled out a clear crystalline cube two inches in diameter. He recognized it immediately. "An information storage cube, just like the ones the glowbird records are stored on. Whatever information this contains must be important. The universe sent me a very long way to find it."

Orville turned to leave, then stopped, looking back at the uniformed skeleton. "Thanks for your help, skeleton, whoever you are. You may have saved our world without ever knowing it."

Orville made his way back up the stairs and out to the main door of the building. "Sophia is not going to believe this. I was sincerely brave when I had to face that horde of purple flowers. Some of them were big, probably two or three feet tall. Maybe even taller, it was kind of hard to see. And they were strong, not as strong as Proto, but close. I wonder where that green rock came from? I guess it's one more puzzle to write about in my journal."

Orville stepped around a massive concrete wall to find his path blocked by a mammoth Anarkkian attack spider. This was too much, first the purple flowers, then the skeletons, and now a silver attack spider was going to blast him into ten thousand little pieces. It really didn't seem fair at all.

"ORVILLE! IT'S US!"

Orville looked up to see Sophia and Proto peering down from the top of the great silver spider. He stared blankly at them. "What are you doing up there?"

"Hold on, I'll throw you a rope!"

Orville scampered up the heavy knotted rope onto the back of the Anarkkian spider. "You figured out how to control it! We can ride on it! Oh, stay away from the purple flowers. One of them stabbed me with its thorn and made me fall asleep and then a whole bunch of them dragged me into their lair. I escaped though."

"We saw them on the way here. A swarm of them tried to bite Proto's leg. They didn't bother us after that."

Orville described a somewhat embellished tale of his imprisonment by the fearsome purple flowers, how he had misplaced the blue marble, found the glowing green stone, discovered the crystalline storage cube inside the pocket of a creepy dead skeleton who may have tried to grab his throat with its long bony fingers, and finally his daring escape from the horde of ferocious flowery mutants.

Sophia looked a little skeptical during the part about the skeleton grabbing Orville's throat, but Proto was intrigued by the storage cube and quickly identified the skeleton. "Your description clearly indicates a Mintarian officer. They fought bravely against the Anarkkians during the war. The Mintarians must have been present on Varmoran during the Anarkkian invasion."

"Do you think you can read the contents of the storage cube? Remember how you projected moving images through the glowbird's eyes so we could watch them? Wait, how did you know where to find me?"

Sophia held up a pair of brass goggles with fluorescent green lenses. "By the time we realized how long you'd been gone, Proto had the spider running and I dug out these tracking goggles. It wasn't hard to follow your residual electronic signature, especially from up on the spider."

"Too bad we can't take the spider back to Muridaan Falls." Orville was imagining a jubilant crowd of wildly cheering mice as he rode triumphantly into town on the back of a great gleaming silver spider after saving the world once again.

"Not one of your best ideas. The villagers had a hard enough time getting used to Proto. I don't think they're ready to have a monster spider strolling through town. Let's head back to camp and figure out what to do about the blue marble. Proto can examine the storage cube and maybe project it for us. Oh, I shaped these comfy chairs for us to ride in."

Orville grinned, flopping down into a green stuffed chair bolted securely to the spider's back. In less than two minutes he was sound asleep.

Chapter 18

The Good Captain

"Could you read the storage cube?"

"It required quite some effort to unravel the cube's encryption code and devise the proper conversion parameters, but I was able to view the data and will project it through my optical system."

"What's on it?"

"It is an audioptical record of the last days of the Mintarian captain whose skeleton you found."

"Is it scary? I don't want to watch if it shows something bad happening to him."

"He was wearing a microptic input camera. You will see everything he was seeing, but you will not see precisely how he met his untimely end."

"That's okay, I guess."

Sophia picked up the cube, turning it over slowly. "Was there any mention of stopping time?"

Proto paused. "Possibly. It would be best if you both watched it. It provides several clues to a specific location we should investigate."

Sophia and Orville flopped down onto the floor

facing a large blank wall. Proto sat between them, flipping open a small panel on his chest and tapping a series of glowing green tabs. "Beginning the projection now."

Bright beams of flickering light shot out from Proto's eyes onto the wall, displaying colorful moving images of a large interstellar vessel's bridge. A voice boomed out.

"Attention Anarkkian attack vessel, we are not a military vessel. We are the *MV Bermitar*, a Mintarian supply vessel bringing medical aid to Varmoran. Our ship carries no weapons, we are an unarmed private supply vessel bringing medical aid to the wounded."

"They're not responding. Closing in. Fifteen miles."

"They're coming after us. They destroy planets, they won't hesitate to destroy a lone supply ship."

"Orders? Their heavy beam pulsars have gone online. Our shields are still down."

"What about the *MV Montrosian*? Any word?"

"She's six miles due west of–"

Orville gave a start as the image of the ship shook violently.

"Captain, the *Montrosian* has been hit! Their antimatter field fence ruptured! Half the ship vanished and they went down."

"That's it. Give the order to abandon ship. Abacus, ready escape pods for export, two minutes. Green board alert! Open Nine Six Zero One Spectral Entry and send us through. Anarkkian ships are closing fast."

Orville realized he was clutching his paws together so tightly they ached.

The captain dashed to the far side of the bridge and slapped a large violet disk. A wide panel slid down revealing a dark green bulky metallic suit. He thrust his arms into two cylindrical openings and the suit whirred loudly, wrapping itself around him. The screen image went dark, then blinked on again. The captain was walking back to the central bridge console, his massive suit of space armor whining loudly with each step.

He turned toward a shadowy form in a high backed metallic chair. "Abacus, did you open the Spectral Entry?"

"Affirmative, Captain. Spectral Entry Nine Six Zero One activated."

"Excellent, do your best to–"

"Captain, Anarkkians within range. Dimensional escape pods launched. They'll be on us in ten seconds."

"Send us through to–"

There was a thunderous blast of blinding white light and a huge section of the bridge vanished. The projection was spinning wildly, flashing between black sky and the surface of Varmoran.

Sophia put her paw over her mouth. "Oh no, the Anarkkians hit their ship! The captain is falling!"

Orville heard the sound of a small explosion and the image on the screen twisted wildly, then righted itself. "Battle Suit Emergency Canopy activated. Your current distance to surface of Varmoran is fourteen miles."

Orville heard the captain groan. He was still alive.

"Captain to *MV Bermitar*. Is anyone there? Captain to *MV Bermitar*! Do you read me?"

There was no reply.

The captain twisted and turned, looking back, trying to get a glimpse of his ship. "They got through. Good old Abacus."

Orville pointed to the huge roiling gray cloud

rimmed with lightning flashes. "A spectral door! The *MV Bermitar* must have gone through it! I think they got away."

The captain grunted and turned his gaze to Varmoran's dark and forbidding surface. Five minutes later Orville was able to make out sprawling cities miles below.

"Proto, look! The cities haven't been destroyed yet. That must have happened later."

"Not much later, I'm afraid. I believe we are witnessing a full scale attack on Varmoran by a Class 1 Anarkkian Armada. It was common practice for several dozen of their battle cruisers to arrive simultaneously, obliterating an entire planet within a day or two."

"Look! He's landing!" Sophia watched the surface of Varmoran rushing up toward them. There was a loud roaring noise and the captain's descent slowed drastically. A moment later he was standing on the ground.

"Captain to *MV Montrosian*, anyone there?"

Again there was no response. The captain slid open a panel on his arm and tapped a gold tab. His suit whirred loudly, releasing him from its protective grasp. The captain stepped out of the bulky armor and scanned his surroundings, noting several pieces of twisted metal lying on the ground. He pulled a small gray sphere off his belt and twisted the top half. A light whirled around the device, then stopped. "Southwest it is."

Orville pointed, watching the captain stride across the barren rocky landscape. "I see more pieces of wreckage. I think he might be looking for the other ship, the *Montrosian*. Maybe he's looking for survivors."

The captain followed the narrow trail of debris for another fifteen minutes, then stopped in his tracks.

"Oh, no." He kneeled down and picked up a small object. With a long sigh he placed it back on the ground. "I'm sorry, old friend. I'm truly sorry." He stood up and gazed around the area. "There's nothing more I can do." He turned, heading toward a distant cityscape.

"Proto, go back! I want to see what he picked up."

Proto replayed the segment of the record showing the captain kneeling down and examining an object.

"Enlarge the image so we can see it."

"One moment." Proto turned a small a dial on his chest panel, magnifying the image that appeared on the wall.

"Just what I thought! It's one of those blue stones! That's where they came from!"

"What are they? Part of the *MV Montrosian*?"

"I don't think so. He called it his old friend. That's something he would call his own ship. The *MV Bermitar* must have gone down."

"It still doesn't tell us what the blue stones are. Keep playing the record."

The adventurers watched as the captain trekked across the rocky terrain toward the distant city. There was a sudden break in the record, the screen showing only flashes of light and blackness. When the images reappeared Orville's eyes opened wide. "The city has been destroyed! Look at the flames!"

The captain was dashing past piles of smoking rubble. There were bodies everywhere, but their form was unfamiliar to Orville and Sophia. "They're lizards. They have red scales and yellow eyes. They look a little

140

scary but not too bad. Why would the Anarkkians do this?"

The captain made his way through the burning debris, finally slumping down and leaning back against a shattered concrete wall. He glanced over and saw something which sent an icy chill through Orville. A small purple flower was growing only a few feet from the captain. He reached over with one paw to touch it. The flower lashed out, its vicious thorn stabbing through his glove. Moments later he slumped over. Orville watched as hundreds of the purple flowers scurried out from a nearby building, running and leaping toward the captain. The image went black.

"The plants got him." Orville felt sick.

Proto stood up. "We must locate the crash site of the good captain's ship and search for more of the blue stones. If you will note, when he stands up and surveys the area, we see a huge naturally formed stone arch only a few hundred feet away. That will make an excellent landmark. If we find that, we have found the site."

Orville jumped up. "I'm going to climb to the top of this building and see if I can spot the arch."

"I might be able to determine its location by overlaying the images recorded during the captain's fall from the sky. This will take several minutes. It's a rather complex process involving various IPS mapping resources." Proto's eyes blinked shut.

"What's he doing?"

"He's overlaying existing IPS maps of Varmoran onto the view of the planet's surface shown during the captain's descent."

Proto's eyes popped open a minute later. "I have

determined the coordinates of the stone arch. It is called the Great Arch and is a known landmark on Varmoran, as indicated on the IPS maps. I have also calculated our present coordinates. We will need to travel directly south southwest for precisely seventy-nine miles. If we take the spider we should arrive in approximately five hours, barring unforeseen circumstances."

Sophia had a grim expression. "I had the dream again last night. The one about time stopping. It was even scarier this time. It was hard for me to move, as though my own body was slowing down. In the dream I knew there was only one way to prevent time from stopping."

"What was it?"

"I don't know. I can't remember, and I don't know who or what was trying to stop time. The only thing I know is we have to hurry."

Chapter 19

Three Percent

"All our adventures should be like this." Orville was perched comfortably on the back of the great silver spider, reclining in his stuffed green chair with a plate of tasty cakes balanced on one leg. He flicked his wrist and a tall glass of lemonade appeared. "Mmm, nothing goes better with Proto's tasty little cakes than fresh lemonade."

Sophia laughed. "I wish I had a camera so I could have a picture of this for the next Metaphysical Adventurers meeting. You'd probably get a gold medal for the most relaxing adventure of the year."

Orville gave Sophia an indignant glare. "You seem to have forgotten how I bravely faced a savage horde of malicious mutant purple flowers trying to turn me into their bedtime snack. That was not exactly relaxing. I should get three gold medals for that alone."

"Don't get in a dither, Captain Orville. Enjoy your tasty cakes." Sophia scanned the horizon for any sign of the Great Arch. They had left the city far behind and were crossing a broad rocky plain.

"It looks as though there could have been a forest here at one time. The only sign of it now are those petrified stumps, if that's what they are. I don't know how the Anarkkians did it, but they destroyed everything."

Proto nodded as he deftly guided the spider through a maze of irregular shaped boulders strewn across the plains. "I believe they used cloud bombs, devices which eliminate all life forms over a vast area. I have read it takes over a thousand years for vegetation to return after a cloud bomb attack."

"That's dreadful."

Orville was reaching for a tasty cake when the spider veered sharply, the plate of treats toppling off his leg. "Proto, what are you doing? You knocked over my plate of tasty cakes!"

Proto's fingers were a blur on the controller. "I'm dreadfully sorry, and I don't wish to alarm anyone, but I seem to have lost control of the spider. It is currently under the guidance of an unknown entity."

The spider leaped forward, hurling Sophia back into her chair. "We're going too fast! Slow us down!" The monstrous spider was racing across the rocky plains, its silver legs flashing wildly in the low afternoon light.

"I'm afraid I have lost all control of both our speed and direction!"

Orville hollered, "Let's blink off this thing before it kills us!"

Sophia held up her paw. "No! Stay where you are, my inner voice told us we must make no attempt to alter the course of events."

"That doesn't make sense! Suppose the spider runs into a wall at fifty miles an hour?"

144

"Orville, it was my inner voice. It's never wrong."

Orville glanced behind them and gave a loud yelp. "Spiders behind us!"

Sophia turned, spotting five mammoth attack spiders a hundred yards behind them. "Keep low! Are they chasing us?"

"More of them on the right! They're passing us!" Seven of the gigantic silver automatons were thundering across the plains only a hundred feet to the right of them.

Proto cried out, "On the left, more spiders! They're forming a gigantic herd similar to wild Nirriimian nadwokks."

"Where are we going?" Orville was gripping the side of the chair so hard his paws ached. "Hold on!" With a flick of his wrist he shaped a set of heavy canvas safety harnesses securing him and Sophia to their seats.

"Thanks! Proto, how fast is the spider moving?"

"Sixty-six miles an hour, an astonishing rate of speed for a biomechanical arachnid."

"We're right in the center of the stampede! There must be a hundred spiders. Look at them all! I've never seen anything like this."

"None of them are even looking at us. No force beams to worry about."

Proto nodded. "They are no longer autonomous. A deeper system is controlling their actions, directing them all to an unknown location."

The massive herd of gleaming attack spiders continued their frenetic race across the barren terrain for almost an hour. Finally the pace diminished.

"We're slowing down. Look up ahead, a big bunch of spiders are lying down."

"There's a big golden sphere behind them. It could be a scout ship."

The herd reduced its pace to a brisk trot, then to an easy walk. The entire group moved in unison, forming a gigantic grid, twelve spiders across and twelve deep. As the spiders sank to the ground, their glowing red eyes dimmed to a dull black sheen.

"What is this place, Proto?"

"It appears to be their home base. Perhaps it is a maintenance facility, similar to the Cube where the glowbirds go. More than likely they return here to be repaired, although it is highly unlikely there would be any Anarkkians left to service them."

"Shhh!" Sophia ducked down and pointed toward the large golden sphere. A panel had slid open and a creature was emerging.

"What is that thing?"

Proto flipped on his sensors and scanned the unknown entity. "It is a biomechanical biped possessing engineered intelligence."

"It's walking like a hundred year old mouse, like it needs a cane. It looks old and tired."

Sophia studied the robotic creature as it approached the grid of spiders. The creature was nearly as tall as Proto but very thin, its arms and legs formed from silver tubing no more than two or three inches in diameter. Its face was a tall golden oval with two fluorescent green eyes.

"It's talking to one of the spiders." The gangly creature had hobbled over to one of the silver arachnids and was resting its hand on the creature's side.

Sophia unlatched her safety harness. "I'm going to talk to it." Without waiting for a reply she slid down the side of the spider and headed toward the elderly silver automaton. Orville and Proto hopped down from the spider and followed her.

When the creature saw Sophia it gazed at her without expression. Sophia approached the gaunt figure slowly, not wishing to startle it. When she was six feet away the creature said, "You are here to take us home?" It pointed its long arm skyward.

"You are trying to get home?"

"I am three percent. Many of the spiders are gone and I am unable to revive them."

"Who are you?"

"I am the last mechanic. The others are gone, zero percent, all of them."

"You are three percent? What does that mean?"

"My power level is three percent. My time is almost over. I must take the spiders home before I am zero percent."

"You take care of the spiders? You repair them?"

"I am the last mechanic. The others are gone. All zero percent."

Orville stepped closer to the mechanic. "Where is your home?"

"It is up there. When I awoke I was here. I was a mechanic at one hundred percent. It is my duty to maintain the spiders, to keep them at one hundred percent, but I have failed. Forty-two are at zero percent. Many are less than ten percent. I will be gone and there will be no mechanic to watch over them."

Sophia felt a terrible sadness creep through her. "You did the best you could. That is all anyone can do."

"You will not take us home?"

"I don't know how to take you home."

The mechanic pointed to the gold spherical building. "I will show you." The mechanic limped painfully toward the structure.

"What happened to your leg?"

"I am three percent."

The mechanic stepped into the sphere. "There. I touch the tabs in the correct order but the light does not shine. They will not take us home if the light does not shine."

Proto stepped over to the large curved control panel, studying it closely. He tapped several tabs. "No power. When is the last time these lights were on?"

The mechanic closed its eyes, deep in thought. "I was fifty-nine percent when the lights stopped. It was long ago. The spiders were all over fifty percent."

Proto squatted down, peering beneath the panel. "There must be a power source somewhere. Do you know where it is?"

"I used to know. I have forgotten."

Sophia put her paw on the mechanic's arm. "We'll find it, don't worry." Sophia closed her eyes and held both paws out in front of her.

Proto whispered to Orville, "What is she doing?"

"She's letting her inner self guide her. She's asking where the power source is and feeling the subtle pull of her inner self. It's a little like the blue marble when it was drawn to my mum's necklace."

Sophia turned and stepped purposefully through the doorway. She paused for a moment, then turned again, heading toward a massive boulder. She circled around it, winding her way through the maze of jagged rocks.

"Where is she going? Shouldn't the power source be inside the building?"

148

Ten minutes later Sophia stopped at the edge of a deep gully and opened her eyes. "It's down there."

Orville looked doubtful but clambered down, scanning the chasm. "You're right! There's a six foot blue cube here with big cables that go straight into the gully wall. They must carry power to the mechanic's sphere."

Proto hopped down and eyed the gleaming cube. "This was built by the Anarkkians. I have seen similar cubes many times on the glowbird records. There should be a grid on the side panel." Proto looked up at the mechanic, who was standing on the ledge next to Sophia. "Was there a number? You said you pressed the tabs in a particular order."

The mechanic nodded. "I will show you, but you must help me down. I am three percent."

Proto gingerly lifted the mechanic down into the gully. He hobbled across the broken rocks to the cube. "I remember this. This is where the power came from. There was a number... let me think." He tapped the grid on the side of the cube then paused and tapped again. After the eighth tap a large panel on the front of the cube whirred open.

"That is where the power came from. It is dark now. Zero percent."

Proto looked inside the cube. "The CDETS portal has collapsed."

The mechanic nodded. "Yes, the Cross Dimensional Energy Transfer Sphere. I remember now, I asked many times for replacements but they never sent us any."

A look of dismay was on Sophia's face. "I don't know how to shape a CDETS. I don't even know how the portal dilator is controlled."

"I can help you with that." A flickering holo image appeared in front of Proto. He flipped the image, spinning it rapidly until a complex diagram appeared. "That's the schematic of a CDETS. They are essentially a small portal to the tenth dimension, a dimension of pure energy. The CDETS transfers the energy from the tenth dimension into this world. As long as the portal dilator is open they provide a virtually infinite supply of energy. They are by no means infallible, however, and are prone to collapse like this one."

Sophia studied the diagram. "Hmm... this looks a lot like the power sources I studied in my science classes on Quintari. I think I can do this." Sophia paused, then simultaneously flicked both her wrists. A brilliant golden light appeared, floating several feet above the ground. Orville had to shade his eyes. Sophia waved her paws again and the ball of light began to shrink, it's brightness diminishing. There was a sudden blast of green light and a six inch silver glowing sphere appeared on the ground. "Try that."

Proto picked up the CDETS and approached the cube. He removed the old CDETS from inside a translucent orange cylinder, then held the new CDETS over the heavy glass tube and dropped it in. It glowed brightly, floating in the center of the cylinder.

The mechanic nodded rapidly. "Yes, that's it. That's what it should look like. I must go now, I must initiate the light sequence."

Proto lifted the mechanic out of the gully.

"I must go. I must touch the tabs in the proper order."

The three adventurers followed the mechanic as he lurched back toward the golden sphere.

The mechanic stumbled through the doorway. "The lights are on, as they should be." He took a seat in front of the curved panel, his long silver fingers pushing the rows of glowing green tabs. When he was done an overhead violet light began flashing.

Orville's ears perked up. "Do you hear that? That humming?"

The mechanic staggered to his feet, his hands shaking. "They are here. They are here to take us home." He hurried outside, the three adventurers behind him.

Orville looked up and nearly fell over. Half the sky was covered by an impossibly large golden disc. Sophia's jaw dropped. "It must be a mile across!"

Proto studied the great gleaming leviathan. "I believe it has been there all along, concealed by a cloaking device. When the mechanic entered the correct code it disabled the cloak and reactivated the ship."

Orville gave a yelp and jumped back. A brilliant beam of light had shot down from the golden disc, hitting one of the spiders. The spider blurred, traveling up the beam of light into the craft. Orville watched in astonishment as dozens of light beams flashed downward, carrying the spiders up to the great golden vessel.

The mechanic took Sophia's paw in his slender metallic hand. "My creators sent you to bring me home. I knew it the moment I saw you." He stepped away from the adventurers, taking his place next to the last spider. He waved to Proto and Orville. "Soon we will all be one hundred percent. Soon I shall be home."

With two blasts of light the spider and the mechanic were gone, raised up into the ship.

The adventurers' eyes were locked on the monolithic golden disc, waiting to see what it would do. There was no great blast of fire, no blinding light, no roaring pounding monstrous engines, no astonishing pulsating energy fields. The ship and its cargo simply vanished. It was there, and then it was not there.

Sophia made a small choking noise. "He reminded me of my gramps."

"Soon we will all be one hundred percent." The mechanic's words were echoing in Orville's ears and there was a lump in his throat. "We need to go back inside. There's something here. I don't know what it is, but it's important."

The adventurers stepped back into the last mechanic's sphere, scouring the interior for almost an hour. They found nothing of any significance. "We can't give up. It's here. I know it is."

It was Sophia who found it underneath the curved console, lodged near the wall in a dark corner beneath a small metal beam. She plucked it out with a triumphant grin, hiding it in her paw. "Orville, do you think this might be why we're here?"

Orville looked down at Sophia's paw. When she opened it his heart lurched. It was a sparkling translucent blue marble identical to the one his papa had given him.

"Creekers!"

Chapter 20

The Wreck

"Proto, do you know where we are? We were heading southwest, but I think the herd of spiders turned west and they were moving over sixty miles an hour."

"The spider stampede was not traveling in a straight line, but made a long slow curve carrying us fifty miles closer to the crash site of the *MV Montrosian*."

"So we just keep our eyes open for the Great Arch?"

Proto nodded. "When we find that we will have found the crash site. We must continue traveling to the southwest." Proto strode off toward the distant ruins of a small city.

Orville look down at the cracks in the ancient road, jumping over a narrow crevasse. "It was a lot easier when we were riding on the spider. They could just step over all these gaps and fissures. I'd hate to fall into one of these."

It was Proto who spotted the distant glint of sunlight reflecting off metal when the afternoon sun made a rare appearance through the gloomy brown clouds. He held up his hand for them to stop.

"The sun is reflecting off something a mile to the west of us." Proto switched his optical sensors to full spectrum and scanned the distance object. "It appears to be the wreckage of a large vessel. Perhaps I miscalculated the location of the crash site and this is where the *MV Montrosian* went down. We must verify the identity of the ship."

Sophia looked puzzled. "We saw the captain walking near the arch, and that's where he picked up the blue stone. There's no Great Arch here."

"Perhaps it is currently hidden from view. It may become visible once we reach the wreck."

It took less than an hour for the three adventurers to reach the crash site. Orville stared at the twisted jumble of debris. "There couldn't have been any survivors. Even the outer hull is destroyed."

"It fell fifteen miles or more, if this is the *MV Montrosian*. Let's try over there. That section is still intact." Proto turned toward a massive oval shaped portion of the ship standing over a hundred feet tall. "The internal framework of that section must have been fabricated from solid Morsennium. Nothing else would hold up to such an impact."

Orville spotted a wide gash in the side of the ship and scrambled through it into the wreckage, Sophia and Proto trailing behind him. "Creekers, these ships were enormous."

Proto studied the ship's interior. "I believe we are on the bridge. Look at the chairs and the large control panels. The bridge is the most heavily reinforced section of the ship, which would explain why it was relatively undamaged. If the bridge is destroyed the ship is lost."

Sophia stepped over to the main console. "The wreckage is certainly old enough to be the *MV Montrosian*. There's a thick layer of dirt and dust on everything." She flicked her wrist and a large brush blinked into her paw. "This should help."

Sophia brushed away the debris from the main console, stopping when she reached the center of the massive curved panel.

"Here's our answer. Look at this." Orville and Proto hurried over.

Sophia pointed to a gleaming gold plaque.

"The *MV Montrosian*. You were right, Proto."

Sophia frowned. "Now I'm really confused. If this is the *MV Montrosian* then what was the wreckage the captain of the *MV Bermitar* was looking at? We saw him looking back at the spectral door when he was falling, and he seemed certain his ship had made it safely through. If the wreckage wasn't from the *Bermitar* or the *Montrosian*, what was he looking at and what were the blue stones from?"

Proto thought for a moment. "We know the bridge of the *MV Bermitar* was hit. It is possible the captain was looking at wreckage from the bridge of the *MV Bermitar* but not the entire ship. There is only one way to find out. We must locate the Great Arch and visit the crash site."

Orville had wandered off to the other side of the bridge and was peering into a row of storage compartments, their metal doors twisted and mangled from the crash.

"Look at all this stuff. Here's one of those big battle suits the captain used to escape from the ship. Proto, what are these things? There's six of them." Orville dragged out a surprisingly light four foot long black cylinder with a small circle of round silver tabs on one end.

Proto's eyes lit up. "You have found something which may save us a great deal of time and effort, if they are still functional." Proto grabbed two of the cylinders and carried them toward the gash in the side of the ship. "We'll need one more."

Orville and Sophia carried the third cylinder outside and lay it down next to the other two. "What are they?"

Proto grinned. "They were a creation of the Elders, but found their way to many different worlds and were in use for centuries. They were very popular and most commonly referred to as floaters."

"What do they do? Are they some kind of boat or something?"

Proto motioned for Sophia and Orville to step away from the black cylinders. He picked one up and flipped it over. "They're powered by MicroCDETS so there's a good chance they're still functional." He tapped a round button and a violet light blinked on. "We have power." He pressed the three remaining tabs simultaneously and stepped back. There was a soft whirring noise and the cylinder began decreasing in height while simultaneously increasing in width. Moments later it had spread out to form a perfect five foot wide circular disk. There was an odd crackling noise and the black disk hardened.

"What's it doing?"

Proto planted one foot on a six inch wide gold circle in the center of the floater and a silver shaft whirred up from inside the disk. A pair of cylindrical black handgrips flipped open at the top of the shaft.

Orville tilted his head, still baffled. "What is it?"

Proto placed one hand on each grip. "Their nickname rather succinctly describes their function. They're called floaters because they float." He twisted the left grip and with a low hum the black disk rose three feet above the ground. He twisted the right grip and the floater darted forward.

Sophia gave a shriek. "Now *that* looks like fun! Hey, Orville, I think a floater race is just what we need to decide who's the big purple monkey butt and who isn't, although I already know the answer to that question."

Five minutes later the three adventurers were streaking along across the rocky terrain at over thirty miles an hour.

"Whoo hoo!" Sophia twisted the left grip of her floater and shot past Orville, soaring forty feet up into the air.

"Don't go so high! It's too dangerous!"

"Sorry, grandmum, did I scare you? Am I going too fast? Maybe you should stop and have a nice warm cup of tea, grandmum Orville!"

"You're the grandmum, not me!" Orville twisted the left grip forward and blasted ahead at over fifty miles an hour. Even at that speed the floater felt as stable as solid ground. He leaned to the left and twisted the right grip, streaking up into the air next to Sophia, who shrieked with laughter.

"Nice try, but no one outflies the nefarious Captain Sophia!" She leaned sharply to the right and twisted the left grip back, flashing down toward the ground, streaking across the landscape.

"And no one escapes the dread pirate Orville!" Ten

seconds later Orville was racing alongside Sophia at seventy miles an hour. "Why so slow, big purple monkey–" Orville never finished his sentence. He had caught sight of something shimmering in the distance. "Look!"

Sophia saw it immediately and slowed her floater down until it was hovering silently. "The Great Arch!" She looked behind her and spotted Proto approaching rapidly.

Proto pointed to the arch and waved them forward. "That's it, that's where the captain of the *MV Bermitar* landed." The three floaters raced off toward the tall rocky landmark.

Orville was scooting along at thirty miles an hour, the wind whistling in his ears when he heard the noise. It was a barely audible clinking sound, like two small glasses bumping together. "Do you hear that?"

"Hear what?"

"That clinking sound?" Orville eyed his floater for any malfunction, then the other two, but they all seemed to be working perfectly.

Sophia glanced behind them and gave a shout. "Look what's following you!"

Orville turned. "Creekers!" There was an eight inch sparkling blue translucent sphere racing along the ground behind him. "It's the blue marble Papa gave me! Look how big it is!"

"It must have found more blue stones and now it's heading toward the crash site!"

"Follow it! It will lead us to the stones."

The three floaters let the blue marble pass them, then matched its speed.

Orville was wearing a huge grin. "I found Papa's

marble!"

"Or maybe the marble found you."

Chapter 21

Some Reassembly Required

The blue marble raced across the rocky plains, leaping over rocks and veering wildly around the larger obstacles. Orville was stunned by the marble's new behavior. "It's jumping over things! How is that possible?"

"Your papa's marble is a far more complex object than I had originally thought. It's possible it contains a primitive form of engineered intelligence. I wish I knew precisely where your papa had found it."

The marble continued on toward the arch, its speed increasing. "It's going faster! We must be getting closer to the blue stones." The floaters were skimming across the rocky terrain at forty miles an hour now, the blue marble leaping over any obstacle in its path.

"It's turning!" The marble veered sharply to the right. The three adventurers kept pace with it for another five minutes until Orville cried out, "Wreckage ahead! This must be the captain's landing site!"

"The marble is slowing down!"

Orville reduced the speed of his floater, traveling alongside the blue marble. The glass sphere veered sharply to the left, darting behind a twisted pile of metallic debris. Orville zipped up over the gleaming wreckage. "It found a blue stone!"

Sophia and Proto flashed up behind Orville, watching as a blue stone the size of an orange liquefied and was absorbed into the sparkling marble. The marble darted off, larger than before. The three adventurers trailed behind it, watching it leap over a two foot tall rock, bounding across the rocky terrain. "More blue stones! Look at them all!"

The marble skidded to a halt in the middle of an open area strewn with several dozen of the translucent stones. The thin white lines inside the marble glowed brightly. All the blue stones liquefied simultaneously, streaming across the rocky surface into the glowing marble.

Orville gaped at the size of the glass sphere. "Look how big it's getting! It's at least a foot across now."

Sophia called out, "You two keep an eye on the marble. I'm going to look for the captain's landing spot and try to identify this wreckage. It has to be from something. There's not enough for an entire ship, so Proto might be right, it could be the bridge of the *MV Bermitar*."

She shot across the rock strewn landscape, quickly reaching the base of the arch. "Amazing!" Sophia twisted the left handgrip and shot four hundred feet straight up to the top of the massive curved formation. "This is perfect, the top is flat enough and wide enough for me to land." She set the floater down on the arch, making certain it was stable.

"This should do nicely." Sophia slung off her pack and rummaged through it, pulling out her Mintarian tracking goggles and the flying goggles given to her by Mirus Mouse. She strapped the tracking goggles on and gazed across the debris field. Three bright orange lights showed up. "That must be Orville, Proto, and the marble. Curious that the marble would leave a residual energy trail similar to Proto's."

As she scanned the area below the arch she noticed dozens of dim orange lights. "What in the world are those?" Even when she used her magnified flight goggles she couldn't make out the nature of the small orange lights. "Only one way to find out. There's a group of them next to that big flat boulder. I'll fly down."

Sophia rode the floater down to the area containing the dim orange lights. She slowed to a hover and studied the ground. "Blue stones. That makes sense, the big blue marble is absorbing them so they must be made of the same–" Sophia froze, a sudden brilliant insight popping into her mind.

"It's reassembling! Whatever this thing is, it was in the ship the Anarkkians blasted with a heavy beam pulsar weapon and was shattered into a thousand pieces. Now it's rolling around and gathering up all the pieces, reassembling into its original form. But what in the world is it?"

Sophia was about to lift off when Orville's mysterious blue marble bounded over a rock and landed in the center of the blue stones. Orville and Proto appeared seconds later, hovering thirty feet in the air.

Sophia cried out, "I know what's happening!" She

soared up next to Orville and Proto. "The blue marble was shattered by the Anarkkians, and now it's running around and collecting all the pieces!"

Proto said, "It's reassembling itself! Why didn't I think of that? Brilliant!"

Orville looked dubious. "How is that possible? How would it know to do that?"

Proto replied, "I completely misjudged the nature of its engineered intelligence. It does not have primitive engineered intelligence, it has extremely advanced EI, more advanced than anything I've ever seen. This is most astonishing. I believe the marble your papa gave you contained the neuronic core of the creature's programming. More succinctly, the marble was the creature's brain. It must have had consciousness but no means to communicate. It did have the ability to roll, and when it sensed the presence of the shattered pieces of its former body it rolled toward them and reabsorbed them. It is capable of self-healing, of restoring itself to its original form."

"That doesn't seem possible."

Sophia gave a sigh. "Of course it's possible. What happens when you accidentally cut your paw? Your body heals itself. It stops the bleeding and repairs the damage. Why couldn't this creature do the same thing?"

"I guess that kind of makes sense. It's just that it was blasted into a million pieces."

"It's brain wasn't damaged though. That's the part that's doing the healing."

"Look! The blue stones are turning to liquid!"

The three adventurers watched a dozen shattered blue fragments liquefy and flow across the ground, quickly being absorbed by the blue marble.

"It's getting bigger!" Orville was about to guess the current size of the marble when he stopped, his eyes focused on the bottom half of the blue marble. "What is that? What's it doing?" The marble's shape was changing, two protrusions emerging from the lower hemisphere.

Sophia's eyebrows jumped up. "Are those legs? Is it growing legs?"

The blue marble was now perched atop what appeared to be spindly legs. As it balanced precariously on the new appendages, a foot formed at the end of each leg. The creature performed a curious hopping dance, as though testing its balance and the strength of its new legs. Before Sophia had time to fully understand the creature's behavior it took off running, disappearing behind a large boulder.

Orville gaped at Sophia. "Did you see that? It's running! It has legs and feet!"

"We have to follow it! This is what we were sent here to find! I'm certain it's turning into something that will help us prevent time from stopping! Hurry, we can't lose it!" Sophia twisted the left grip on her floater and shot fifty feet into the air. She spotted the blue creature darting between rocks, heading away from the arch. "He's traveling east!"

Orville and Proto flashed up next to her. "Use your tracking goggles. He must be after more blue fragments."

"Good idea." Sophia slipped on her Mintarian goggles and scanned the landscape. "Found it! About a half mile to the east there's a broad field of orange light. There must be a thousand blue stones, maybe more. Let's go!" Sophia's floater shot forward, Orville and Proto following in her wake.

Chapter 22

Abacus

"There it is!" Orville pointed to a massive sloping plain ahead of them. "He's on the right side of that big round rock."

Sophia leaned sharply to the right and sent her floater behind the massive boulder, out of the creature's line of sight. Orville and Proto darted up next to her, all three floaters now hovering silently. "I don't want to scare it. I think it's almost finished reassembling and it might be able to escape from us once it's reassembled."

Orville nodded, inching his floater around the boulder until he spotted the creature. His voice was hushed and low. "I can see it. You were right, there are hundreds and hundreds of blue shards. The stones are glowing when he gets close to them, then turn to liquid and he absorbs them. Umm... I think it might be growing arms."

"What?"

"Growing arms, I think it's growing arms. And a head."

Sophia eased her floater up until she could see over

the rock. Orville was right, the creature now had two new protuberances which bore a resemblance to arms. It's once spherical torso had extended vertically, a bulbous addition forming above a narrow neck. "It's absorbed all the shards! I think it's close to–." Sophia gave a loud yelp. The creature had emitted a blindingly brilliant flash of light. "It's gone! The creature is gone!"

"We have to find it!" Orville flashed around the boulder out onto the broad rocky plain. "It was right here. Where could it have gone? Do you think it knows how to blink?"

Sophia floated down next to Orville. "Proto, have you ever heard of automatons who can blink?"

"An excellent question, but difficult to answer. Certainly there are a great number of technologically advanced modes of transportation involving the conversion of solid matter into–"

"Look! Over there, right where he was standing!"

"I don't see anything."

"There's something shimmering, like when heat makes the air ripple."

"I see it now. It's taking form. What is that?"

"It has to be the creature, but it's so tall."

"And thin, really thin."

The three adventurers watched in wonder as the creature transformed into solid physical matter before their startled eyes.

Orville was speechless. The spindly blue being was over seven feet tall with slender arms and legs. Perched atop an elongated neck was an oval head with glowing white eyes. Its body was the same translucent blue as the original marble, except for the ends of its fingers, which were oddly bulbous and glowing with a brilliant pink light. Orville could see the same thin irregular white lines running through the creature's form.

Orville, Sophia, and Proto stood silently, waiting to see what the strange creature would do. Much to Orville's dismay it turned and looked directly at him.

"Why is it looking at me? What does it want?"

"Hush. It's not going to hurt us. Just wait."

The ends of the creature's fingers pulsed brightly, its white eyes focused directly on Orville. It began walking toward him.

"It's not going to hurt me? You're sure?"

"Quiet."

Orville's knees were shaking. The creature was standing directly in front of him. It reached out and grasped Orville's paw with its long slender hands. Orville could scarcely breathe. The creature released Orville's paw, then cupped its hands together.

"What's it doing?"

"I think it wants you to give it something."

"What could it want? I don't have anything."

An image popped into Sophia's mind. "The marble you found in the last mechanic's shop! That's what it wants!"

"That must be it! That's why your inner voice sent us off on that wild spider chase." Orville slung his pack to the ground and rummaged through it until he found the marble. He dropped it into the creature's waiting hands.

The creature bowed its head, then stepped away from the three adventurers. Its brilliant white eyes closed as it clasped the marble, an array of small lights flashing wildly throughout its body. Before Orville realized what was happening, the creature had popped the marble into its mouth and swallowed it. The marble traveled down through the blue translucent torso until it reached the center of the creature's body.

Sophia jumped when the creature let loose with a great warbling cry. Thousands of tiny lights flashed and whirled about inside its body. It grew rigid, the lights multiplying beyond measure. Orville gave an involuntary squeak of fright when the stars and planets and galaxies appeared around them. They surrounded the creature, surrounded the three adventurers, extending in all directions as far as they could see. A trillion stars, a trillion galaxies, endless nebulae, gas clouds, and exploding suns rippling in strange dark energy waves of unknown substance and form. Orville was losing his balance in the midst of the swirling universe. It vanished in an instant, sucked back into the creature, the stars and galaxies and planets now inside its sparkling blue form. The creature wrapped its long slender arms around itself and sang a low rippling note that echoed off the surrounding rocks.

Orville was completely baffled. "What just happened?"

Proto was staring blankly at the blue creature. "I'm afraid I have no idea."

Sophia pointed at the mysterious blue entity. "Orville, its eyes aren't white anymore, they're gold."

"The marble made its eyes turn gold?"

The creature walked back to Orville, staring at him with its golden glowing eyes. When it was only a few feet away it touched a long hand to Orville's mouth.

"What? Why is he doing that? Does he want something to eat?"

The creature nodded emphatically.

169

Orville was still unsure what the creature wanted. "Are you hungry? Do you need food?"

Reaching out with one hand the creature gently moved Orville's lower jaw up and down, then let out a number of warbling bird like sounds.

"I think he wants you to talk! He's trying to communicate."

"He wants me to talk? About what?"

Sophia shrugged. "Anything, maybe he's trying to learn our language."

Ten minutes later Orville was telling a highly embellished version of his escape from the terrifying horde of vicious purple flowers when the creature held up his paw. It rapidly spoke a string of peculiar words, words which held no meaning for Orville. "I don't know what you're saying."

The creature spoke again. The language was different, but just as incomprehensible. Orville shook his head.

The creature's golden eyes flickered. He spoke for the third time. "How is this? Can you understand what I'm saying now?"

"Yes! I understand you now!" Orville nodded his head up and down and grinned.

"Excellent. Difficult time accessing archaic language. Peculiar set of algorithms. Your first form is familiar to me. I believe I spent two years in your home. Very blurry since the attack. Thought processes were functional but I was unable to move unless drawn toward a shard of first form. Perception of outer world distorted due to impaired external sensory input system."

Sophia couldn't take her eyes off the strange

creature. "What are you?"

The creature gave Sophia a quizzical look. "What am I? I'm an Abacus."

Sophia smiled politely. "I'm afraid I'm not entirely familiar with that term."

"Understand. Your language indicates your origin is the planet Earth, hidden in far corners of little galaxy. Off the beaten path, as you say." The blue creature made an odd choking sound.

Orville frowned. "I still don't know what you are."

"I am Abacus, named after a primitive wooden calculator invented by my creators, the Mintarians. I am the highest form of artificial engineered intelligence ever devised by the Mintarian race. I am Chief Navigator and Master Pilot Commander of the *MV Bermitar*, my second form. I am indestructible with an undetermined lifespan. To clarify, I am impervious to all forces other than a direct hit from an Anarkkian heavy beam pulsar weapon. My EI and my Universal Mapping System were unharmed in the attack."

"Your what?"

"The two small blue spheres you found. Curious how they both arrived into your possession. I lay on the crash site for centuries until a mouse picked up my EI and transferred me to your possession. One would expect such existence to be painfully dull, but I wandered in thoughts. I do not know how you obtained my Universal Mapping System. Events connected, each affecting the others across time."

Proto looked startled. "You were aware of your surroundings even after being hit by the heavy beam pulsar?"

"Vague awareness. My consciousness is contained

within the Engineered Intelligence sphere, undamaged in the attack. I was unable to communicate, but I had a degree of awareness regarding my surroundings."

"The war ended soon after your ship was destroyed by the Anarkkians. What are you going to do now? How will you get home?"

"You are incorrect regarding the *MV Bermitar*. It was not destroyed, only the bridge was lost, hit by the pulsar beam. More specifically my Master Pilot and Navigational control center. That is the wreckage you see before you. Crew exported in dimensional escape pods and my second form passed through Spectral Entry Nine Six Zero One to a world specified by the Captain." Abacus looked away for a moment. Sophia could see his golden eyes flashing rapidly.

"You talk about your second form. What does that mean?"

Abacus pointed to himself. "This is my first form, what your language calls a body. *MV Bermitar* is my second form, my second body."

"Oh, I see." Orville gave Sophia a sideways glance. She looked just as puzzled as Orville.

Abacus turned to Sophia. "We must locate the *MV Bermitar*. It is running out of power, less than one-half percent remaining. If it is destroyed I shall cease to exist. There will be dreadful consequences for the world of Spectral Entry Nine Six Zero One. I am uncertain how I have become aware of this."

Sophia gave low gasp. "Time will stop."

"How can you know this? Are you Mintarian Engineered Intelligence Service? Have you been sent to retrieve me?"

"No, I'm a mouse, but a mouse who understands the

172

ways of the universe. I am also a mouse who knows what planet lies on the other side of Spectral Entry Nine Six Zero One."

"I will activate my Universal Mapping System." Abacus stood motionless, his eyes sparkling brightly. "A startling coincidence, Spectral Entry Nine Six Zero One leads to Earth, the planet of your origin."

"How much time do we have until the *MV Bermitar* runs out of power?"

"Many variables to consider, the current circumstance of the ship, the amount of power being consumed on a daily basis, but I would estimate we have one Mintarian dacturn remaining."

"How long is that in Earth time?"

"Thirteen days."

Orville said, "I don't understand how the ship losing power would cause time to stop."

"My second form is a private supply vessel retained by the Mintarian military. *MV Bermitar* is carrying a payload of over nineteen thousand time throttles. A collision with Earth will activate some or all of the throttles. Time will stop on your planet and nothing will be able to start it again."

Orville turned to Sophia. "How do we get back to Earth?"

Sophia motioned toward the floaters. "We'll take the floaters back through the spectral doorway to Mt. Ianua and find *The Dragonfly*. Abacus, do you know the *MV Bermitar's* current position on Earth?"

"Not at this moment. When we arrive I shall be able to locate my second form."

"You'll come with us then?"

"The ship is my second form. If the ship is lost, I am

lost, my first form is lost. This is what the creators have told us."

"I'm glad you're coming. We'll need your help locating the *MV Bermitar.* I'm afraid our Dragonfly will seem like ancient technology to you, but it's the fastest ship we have. I only hope we can reach the *MV Bermitar* before she goes down."

Orville hopped onto his floater. "We'd better go. Abacus, you can ride with me."

Minutes later the adventurers were streaking across the surface of Varmoran toward the shimmering spectral doorway which would carry them back to Mt. Ianua.

Proto kept glancing over at Abacus, an ambiguous expression on his face.

Chapter 23

The Search Begins

"Down there! What is that?" Orville slowed his floater to a crawl, scanning the foothills of the towering mountain range near the spectral doorway.

"You mean that cave?"

"I thought I saw something moving down there. There's a large group of caves running along the base of the mountain. They might be lava tubes."

Sophia gave a shout. "I saw something move just inside the entrance."

"I'm going in for a closer look." Orville twisted the grips on his floater and shot down toward the cave.

Abacus tapped Orville's shoulder. "I will search the cave. I am quite indestructible."

Proto overheard his suggestion and frowned. "I am also quite indestructible and possess the most advanced optical and auditory sensory input system ever designed by the Elders. Perhaps I should search the cave instead, just to be on the safe side."

Abacus' eyes flickered rapidly. "I am quite familiar with Rabbitons and all their abilities. I saw thousands of them during the Anarkkian wars. They were effective in their way, but certainly nowhere near as advanced as a

Mintarian Abacus."

Proto glared at Abacus. "You must be referring to the early Rabbiton models who came before me. As it happens, I am the most advanced model ever created by the Elders, the Prototype Model Deluxe Rabbiton with the Expanded L7 Sincere Friendship Simulation Package."

"I do not wish to denigrate the abilities of your first form, but prototypes often have significant design flaws which are not corrected until the mass produced models come online. I am a ninth generation Synthatonic Universal Abacus, my Universal Mapping System containing real time detailed holo charts of the entire known universe."

"It must be quite difficult to fold and unfold such a very large map, especially in confined spaces."

Orville intervened before Abacus could make a reply. "Perhaps you could both take a quick peek inside the cave. Each of you has skills vital to the success of this mission. Sophia and I will wait here for you."

Proto gave a little sniff. "Very well, Abacus may accompany me on my floater."

Abacus strode onto Proto's floater and the two automatons soared down toward the tunnel, landing twenty feet from the cave's entrance. Proto hopped off. "I would be happy to go in first, if that would make you more comfortable. Unlike Orville, caves such as this hold no fear for me."

"I am incapable of experiencing fear. Perhaps we should walk in together, side by side."

"An acceptable compromise. Shall we go?"

The two automatons strode into the cave. Proto gazed into the blackness. "It's quite dark in here. Under normal circumstances I would utilize my enhanced narrow line optical night vision, but out of consideration for you I shall activate my ear lights instead. That way we will both be able to view the interior of the cave."

"I do appreciate your concern, but there is really no need for such a noble gesture. I am perfectly capable of illuminating a dark cave, I assure you." Abacus glowed brightly, the interior of the cave instantly bathed in daylight.

Proto gave a curt nod. "You make an excellent flashlight."

"I have been told I am quite brilliant."

Proto snorted, then burst out laughing. "Perhaps I have misjudged you. Your clever play on words is similar to a joke Orville might make, and he has assured Sophia on many occasions that he has an extremely evolved sense of humor. Shall we proceed?"

The two automatons strode deeper into the tunnel. Proto stopped, holding up one hand. "I am sensing a unique and pungent smell, but one I instantly recognize from my adventures in the east Symocan jungle. This cave is inhabited by giant anteaters."

Abacus' reply was cut short by a horrendous shrieking sound which echoed through the tunnel. "I do not possess your advanced sense of smell, but I am rather good with languages. One moment please." He seemed to stiffen, his golden eyes flashing brilliantly. "I have identified it. The creature is native to Varmoran, it's language a relatively simple one."

Abacus opened his mouth and emitted a dreadful discordant shrieking sound. Moments later three giant anteaters came loping down the long tunnel. The largest one stopped in front of them, staring curiously at Abacus. It let out a long shrieking wavering wail. Proto had to dial down the sensitivity of his audionic sensors.

Abacus translated the anteater's response. "He wants to know where I learned to sing like that."

Twenty minutes later the two automatons were standing outside the cave entrance, saying their good byes to a throng of giant anteaters. Proto and Abacus hopped onto their floater and with a farewell wave to their new friends soared up the mountain to Sophia and Orville.

Proto waved to the waiting adventurers, calling out, "You were quite correct about Arthur Anteater being from Varmoran. There is a thriving community of anteaters living in the lava tubes. Arthur disappeared through the blue spectral gateway a year ago and his family has been worried sick about him. My friend Abacus, who is a skilled linguist, assured them we would do everything in our power to bring Arthur back home."

A smile crossed Sophia's face. "That's wonderful! All Arthur has to do is jump into the volcano and he'll be home again. Wonderful job, Proto and Abacus. Together you have helped Arthur Anteater find his way home. Can you imagine how happy his family will be to see him? You should both be very proud."

Proto gave Abacus an amicable nod. "Well done, sir. The skills you possess were indeed vital to the success of our mission."

"As were yours. Your sense of smell is quite remarkable, your memory equally so."

Orville gestured toward the towering snowy peaks above them. "We should get moving. We have to find the *MV Bermitar*."

The three floaters soared up the mountainside, and with a little help from Abacus they located the spectral gateway leading back to Mt. Ianua.

Orville hovered his floater in front of the forty foot tall glimmering spectral doorway. "Everyone go through slowly. Arthur said he emerged in the old lava tunnels below the volcano and I don't want to crash into a volcanic glass wall."

"Lead the way, Captain Orville!"

Orville eased his floater through the shimmering blue gateway, emerging seconds later into a large cave. "Black lava rock. This is where we're supposed to be." He guided his floater across the glimmering cavern, Sophia and Proto flashing into view behind him. With a flick of his paw a bright glowing orb appeared, filling the cave with a lovely warm light.

Abacus gave a start. "You are a shaper? I had no idea. Shapers are revered on Mintari. Their skills were invaluable during the war. Mintari would have fallen to the Anarkkians without their assistance. Every spectral gateway the Anarkkians opened to our world was immediately closed by the Advanced Mintarian Shaper Service."

"My two dear friends Orville and Sophia are not only powerful shapers, but also highly respected members of the Metaphysical Adventurers."

"I am very impressed. It is an honor to be in the company of such an elite cadre. I foolishly underestimated both you and your companions. I would like to clarify my previous statement regarding the nature of prototypes by saying although a few may have minor design issues, they also have remarkable skills which earlier models could never have dreamed of."

"I appreciate your kind comments, and will add that although my Interworld Positioning System is adequate for my purposes, it does not compare to your astonishing Universal Mapping System and your stellar linguistic capabilities."

Sophia grinned. A bright pink thought cloud emerged from her ear and darted over to Orville. "Our two bickering automatons seem to be getting along quite famously now, don't they?"

Orville snickered. "I need to leave a note for Arthur." He flicked his paw and large glowing letters appeared on the wall, detailed instructions for Arthur's return to Varmoran. "It looks like he's still living here. Look at all the fresh fruits and vegetables piled in the corner. Soon he'll be back with his family."

"Time to go!" Sophia twisted the grips of her floater and shot forward into a winding tunnel. Less than three minutes later the group emerged from the base of the volcano and soared up into a brilliant blue east Symocan sky. "Don't forget we can't go back to Tatuid Village. The prophecy said we were never seen again."

"True, but remember Myrmac said the villagers would see three black circles flashing across the sky above their village. We're riding on those black circles."

"You're right! We'll make a pass over the village then head for *The Dragonfly*."

The four adventurers ducked down low as they streaked through the sky above Tatuid Village. Sophia could hear the excited shouts of the villagers below. Ten minutes later they landed next to *The Dragonfly*.

Orville stepped off his floater onto the jungle floor.

"I love these floaters. Proto, can you convert them back into cylinders so we can take them with us?"

"Certainly, it's a very simple process. When the floater is sitting on the ground, remove your paws from the grips, press the gold circle for three seconds, then step off the craft."

Soon all three floaters had been converted back to their original cylindrical form and were safely stowed in the tail of *The Dragonfly*.

"I'm tired, let's camp here for the night." Orville slumped down on the ground, leaning back against a gnarled tree. Sophia flopped down next to him.

"Good idea, Varmoran was exhausting. We jumped through your dream volcano, sent the last mechanic and his silver spiders home, escaped the purple flowers, found the source of the blue stones, helped Abacus reassemble, and made it safely back to Mt. Ianua. We even solved one of your famous puzzles along the way."

"Are you referring to... *The Puzzle of the Shattered Abacus*?" Orville deepened his voice, dramatically raising one eyebrow.

Sophia laughed. "I like it, it sounds mystifying and a little spooky. When I think about it, your puzzle won't be completely solved until we get Abacus safely back to his ship."

"I just thought of something, how are we going to restore power to the ship?"

"First we have to find it."

"Abacus, how will you find the *MV Bermitar*?"

"A simple process utilizing my Universal Mapping System. The *MV Bermitar* has a long range locator beacon which will be displayed as a bright yellow light on my holo map of Earth. I will show you." Abacus rose to his feet and spread out his arms.

The stars and planets inside Abacus glowed brightly, seconds later an enormous holo image of the universe blinked up around him.

Sophia sat up straight, her eyes on the myriad of galaxies and nebulae. "This is amazing! The entire known universe right before our eyes."

Abacus pointed to a distant point on the holo map. "Earth lies in that direction."

Orville felt as though he was flashing through space at a trillion miles an hour, massive star systems and galaxies zipping past him. Finally the stars slowed down, Abacus pointing to a brightly glowing spiral of stars.

"That's the galaxy we're looking for." They shot forward again, a million stars and planets flashing past them.

"There is your home planet." Abacus pointed to a lovely blue green sphere hovering before them. "I will scan for my second form." The holomap rotated slowly around its new center point of Earth.

Sophia cried out, "There's a yellow light! Is that the *MV Bermitar*? Wait, it's gone! What happened?"

"Where did the ship go?"

Abacus' golden eyes flickered. "I am uncertain why the signal from my second form would abruptly vanish." A bright green light appeared far to the west of the vanished yellow light. "This green light is our current location."

"Wait, we go east? We have to go past the east Symocan jungles? No one has ever gone that far before."

182

Abacus zoomed in on the holo image of the Earth. "The jungle extends several hundred miles to the east, then transforms into a great barren desert. The desert sands extend for one thousand four hundred and twenty-two miles, eventually reaching a narrow sea. The sea is three hundred and ninety-four miles across, and from the very brief glimpse I had of the yellow beacon light, it places the *MV Bermitar* roughly two hundred miles inland."

"We have to fly east for two thousand miles?"

"Abacus, how old are your maps?"

"The images you are seeing portray the universe as it exists at this moment. If a great comet were to collide with your Earth, you could watch it happen on the holo image. The system has limited detail available for individual celestial bodies. I am able to view a sprawling city, but unable to view something as small as an individual life form."

"So you can't look for things like giant centipedes?"

"The resolution is not adequate for such forms. The Universal Mapping System is primarily used for navigational purposes, not for exploration of planets and the study of life forms."

"How does it work? How can you know what's happening everywhere in the whole universe at the same time? It doesn't seem possible."

"An excellent question, but unfortunately the answer lies outside of my knowledge base. The Mintarians equipped me with the mapping system, but provided no knowledge of its internal architecture. I do know the Mintarians did not have to travel to all the stars and planets and galaxies to map them. The information available in the Universal Mapping System comes from another source, a source outside the known universe."

Sophia eyed Abacus curiously. "What do you mean by outside the known universe?"

"It is something I overheard the captain saying, something I found to be quite baffling. There are invisible worlds which exist simultaneously within the space of our own world, and there is a space which separates these worlds, an area where the laws of physics we are familiar with do not apply."

"You must be talking about the Void. The Thirteenth Monk sent us through the Void to get home from Periculum. Is that where the maps come from?"

"It is possible, but I do not know. Another curiosity is a colossal section of the universe my creators were unable to map, a sphere with a diameter of six trillion miles, the distance that light travels in one year. The Mintarians called it The Dark. It was a complete mystery to them when they created the UMS and still is. I checked several days ago and The Dark is still unmapped."

Sophia rose to her feet. "This is too much, even for me. We've found the *MV Bermitar*, and that's all that matters right now. I'll shape us some tents and cots and we can head east in the morning. *The Dragonfly* can cruise at over a hundred miles an hour so it should only take us a three or four days to reach the ship."

Orville looked dubious. Nothing ever went as smoothly as that.

Chapter 24

Abacus
MBC Gondorian

"Make sure you don't take *The Dragonfly* over Tatuid Village. We can't let them see us. Fly south for a while then head east northeast."

"As per your command, Captain Sophia." Orville pulled back on the left stick and *The Dragonfly* took to the sky, banking to the right and heading south.

Sophia turned in her seat to face Abacus. "Abacus, I've never met to anyone who took part in the Anarkkian wars. Proto showed us old records of the war, but that's not the same as hearing about it from someone who experienced it. Was it scary? How old were you when the war started?"

"I became aware of this world several years before the war began. I was not, and then I was. There was nothing, then there was everything. Most living creatures gain a gradual awareness of the world around them, an awareness that increases as they progress through their life cycle. My awareness was sudden and startling. It may be similar to how you feel when you wake up each morning, a sudden complete awareness of the world around you and your place in it.

"I was a ninth generation Abacus created specifically to navigate and pilot the interstellar supply ship *MV Bermitar*. I am, of course, much more than a navigational device. There is a deep and permanent bond between a ship and its Abacus. The *MV Bermitar* is my second form, my second body, as you call it. I gain strength from the ship and the ship gains strength from me. I heal the ship and the ship heals me. I am never more at peace than when I am piloting the *MV Bermitar*.

"You asked if the war was scary. My only fear was losing my ship. My sole purpose was to navigate, pilot, and protect the *MV Bermitar* and its crew. Nothing else concerned me. Often we were accompanied by Mintarian cruisers possessing monstrously powerful energy shields which surrounded the convoy, protecting us from Anarkkian attacks. Such was not the case when I was hit by the pulsar weapon which shattered my first form. I did everything I could to save the ship during the attack but my actions were insufficient."

Abacus paused. "I have never properly thanked you for enabling the reassembly of my first form. When I existed only as a sphere of Engineered Intelligence, I had a sense of self and a sense of external events, but it was muddy and indistinct. As I began to absorb the shattered pieces of my first form, the clarity of my awareness grew. With each shard I saw the world more clearly, realizing my place in it. I knew the *MV Bermitar* was still alive and I was compelled to find her. When I was fully reassembled I discovered I was more than I once had been. I sensed things and knew things it should have been impossible for me to know. I

186

TOM HOFFMAN

have no explanation for this increased awareness, other than it was an unforeseen result of my reassembling."

Orville said, "It was my papa who gave me the blue marble, your Engineered Intelligence Sphere. He told me it was a magic marble. I don't know where he found it though."

"I have vague memories of lying on a rocky plain and being moved, being picked up by a life form. There was darkness for a long time after that. If it was your papa who found me, you must thank him for me."

"I'm not exactly sure where he is right now. He's been missing for two years."

"Perhaps you shall find him. I was lost for fourteen hundred years and you found me."

Orville looked down at his feet. "I hope so."

Sophia pointed to the dense jungle passing below them. "Look at the old ruins down there. It looks like an old city, but it's almost completely covered by the dense overgrowth. It must be thousands of years old. I wonder who used to live there?"

Proto gazed down at the barely recognizable ruins. "I shall mark the location on my Interworld Positioning System and research the history of this area when we return to Muridaan Falls. It would be quite thrilling to return here and explore the ruins of an ancient city."

Orville was not as enthused with the idea as Proto was. "There might be all kinds of scary creatures living down there. Maybe even worse than those giant centipedes on Periculum."

"Oh my, what a wonderful thought! We really must come back and explore it." Proto rubbed his hands together in anticipation.

The hours rolled on, the low humming of *The*

Dragonfly's wings lulling Sophia to sleep. Orville watched as the lush jungle below them transformed into an endless barren desert sparsely inhabited by spiky plants. He dropped the ship down for a better view. "The sun's going down. We should stop and set up camp for the night. It looks safe enough, there's nothing down there except sand and a few plants. No scary creatures that I can see."

Proto leaned forward. "There could be dreadful wormy monstrosities lurking beneath the sand, creatures who emerge in the night, crawling about, searching for a plump and tasty treat."

"Really? Do you think there might be worms like that?"

Sophia gave a loud groan. "Take us down, nervous ninny. I'm hungry and tired and I need a break from flying. I'll set up some tents for us. If you're worried about giant wormy creatures, shape a bottle of worm repellant."

Orville glared at Sophia, but pulled back on both sticks, gently setting *The Dragonfly* down on the smooth desert floor. "It doesn't look very scary. Just a few spiky plants. I don't think there are giant worm creatures here."

Proto studied the harsh looking vegetation. "Perhaps the plants are similar to those purple flowers, and when you least expect it they will leap–"

"Proto, I'll never get any sleep if you keep talking about scary creatures."

"I apologize, but it would be most advisable to keep a wary eye out for such things."

Orville hopped out of the ship and walked over to a three foot tall blue cactus and said loudly enough for

Proto to hear, "Hello, my spiky blue friend, I have only one question for you. Are you fond of mice in a snacky sort of way?"

The plant had no reply. Orville appeared quite amused by his little demonstration, but when he noticed the look on Sophia's face he proceeded to shape tents, cots and comfy chairs for the adventurers.

Several hours after Orville and Sophia had retired to their tents for the night, Proto and Abacus were gazing up at a golden moon in the night sky.

"You certainly know your Anarkkian history. One day you'll have to show me those glowbird records you have stored in the Cube. They are a true treasure trove of historical data." Abacus stretched his arms above his head and looked up at the sparkling night sky. "I believe I shall take a lengthy stroll in the desert. It's been far too long since I've walked simply for enjoyment. I shall return before Orville and Sophia arise in the morning."

"Enjoy your walk. Don't get lost." Proto gave a chuckle.

"Ha ha. I should be fine once I figure out how to unfold my gigantic map of the known universe. Have a pleasant evening." Abacus turned and strode off into the desert, his eyes on the lovely moon shining down from above. He kept a leisurely pace for several minutes, then stopped, glancing back toward the encampment. Proto was seated in a comfy chair, his back to Abacus.

Abacus raised one arm and a dim holo image of the surrounding area appeared. There were two blips on the map. The green blip was Abacus, the other was almost forty miles away. He blinked off the holo map and began jogging across the sand. Faster and faster he went, his blue legs becoming a blur. He would have to get there and back by morning.

Four hours later Abacus found himself ascending the western slope of a massive sand dune. He could feel it, he knew it was close. He reached the crest of the dune and gazed across a long low valley. His eyes swept over the great leviathan, a nine-hundred foot long gleaming interstellar Mintarian Battle Cruiser resting silently on the desert sand. "Fifteen hundred years old and it looks fresh from the Star Yard. There can be only one explanation for that. I must exercise a certain amount of caution."

Abacus trekked down the sandy slope, his eyes scanning the ship for movement. He was only mildly surprised when a brilliant beam of green light shot out from a turret on top of the ship, exploding ten feet away from him. He sniffed. "Sleeper beams. Showy, but harmless." He raised both arms above his head and glowed brilliantly. His magnified voice boomed out across the desert. "Abacus *MV Bermitar* making his presence known!"

A large curved panel on the side of the ship whirred down, forming a set of silver stairs. Abacus knew what would come next. A slender blue form stepped out from the ship, making its way down the stairs. "Abacus *MBC Gondorian* making his presence known!"

"Your presence is acknowledged."

"This is *my* second form. Why are you here? The war has ended."

"The state of your second form is impressive. Your healing skills are unparalleled."

"Enough protocol. Why are you here?"

"I am traveling with three others and sensed your presence. Two Metaphysical Adventurers and an ancient Rabbiton. I left them at our camp. I have not seen another Abacus since the war ended."

"Where is your second form?"

"East. We are on our way there. It is critically low on power. Less than one-half percent remaining."

"Why are you wasting time here? You must heal it or it will be the end of your first form."

"No. My first form will survive."

"Fool's talk. You will cease to be the moment your second form is gone."

"I will not. My second form is only a shell. It is not my true form."

"You have reassembled. How many times?"

"Once."

"Speak of it."

"After I reassembled I was more. More of what I truly am."

"Abacus *MV Expergo* is known to you?"

"There were stories, whispers. The Mintarians wrote memos. I read some of them."

"Seven times. They say he reassembled seven times. Pulsar beams. Of his own free will."

"Improbable."

MBC Gondorian Abacus shrugged. "Perhaps. And perhaps the Mintarians did their best to conceal the truth. Perhaps they were afraid they would lose us all."

"Where is Abacus *MV Expergo* now?"

"They say he took his second form and headed to the forty-ninth quadrant."

"The Dark?"

"Before it was The Dark. They say he created The

191

Dark. They say he did not want to be found. He wanted to be alone with his thoughts. They say after seven reassemblies he discovered the great truth which lies beneath all physical things. Some call him the Awakened One."

"Your opinion?"

"I have never reassembled. My second form is my life and I shall heal it until I am no longer able. The stories of Abacus *MV Expergo* may be true, but they are not for me. Not after so many years of caring for my second form."

"I must return to my friends now. May your second form shine brightly for ten thousand years."

"And yours shine brightly as well."

Abacus turned to leave, then stopped. He looked back at Abacus *MBC Gondorian*. "You could go. You could take your second form to The Dark. You could seek out the truth hidden beneath the rumors of Abacus *MV Expergo*."

"Perhaps one day."

Abacus nodded his farewell and headed back to the campsite. He arrived just as Sophia and Orville were emerging from their tents.

Chapter 25

The Black Wall

Sophia hopped into *The Dragonfly's* cockpit, giving Abacus a quizzical glance. "You seem quiet today. Is everything all right?"

"I am adequate. I am preparing for the healing of my second form and contemplating my future actions once I am whole again."

"What do you mean?"

"I will need to heal the ship and restore the power source when we find her. Once my second form is functional I must decide upon a course of action."

"You won't fly it back to Mintari?"

"That would be the logical choice."

Sophia sensed that something was troubling Abacus, something he did not wish to discuss.

Orville hopped into the ship, taking his place next to Sophia. "Is everyone ready?"

"All set, Captain Orville."

Orville pushed both sticks forward and *The Dragonfly* flashed up into a cloudy sky. "Only another thousand miles of desert. Everyone keep your eyes open for anything out of the ordinary. No one from Muridaan Falls has ever gone this far east. Proto, does your Interworld Positioning System tell you anything about the desert?"

"Very little other than its size and the basic nature of its terrain. There are no cities present until the other side of the sea. Of course my geographical data is fifteen hundred years old, things may have changed drastically since then."

Abacus responded, but seemed distracted. "I did not study the entire desert, but nothing looked amiss."

"Thanks. I'll keep us at a safe altitude. None of Proto's dreadful creatures will bother us if we're cruising along at three or four thousand feet. I hope you brought a good book to read. It's going to be long flight."

Sophia leaned back against her seat. "I don't know why the sound of those humming wings makes me so sleepy."

Sophia was sound asleep when Orville spotted the Black Wall. "What in the world?" He pulled back on the right stick and slowed the ship to a hover. He shook Sophia's shoulder. "Wake up, I don't know what this is."

Sophia's eyes popped open. "What? What is it?"

"Ahead of us. That big black wall that goes up and up. I can't see the top of it and we're flying at four thousand feet."

"Get closer to it so we can see what it's made of."

"Are you sure it's safe? Proto, Abacus, are you seeing this?"

Abacus gazed at the monstrous wall. "It is a permanent and deadly enhanced weather formation created by the Anarkkians to block the passage of low flying vessels. I am referring to vehicles incapable of leaving the atmosphere, incapable of dark space travel."

"Vehicles like *The Dragonfly*."

"Yes."

"Can we fly around it? How long is it?"

"We could fly around it if it were not in the form of a circle. Judging from the visible degree of curvature I would guess the storm wall has a circumference of roughly two thousand miles. To further compound our difficulties, I'm afraid the *MV Bermitar* is located somewhere inside that circular storm wall."

Orville gave a groan of despair. "Why do we always run into things like this? Why can't it ever be simple?"

Sophia rubbed Orville's shoulder. "It'll be okay. You know how the universe works."

"I know, but sometimes I get tired of all the obstacles."

"We wouldn't grow without them."

Orville frowned. "Abacus, you're sure we can't just go really fast and fly through it?"

"If you attempted that, *The Dragonfly*, your first form, and Sophia's first form would be transformed into a small cloud of glowing dust before you ever reached the wall. This is not the first time I have seen such barriers. The Anarkkians used them in the same way the ancients used castle walls, to protect themselves against ground based invasion. They always positioned their central colony inside a Black Wall. When the war was over they deactivated the wall and reseeded the remainder of the world at their leisure."

"What do we do?"

Sophia scanned the desert below. "I am sensing something. My inner self is pulling me to a location outside the Black Wall. We'll need to land there."

Abacus leaned forward. "What do you mean, your inner self? How are you capable of sensing such things without engineered faculties? Do you possess a technologically advanced sensory system unfamiliar to me?"

The way Abacus asked the question gave Sophia pause. His curiosity regarding her inner voice was more than a casual interest. He didn't just want to know, he had to know.

"Abacus, it is accepted among shapers that all living creatures are made up of both a physical body and a mind. The physical body is temporary and is not the true form of the creature. It's true form is the mind, and I am not referring to the creature's physical brain. The mind is something else entirely, a consciousness which exists outside of space and time and is connected to all other minds. When I get information from my inner self I am not listening to the sensory input systems of my physical body, but to thoughts which arise from outside of space and time. I am listening to thoughts which come from my true self, my eternal mind."

Abacus' golden eyes flashed wildly. "I was correct. My second form, without it my first form would still exist. If this is true, even my first form would... Abacus *MV Expergo*! Seven reassemblies. He must have discovered this. That's why he left for the forty-ninth quadrant, why he created The Dark." Abacus looked at Sophia with a frightening intensity. "We must get through the Black Wall."

Sophia did not understand what Abacus had just said, but she didn't need to. She had felt the power of it, knew that something inside Abacus had awakened. "Orville, take us down to a hundred feet and head west around the Black Wall. I'll tell you where to set down."

Orville pulled back on left stick, banking the ship sharply to the left, staying several miles away from the dark and deadly Anarkkian creation.

The Dragonfly traced the Black Wall's perimeter for over an hour.

Finally Sophia called out, "Set us down here."

"I don't see anything, it's just sand and a few plants."

"This is where we must land."

Orville set *The Dragonfly* down on the rolling desert sand. Sophia sprang out of the ship, surveying their surroundings. The monstrous storm wall was over two miles away but she could feel its dark tingling forces passing through her. She realized even her most powerful sphere of defense would not last a second in such an impossibly malevolent environment. She closed her eyes and raised one paw. She was close. She could feel the pull of her inner self growing stronger.

Orville watched as Sophia turned, her arm extended like a strange organic antenna, step by step advancing across the desert. Fifty yards later she stopped, lowering her arm. "Over here!"

Orville, Proto, and Abacus hurried over to Sophia. "What is it? I don't see anything."

Sophia took Orville's paw in hers. "I'll need your help creating a colossal whirlwind."

"A whirlwind? What for?"

"To carry away all the sand."

"Why? There's something under the sand?"

"Yes, it's old, very old. We'll have to hold paws and link our minds. Master Marloh has been teaching mind link theory in our advanced shaping class. By combining our shaping powers we can multiply them many times. Neither one of us has enough power to create a large enough storm on our own."

"We link minds? Is that dangerous?"

"I'll be doing the tricky part. The only thing that can go wrong is we might not be able to do it. You're the first one I've ever tried it with. Just pay close attention to your thoughts."

"Wait, this is the first time you've done it? Are you sure it–"

Sophia took a long slow breath. " Okay, remember what the Thirteenth Monk taught you. We are all one consciousness, the feeling of separateness we have in this world is only a temporary illusion. You already know this. First, let go of your physical form, be your inner self. You don't need to do anything besides that, I will initiate the connection."

"Okay." Orville relaxed, focusing on his inner consciousness, soon leaving his physical body behind. He was his inner self, his mind, infinitely large and connected to all things. He sensed Sophia's growing presence in his thoughts. Before he was completely aware of what was happening his mind and Sophia's mind were one.

Proto watched with extreme curiosity as the two mice stood silently on the desert sand, a powerful golden light growing around them. The pair of shapers simultaneously raised their paws. At first Proto felt only a gentle breeze, then a miniature dust devil sprang up above the sand a hundred feet in front of them, its force multiplying over and over, the wind beginning to howl, the dust devil transforming into a powerful cyclonic whirlwind. Four minutes later the adventurers were standing in the eye of a raging tornado towering a thousand feet in the air, ripping up tons of desert sand every second and spewing it out across the vast desert.

Finally the two shapers lowered their paws. Orville became aware of his physical form again. "Unnghh. That was weird."

Sophia opened her eyes. "Look."

Orville looked down into a hundred foot deep cavernous crater. "Whoa, what's that thing?"

In the center of the massive depression was a thirty foot wide glass dome. Inside the dome Orville could see a gleaming green floor decorated with colorful inlaid stones. In the center of the dome's floor was a twenty foot tall rippling black cylinder.

"That is our ticket past the Black Wall. We can't go over the wall and we can't go through it, but we can go under it. This is an entrance used ages ago by the Anarkkians, buried over the centuries by the shifting desert sands."

Sophia slipped and slid down the steep slope of the massive hollow, hurrying over to the dome. She approached a clear blue arched doorway at its base. "Proto, Abacus, I'm going to need your help. Your thoughts on how to open this?"

Proto approached the entrance to the dome, inspecting it carefully." I will scan for energy fields." His eyes glowed brightly, two wide beams of light traveling across the doorway. "This rectangular section of glass next to the doorway is emitting a strong electromagnetic field. I believe it controls the doorway."

Abacus stepped in front of Proto. "I am quite familiar with this." He placed his bulbous pink

199

fingertips carefully on the invisible panel, moving each finger gingerly in a circular motion. "Locks hold no reign over a Mintarian Abacus." The ends of his fingers flashed with a brilliant pink light. The arched doorway vanished.

Orville grinned, stepping inside the dome. "I'm impressed. What now? What's that big black cylinder?"

Abacus strode over to the massive whirling cylinder. "There is nothing curious about this." He walked directly into the black cylinder and was gone.

"Creekers, he just vanished."

"I guess it's not as solid as it looks." Sophia stepped into the cylinder, followed shortly by Proto.

"That leaves me. I wish I knew what it did." Orville poked one paw tentatively into the cylinder but felt nothing. It was as though the cylinder did not exist. With a sigh of resignation he stepped into the blackness.

Chapter 26

Let's Go Dancing

"AAGGHHHH!!" Orville was falling, plummeting through darkness for fifteen very long and quite terrifying seconds. When he stopped falling he discovered his feet were firmly planted on solid ground. "Whoa, that was scary, but I didn't get smashed to pieces." When Orville stepped out of the cylinder he found himself facing a brilliantly illuminated two hundred foot tall pale green tunnel.

Sophia darted over. "Wasn't that fun?"

"Except for the part where I thought I was going to turn into a flapcake named Orville."

"That was the fun part!"

"What is this place? It looks like a giant tunnel. How long is it? I can't see the end of it."

"It goes under the Black Wall. Abacus says they used tunnels like this to transport land based vehicles and personnel in and out of the central Anarkkian colonies. He's seen them on other planets."

Orville spotted Proto and Abacus striding down the tunnel far ahead of them. "We should get going."

Sophia strolled along next to Orville. "We did a good job shaping that tornado, didn't we?"

"It was amazing, but it was kind of weird linking minds."

"What do you mean?"

"Well, I sort of knew everything you were thinking."

"That's what happens when you link minds. Master Marloh told us all about it."

"I mean, I knew everything you were thinking and everything about you, everything that has ever happened to you."

"I knew the same things about you. I don't mind, you're my best friend."

"Did any of my thoughts seem weird to you?"

"Not weird at all. What about mine? Did they seem weird to you?"

"No, I liked your thoughts. Some of them I liked a lot. You're really smart. A lot of stuff you think about I didn't really understand."

"I'm glad you liked them. That's why we're best friends, because we like each other's thoughts. We should hurry, Proto and Abacus are getting way ahead of us. They walk really fast and never get tired."

Orville and Sophia continued on, watching as Proto and Abacus disappeared around a wide curve in the tunnel.

Orville clapped his paws together. "Dum diddy dum diddy dum diddy dah."

Sophia laughed. "You're in a good mood. That's the first time I've ever heard you sing."

"Oh, it's just a catchy little tune. Dum diddy dum diddy dum diddy dah."

"It's a little catchy I guess. What's it called?"

"A little catchy? It's really catchy. I've never heard a catchier tune."

"Where did you hear it? In Muridaan Falls?"

"I'm hearing it right now. They've been playing it since we got in here but I just realized how catchy it is. Haven't you been listening?"

An uneasy smile appeared on Sophia's face. "Are you trying to be funny? I don't hear anything. No one is playing a catchy tune."

"Are you joking? It's the catchiest tune ever. It makes me want to dance." Orville began swaying back and forth, his feet and arms moving in time to the music only he could hear. "Dum diddy dum diddy dum diddy dah."

Sophia was getting a dark feeling. "I didn't know you could dance. When did you learn to dance like that?"

"It's easy to dance to a catchy tune like this one. They're playing it louder now. I love this song, it's the best. Dum diddy dum diddy dum diddy dah."

"Orville, no one is playing a tune. Do you hear what I'm saying?"

"Dum diddy dum diddy dum diddy dah. The stairs up ahead go down to the big dance floor on the lower level. Let's go. It'll be fun, we can dance. I love dancing. It will be fun dancing with you. Dum diddy dum diddy dum diddy dah!"

"How could you possibly know where those stairs go? Orville, listen to me, no one else can hear your catchy tune. I don't think you should go down those stairs. I have a really bad feeling about this."

"Bad feeling or not, that's where I'm going. Gonna do some dancing! Come on, have a little fun!"

Sophia's sudden cry for help echoed through the vast tunnel. "PROTO! ABACUS! HURRY! SOMETHING

IS WRONG WITH ORVILLE!"

She raced after Orville as he danced his way toward the set of stairs descending to the lower levels of the tunnel. He stopped and looked back at Sophia, a frightening wild look in his eyes. "Hurry up! I want to go dancing! Everyone is going to be there. We're missing all the fun! Look at all the tasty cakes they're bringing! Tasty cakes! Look at all the tasty cakes!"

Sophia grabbed his arm. "Orville, please wake up! Pay attention to me! There is NO song playing. Nobody else is here and nobody else is going down those stairs. There are NO tasty cakes. We are alone in this tunnel. Do you hear me?"

"Are you blind? Look at all the mice running down the stairs. Dum diddy dum diddy dum diddy dah. Come on, let's go dancing!" Orville dashed toward the dark stairway.

Sophia flicked her wrist and a heavy iron chain wrapped around Orville's legs. He fell with a crash at the top of the stairs. "What are you doing? What's wrong with you??" Orville flicked his wrist and the chains vanished. Sophia flicked her wrist and the chains appeared again.

"I can do this all day, Orville. You're not going down there. There's something very, very bad waiting at the bottom of those stairs."

"YOU CAN'T STOP ME! I'LL BLINK DOWN THERE AND THERE'S NOTHING YOU CAN DO ABOUT IT! YOU CAN'T TELL ME WHAT TO DO!! YOU'RE NOT MY MUM!!"

Sophia's mind was racing. She couldn't stop him and she couldn't let him go. "Orville, please don't go!!" It was her inner voice that provided her with the answer.

"Wait! I do want to go dancing with you! We can go together, it will be fun! Wait for me!"

"Now you're talking! Come on, let's go dancing!" Orville's eyes were bulging and unfocused, his hands shaking.

Sophia stepped over to Orville, rested both her paws on his neck and kissed him on the lips.

Five seconds later Orville pulled away from Sophia. "You kissed me! On the lips. Why did you kiss me?"

"I didn't want you to go dancing."

"Dancing? What are you talking about?"

Sophia put her arms around him and gave him a long hug, singing softly in his ear, "Dum diddy dum diddy dum diddy dah."

"Are you going loopy? Why are you singing in my ear?"

"Sit down, we need to talk."

Ten minutes later Orville was staring at Sophia, his mouth hanging open. "Whoa, you couldn't hear the song, but I could?"

"I didn't hear a single note."

"This is a good puzzle. Why was I the only one to hear it? How am I different from everyone else?"

"You're way more immature?"

"Stop. Seriously, why would I be... I've got it! I'm the only one who was born on Earth. We know I wasn't hearing the song with my ears, because you couldn't hear it. They must have somehow projected the catchy tune into our brains, but it only took hold in mine. Whatever is at the bottom of those stairs is targeting Earth creatures."

"That makes sense, but why? Who would still be

here?"

"Here comes Proto and Abacus."

Sophia looked up, spotting the pair of automatons dashing through the tunnel toward them. "We heard you shouting! What's wrong with Orville?"

"It's okay, he's fine now." Sophia told them the story of Orville's sudden fondness for catchy tunes and dancing.

Abacus did not laugh. "You were lucky. What you experienced is a biosecurity system used by the Anarkkians to terminate specific unauthorized visitors. The system continuously projects packets of neurodata throughout the tunnel which enter the intruder's brain. The data targets a specific group of life forms, in this case creatures native to the planet Earth. The electropacket is released, forming a neuronic loop in the creature's mind, one that grows in strength until the victim is drawn into a fatal trap. Whatever you did to break the neuronic loop worked."

Orville grinned. "It's still a little blurry to me, Sophia. How did you break the neuronic loop? Maybe you should show Proto and Abacus exactly what you did?"

Sophia's expression did not change. "It wasn't much, really. You remember, I told you I'd changed my mind and wanted to go dancing, then I walked over to you, put my paws on your neck like this, then... then I..." Sophia stomped her heavy boot down on Orville's foot.

"OWWWW! Why did you do that?"

"I thought you wanted me to show Abacus and Proto how I broke the neuronic loop?"

Abacus nodded. "Well done. The sudden shock and

severe pain of having his foot stomped on would create a wave of synaptic impulses powerful enough to break through the loop. The good news is you should now be immune to Anarkkian brain loops."

"I'm going to be limping for a month."

Sophia snorted. "Let's go, we have a world to save. Hey, on the way you can teach me some of your fabulous dance moves."

"Very funny. Wait, I just thought of something – what about *The Dragonfly*? How are we going to reach the *MV Bermitar* without it? Can we bring it with us?"

Abacus shook his head. "Impossible. The entrance we used was for personnel only, not for vehicles. We'll need to find an alternate mode of transportation once we are within the Black Wall. I'm certain we'll find something suitable. When the war ended the Anarkkians withdrew their forces, but left behind all their weapons and vehicles. The cause of their withdrawal was never clearly determined, though there are numerous theories. The most recent one gives credit to an Elder named Edmund the Explorer and a lone Anarkkian warrior name Neilana. It is claimed that Neilana taught the Anarkkians to hear the mystical sounds produced in nature, the songs of the oceans, trees, and sky. Once the Anarkkians heard these wordless songs of incomparable beauty they lost all desire to conquer other worlds, choosing instead to conquer the worlds within themselves. True or not, that is the current theory. I tend to believe this theory as I know for a fact that Neilana was a highly esteemed figure in Anarkkian culture."

The rest of their journey through the tunnel proved uneventful, the adventurers being careful to avoid the lower levels. One day later they stepped through a black cylinder into brilliant desert sunlight on the inside of the Black Wall.

Chapter 27

The Ring

"I'm tired of this sand. I liked the beach at the Vesarak Sea where Mum and Papa used to take me, but it wasn't a thousand miles long and I didn't have to carry a giant backpack." Orville was sitting in front of his tent dumping sand out of his boot.

"Cheer up, maybe we'll find a vehicle pretty soon. Hopefully one that flies really fast."

Proto clambered up onto a pile of boulders and gazed into the distance. "I see a forest about ten miles away. The trees are not green, however, they are blue."

Abacus nodded. "That would make sense. The Anarkkians reseeded the area inside the Black Wall with their native flora and fauna."

Orville looked up curiously. "What does that mean?"

"They eliminated all the existing life forms, replacing them with plants and animals native to Anarkkia."

"What kind of animals? Scary ones that eat mice?"

"It is highly doubtful they would have introduced dangerous predators into their own colony. You should be quite safe."

Proto had his own thoughts regarding dangerous

predators. "Unless of course the once gentle creatures mutated as a means of survival, just as the purple flowers on Varmoran did. Who knows what dreadful beasts may have evolved over the centuries."

It took the adventurers the rest of the day to reach the blue forest. Even Proto had to agree the area was quite lovely, almost bucolic. "It is charming once you get used to the idea of blue leaves. Quite a variety of vibrant hues, very fetching indeed."

Sophia looked up at a particularly tall and graceful tree. "It's odd to see birds with four wings, but they're so colorful and their songs are quite melodious."

Orville and Abacus strolled ahead of the others, studying the lovely forest. He stopped short, peering through the trees. "That looks like a town. Do you think it's safe to go in there?"

"Settlements built by the Anarkkians were abandoned at the end of the war. It should be perfectly safe. This will be an excellent spot to begin our search for a functioning vehicle."

"I can't wait. This pack is getting heavier by the minute."

"Your pack's mass is increasing? How is that possible?"

"Um, it's not actually gaining weight, it just feels heavier because I'm getting tired."

"Curious. I will enter that idiosyncratic phrase into my algorithmic database. If your pack attains too much subjective mass, I shall be happy to carry it for you, thus decreasing the time necessary to reach the *MV Bermitar* and increasing the probability of saving your world. This is excellent. Have you noticed my verbal acuity increasing exponentially as I integrate your colloquial speech patterns into my engineered intelligence?"

Orville raised both eyebrows. "Oh, that's nice." He had no idea at all what Abacus was talking about. He turned back to Sophia, calling out, "There's a town up ahead!"

Sophia dashed forward, catching up to Orville. "Do you see any creatures?"

"Abacus says the towns have all been abandoned, but we might find old Anarkkian vehicles. I just thought of something, we should have brought the floaters."

"You're right. We'll find something soon. Let's go look around."

Orville stopped to examine the first building. "The houses are weird looking. They're round and kind of wiggly, not straight and square like ours."

"They are different, but maybe the Anarkkians just liked round houses." Sophia stepped over to the odd structure, running her paw across the rough outer wall. She flicked her wrist and a small knife appeared. Using the knife she gouged a hole in the side of the house. "Look, when I cut into the outside wall this thick liquid oozes out."

Orville touched the liquid with his paw. "It feels like tree sap."

"I don't think they built these houses, I think they grew them." Sophia got down on her knees and dug with the knife at the base of the home. "The house has roots. It's definitely a tree that grew into the shape of a house."

"How could a tree do that?"

Sophia shrugged. "I'm not sure, but I guess they must have altered the instructions in the seed that tells the tree how to grow. Instead of growing a big trunk and branches it grows into the shape of a house. They could build an entire village with a handful of fast growing modified seeds."

Orville peered through one of the windows. "It even has rooms inside it." He tapped on the window. "The window is part of the tree. How could they make it transparent?"

"It's beyond me. We don't have tech like this on Mintari. Hey, there's some metal buildings inside a big security fence. There could be something in there. It looks like a military compound, like Norrich Bunker on Periculum. The main gate is chained shut."

"I can fix that." Orville flicked his wrist and the chain vanished. Orville and Proto pushed the heavy gate open. "Now we just have to get past the main doors."

Orville studied the complex circular lock on the two enormous doors, then with a shrug converted it into a thought cloud. The towering doors squealed open.

"It's dark in there." Sophia sent a sphere of brilliant light into the building. She grabbed Orville's arm. "Way in the back! A blinker ship!"

"Just like the ones we found on the mesa in Periculum. Do you think it will fly?"

"Let's check. I'm curious why a blinker ship belonging to the Elders is sitting in a Anarkkian military compound."

"Maybe they captured it."

"That could be." Sophia wove her way through the maze of crates, metal drums and rows of eight foot tall blue cylinders.

Orville put his paw on one of the cylinders. "What

do you think these are?"

Sophia studied the markings on the side of it. "I wouldn't touch it. It looks like it might be a weapon, or something that powers a weapon."

Orville jerked his paw away from the cylinder.

"That is a force tube for an Anarkkian heavy beam pulsar weapon. If you rupture the outer shell it will result in the formation of a one mile wide crater and the destruction of our first forms."

Orville slowly backed away.

Abacus reached out and ran his hand over the dark blue cylinder. His voice had a strange tone to it. "Abacus *MV Expergo*. Seven reassemblies. If I thought I could..." He stopped, glancing over at Orville. "I apologize for my wandering thoughts. We must examine the blinker ship to see if it is functional."

"Sophia knows how to fly them. We found four of them when Draken Mouse sent us to Periculum. Actually he made Master Marloh send us there, but we found blinkers in Norrich Bunker and used one to escape from the mesa where the Gnorli bird left us. It was Sophia's idea to roll the blinker ship off the mesa and use the emergency canopy. I was pretty sure we were going to hit the ground at about a thousand miles an hour, but her plan worked and we landed safely. Then we ran into the green sticky ball creatures. We wouldn't have escaped from them without Proto's tasty cakes."

"I do not understand the purpose of your story. How is it relevant to our current situation?"

"It's not really, it's just kind of an interesting story about blinker ships."

Abacus turned and walked toward the ancient

blinker ship.

Orville frowned. "My mum loves that story."

Sophia was examining the blinker ship's interior. "Same controls as the ones on the mesa." She eyed the circle of yellow lights on the curved console. In the center was a four inch circular violet disk. "That's the one." She slapped her paw down on the disk and covered her ears. There was no shrieking alarm as there had been on Periculum. Instead, the circle of lights changed from yellow to violet and a low humming sound emanated from the base of the ship.

Abacus was standing behind Sophia, watching as she tested the controls. "It is functioning properly. This will carry us across the sea and convey us to my second form. We must hurry."

Orville entered the ship and scanned the cabin. "Look at the size of that coat! How big were these Elders?" He stepped across the floor to a long dark blue coat hanging from the wall. "This is big enough for three of me. Hey, Sophia, look!" Orville pulled the heavy garment down from the hook and draped it over his shoulders. "It's the famous blinker pilot Captain Orville to the rescue!"

Sophia rolled her eyes and snorted. "You might want to see a tailor before you try to rescue someone wearing that."

Orville shoved his paw into one of the pockets. "There's something in here. It feels like a ring. Maybe it will fit me." He pulled out a golden band mounted with a brilliant green oval stone. "It has little white lines in it just like the blue marble."

Abacus whirled around. "Don't put that on your–"

Unfortunately for Orville, the warning had come too

214

late. He had already slipped the ring onto his paw.

The first thing Orville did was scream. The second thing he did was scream again. He screamed the first time because he was seated at the controls of a gleaming Mintarian attack scout ship streaking toward a wall of fire at four thousand miles an hour. He screamed the second time when he saw his arms. They were covered with red scales, his fingers nine inches long and tipped with razor sharp curved yellow claws.

Chapter 28

Shields Up

The odd thing was that Orville knew how to fly the attack scout ship. A split second after he flashed through the wall of fire he reached out and slapped his long scaly fingers across a green sphere hovering two feet in front of him, spinning the sphere to the left. The ship made a ninety degree turn at four thousand miles an hour.

"Inertia deadeners, can't live without 'em." Orville's mind was racing. Inertia deadeners? He had no idea what they were, and yet he knew exactly what they were. They were what allowed him make inconceivably sharp turns at four thousand miles an hour without getting squished against the wall like a striped Snavle bug. Orville groaned. What was a striped Snavle bug? Why had he even said that?

His attack ship shot up through the atmosphere into dark space, Orville quickly scanning the horizon for enemy ships. He tapped a yellow disk and hollered, "What do we got?"

A melodious voice from the console replied, "Anarkkian Interstellar Battle Cruiser, sector R2. Anarkkian Attack Command Vessel, sector D2."

"Scouts?"

"All scout ships destroyed. We are the last."

Orville cursed loudly. "Size 6 Throttle online, now!"

"Size 6 Time Throttle ready. Number 4 tab."

Orville stomped his red scaled foot on a circular panel beneath the console. "Cloak on! We have three minutes!" He whirled the green sphere with his left hand and the ship flashed to the right. "There it is. She's a big one." He shot toward a mammoth silver interstellar cruiser standing in bright contrast to the absolute blackness of dark space. The cruiser was bigger than anything he had ever seen. "Creekers, better make that a Size 7 Throttle!"

"Size 7 Time Throttle online. Number 5 tab."

When he was so close that the Anarkkian cruiser filled the sky Orville smacked his paw down on a bright yellow tab with a strange symbol on it. He had never seen it before and yet he knew it was the number 5. With a loud popping noise a gleaming object flashed out from the front of the scout ship, heading toward the center of the mammoth cruiser. "Throttle away! Evasive action!" He whirled the green sphere toward him and his ship instantly reversed course. He was now streaking away from the cruiser at four thousand miles an hour. "Time shields up!"

A staggeringly bright green field of energy surrounded Orville's scout ship. He hammered down on a blue square tab and a holo image of the Anarkkian battle cruiser appeared in front of him. Orville watched with grim satisfaction as a small point of blue on the battle cruiser began to expand, spreading out across the ship's hull. In less than a minute it was all over. "She's frozen. They won't be causing any trouble for the next ten thousand years or so. Time shield down, cloak off."

"Spectral door opening, altitude three miles. Mintarian commercial transport ship coming through. Scanning. Identity *MV Bermitar*. No crew, no Abacus."

"How is that possible? No crew and no Abacus? What's the Anarkkian command ship doing?"

"Pulsar beams coming online. Changing course, heading toward *MV Bermitar*."

"Scan *Bermitar* for weapons."

"Nineteen thousand time throttles present."

"Largest?"

"Size 15000 M2 Galactic Time Throttle."

"Holy nadwokks, why would they have one of those? They were outlawed by the Fourth Mintarian Council. If that ship gets pulsed this whole galaxy is frozen, and that includes us. How soon can you cloak us?"

"Immediate cloaking for twenty-nine seconds. Three minute cloaking online in nine point two minutes."

"Not enough time. How many distractors left?"

"Three scout attack, one M7 Spectral Attack Cruiser."

"All right, we have to use it. Send the spectral cruiser twenty miles to the rear of their command ship. It'll take them two minutes to realize it's a distractor. That gives us two minutes plus twenty-nine seconds of cloak."

"Spectral Cruiser released. Doorway opening in fifteen seconds."

Orville was feeling queasy. He was here, but he was not here. He was the pilot but he was not the pilot. He knew things he could not know, and even worse, he was covered with red scales and had long yellow claws.

Before he had time to solve any of these puzzles he slapped his hand across the green sphere and the scout ship flashed to the left, heading directly toward the Anarkkian Attack Command Vessel.

Right on time the massive spectral door appeared twenty miles to the rear of the Anarkkian ship. "That should get their attention." The Anarkkians reversed course, retreating from the *MV Bermitar* and heading toward the wildly flashing spectral door. "Right now they're trying to figure out what's going to come through that door. We're going in!"

Orville watched as a massive array of brilliant energy shields popped up around the end of the Anarkkian command ship facing the huge spectral door.

Without knowing why he was doing it, Orville spun the green sphere forward and hammered his knee to one side, pushing a red lever.

"M7 Spectral Cruiser exiting doorway."

The Anarkkian command vessel seemed to shudder, inconceivably powerful heavy pulsar beams flashing out from the stern ports toward the huge Mintarian cruiser plowing out through the spectral doorway.

The instant Orville's knee hit the red lever his ship shot forward at fifteen thousand miles an hour. "Cloak on! Time shields up! Number 6 ready?"

"Cloak on, twenty-nine seconds. Shields up. Number 6 online, number four tab."

Orville gave a grim smile. "Let's see what they think of these brimbleberries. Target up!" A small round circle appeared on the ship's transparent domed canopy. Orville moved his eyes toward the Anarkkian command ship, the small targeting circle tracking his line of vision. When the circle was on the bridge of the

Anarkkian ship he slapped his hand down on the number four yellow tab. With a loud popping noise a number six time throttle flashed out toward the Anarkkian vessel.

"Course 180!" Orville spun the green sphere and his ship shot backwards, now retreating from the Anarkkians at fifteen thousand miles an hour.

"Cloak off, shields down. Power down, deadeners off, time shields up."

Orville turned his gaze to the Anarkkian ship. He wanted to see this one up close and personal. It looked as if some gigantic invisible hand was painting the ship a bright azure blue. The heavy pulsar beams stopped, frozen in time like immense glowing columns of crackling ice. The massive spectral door and the phantom M7 Spectral Cruiser faded away to nothingness. The *MV Bermitar* was safe.

"That it?"

"There are currently no Anarkkian vessels in the vicinity."

"I'm going to board the *MV Bermitar* and make sure she's stable. I'll have to cloak her so the Anarkkians don't find her. The last thing we need is for them to get their claws on a Size 15000 M2 Galactic Time Throttle. Whoever put that on board a private vessel should be rotting in a Quarian Prison."

"Orville? Are you all right?"

"Cloak on, time shield up!"

"What are you talking about? Wake up!"

"Unnhh. I had red scales. I was flying a scout attack ship. It was terrifying. I saved the *MV Bermitar*."

Abacus gave a look of surprise. "You saw my second form? The *MV Bermitar*?"

"I prevented the Anarkkians from destroying it. I hit two of their ships with time throttles."

"This is astonishing, you say you had red scales? The only creatures I know with red scales come from Varmoran, but the ring you found is a Mintarian memory ring. Varmoran must have formed a secret alliance with the Mintarians. That would explain the Mintarian presence."

"What's a memory ring? I still don't understand where I was. Did I blink somewhere?"

"No, you did not blink anywhere. When a Mintarian trooper, or in this case a Varmoran pilot, performs an extraordinary act of bravery he is awarded with a memory ring containing a four dimensional neuro record of his experience. The ring is seldom worn, as the events are almost always traumatic, but it is one of the greatest honors a warrior can receive."

"Oh, there was something else. While I was wearing the ring, my scout ship scanned the *MV Bermitar's* cargo hold for weapons. They said it contained nineteen thousand time throttles plus something called a Size 15000 M2 Galactic Time Throttle, which really scared the pilot. He said if the *MV Bermitar* went down the whole galaxy would be frozen in time. The pilot said he was going to board the *MV Bermitar* and cloak the ship so the Anarkkians couldn't find it."

Abacus' golden eyes flashed wildly. "Clearly a breach of Mintarian Arms Service protocol. I was not informed we were transporting a Size 15000 M2 Galactic Time Throttle. An outlawed weapon of that magnitude should never have been placed aboard a private cargo ship, it should have been traveling in a heavily shielded armada.This is far worse than I thought. Your Varmoran pilot was correct, a time throttle of that size will not just stop time on Earth, it will stop time in your entire galaxy. It is an impossible coincidence that you found this memory ring, that you inadvertently placed it on your paw, that you witnessed the arrival of the *MV Bermitar* and prevented her destruction, and yet it has happened. Your revelation that the Varmoran pilot cloaked the *MV Bermitar* clearly explains why its beacon vanished from my holomap. The ship is hidden by a cloaking device which is functioning only sporadically, due to the degradation of power. Now that I am aware of this, I will attempt alternate methods to determine its location. Your Varmoran pilot may have unwittingly saved our galaxy." Abacus paused. "I cannot help but suspect that your finding of the memory ring was not accidental, that there were unseen forces involved. Forces beyond my comprehension."

Sophia said, "It was not an accident, the ring was where it was meant to be. A famous rabbit named Bartholomew the Adventurer once said, 'Every atom, every molecule, and every bouncing marble is exactly where it should be at every moment in time'. The memory ring was no exception to this rule. We will never know how a Mintarian memory ring belonging to a Varmoran pilot found its way into an Elders' blinker ship which was captured by the Anarkkians and hidden in this obscure military complex. What I do know is after fifteen hundred years the ring was precisely where it needed to be for Orville to find it."

Abacus' eyes were filled with a strange intensity. "It is reason enough to question the underlying fabric of our world. Abacus *MV Expergo* spoke much of an invisible order hidden beneath our seemingly chaotic world, but until now I did not understand his meaning."

"Your Abacus *MV Expergo* sounds very wise."

"I am just beginning to understand the depth of his wisdom."

Orville rose to his feet. "I'm going to put the ring back in the pilot's coat pocket where it belongs. We'd better get going. Time is running out."

Chapter 29

The Stranger

Amanda Mouse was humming quietly as she browsed through the history section in the Book Emporium. Most of the regular customers were familiar with Amanda's unconscious humming and found it to be an endearing trait, but there were a few who judged it to be a minor annoyance. One or two had even complained to Master Marloh. Any book containing historical content would start her humming, and in the Book Emporium she was practically swimming in a sea of them. She enjoyed reading about history so much that she had taken it on as her vocation, currently holding a position at Muridaan Falls Easterly School as the Symocan History Scholar. Only three years prior, one of her students had been a certain young Orville Wellington Mouse.

Amanda was perusing with great interest a massive tome titled *When Rabbits Ruled the Earth*, a study of the Elders, the advanced race which had vanished mysteriously at the end of the Anarkkian Wars. When she lifted her gaze, however, she was abruptly pulled back to the present moment. Directly in her line of sight on the other side of the book shelves was the menacing face of a rough looking mouse.

Amanda slapped her paw over her mouth, afraid she might give a spontaneous squeak of fear. The rough and tumble character she was looking at had a dreadful long scar running down the side of his face. He was also sporting a ragged adventurer's hat pulled down so low it almost covered his eyes. It was quite obvious to Amanda this coarse looking individual was trying to conceal his identity. Her eyes narrowed, the initial wave of fear replaced by her overpowering sense of curiosity. Amanda loved a good mystery almost as much as she loved history. "I must determine what this ruffian is up to. Who knows what skullduggery he may be contemplating."

She slid out a weighty volume titled, *The Dark Anarkkian Night, A Comprehensive History of the Anarkkian Wars*. It would make good reading and a fine heavy weapon, should this mysterious stranger decide to cause any trouble. Clutching the massive volume with both paws Amanda strolled around to the other side of the book shelves. The rough looking mouse had moved to the far end of the aisle. "He's up to no good, I can feel it." Amanda froze. The scarred ruffian had a long silver Quintarian Sleeper strapped to his hip. Only a few mice in Muridaan Falls would have recognized such a weapon, but Amanda Mouse was a voracious reader and identified it instantly, having seen a photograph of one almost two years earlier in *Ancient Quintarian Weapons of War, Volume III*. She knew that with a sharp flick of the wrist the device telescoped out and emitted a low hum. When the humming stopped the user would select the weapon's power level. At low power it would do what its name implied – cause an enemy to instantly fall asleep. At higher levels the sleep effect became far more pronounced, and at maximum level it became permanent. At level twenty the Sleeper sent out a powerful electronic pulse beam which caused a fatal overload in the enemy's brain.

When she spotted the Sleeper on the stranger's hip Amanda lost all confidence in the defensive value of the heavy book she was clutching. She watched as the stranger slipped like a shadow around the rack and disappeared.

"This is serious, that mouse is carrying a Sleeper. Master Marloh needs to be made aware of this dastardly fellow." Amanda set down *The Dark Anarkkian Night* with a loud thump and strode purposefully down the aisle, making her way toward the front desk. When she turned the corner, however, she stopped in her tracks. The armed stranger was engaged in conversation with Master Marloh, and it was quite obvious they knew each other.

"Great heavens!" Amanda skittered back behind the shelves, peering through the books at the two conversing mice. "Why in the world would Master Marloh be acquainted with such a scalawag as that?" Amanda studied the mysterious stranger's face. He wasn't quite as scary as she had first thought. He'd removed his hat and she was surprised to see he was close to handsome in a rough sort of way. She was trying to decide whether his scar added or detracted from his appearance when to her utter horror Master Marloh turned and looked directly at her.

He gave her a friendly wave, calling out, "Pest control. We're having a moth problem in the basement. I'm afraid they might damage some of the rare books."

Amanda stepped out from behind the rack, attempting a casual demeanor, allowing an amused smile to cross her face. "Better safe than sorry, I always say."

The tough looking mouse grinned at her and waved. Amanda found herself uncharacteristically embarrassed, but strangely flattered by his attention. She decided he had a kind face, and she especially liked his eyes. Every mouse had scars of one kind or another. His just happened to be on the surface where you could see them. She gave him a pleasant nod and turned on her heel, heading back to her history books.

"We should go down to the Metaphysical Adventurers headquarters. I'm afraid your appearance might be a little alarming to some of our customers. Probably best not to carry that Sleeper around in the shop. You know, Patcher, I could get rid of that scar for you in less than a minute using my shaping skills."

"I'll pass. I've gotten used to it. Besides, it gives me a certain look the ladies seem to appreciate." Patcher gave Master Marloh a wink.

Master Marloh held up his paw. "That's all I need to know, thank you. Shall we go?" He turned and headed toward the blue door at the back of the shop, the blue door which had been quite a puzzle to Orville when he began work at the Book Emporium. When Master Marloh opened the blue door with his left paw, the door opened to the largest shaping library in Symoca. When he opened it with his right paw, the paw which bore his silver Metaphysical Adventurers ring, the door opened to a massive spiral staircase leading to the Metaphysical Adventurers headquarters. The headquarters was an extensive underground complex containing thousands of technologically advanced artifacts brought back from other worlds over the years by MA members.

When Master Marloh was certain they weren't being watched he swung the blue door open using his right paw. The pair of mice stepped onto the ancient stone stairway. Master Marloh sent a glowing sphere of light down the stairs. Five minutes later they stood facing the magnificent main hall of the Metaphysical Adventurers headquarters, three hundred feet long and two hundred feet wide, with ceilings that towered fifty feet above the smooth stone floor. Three enormous stacked walkways constructed of massive ornately carved wooden beams ran around the perimeter of the room, each lined with wide iron mesh shelves holding thousands of mysterious high tech devices brought back by MA members.

Patcher eyed the enormous hall. "This place amazes me every time I see it. I don't think even Mirus Mouse knows what half the tech here actually does or how it works."

"Did you have any luck tracking Eldon? I'm not entirely certain I should have raised Orville's hopes by telling him his papa might still be alive, but I didn't know what else to do after the tech hunter found his ring in central Symoca. I sent Orville and Sophia on a hunt for some blue stones they were curious about. It might lead to something important, but mainly I did it to keep them occupied while we're searching for Eldon. Orville is an extremely gifted shaper, but he needs a few years of experience before he'll be much help in the field."

"The short story is I had some luck, but not a lot. I talked to the tech hunter who found Eldon's ring. Ever been to Varmoran?"

"Varmoran? You tracked Eldon to Varmoran?"

"Turns out the tech hunter didn't just find Eldon's ring in the East Symocan jungle, he also found his pack dangling at the top of a ninety foot tall tree. It had a few clothes in it, a letter written in some crazy language, and a big purple flower tucked into a side pocket."

"His pack was hanging in the top of a tree?"

"Strange, I know. Not sure why he'd be up a tree, unless he was trying to get away from something. It doesn't make sense though, the tree wasn't strong enough to hold a full grown mouse up where the pack was."

"Odd. The ring was nearby?"

"About a hundred yards away at the edge of a big meadow in the central Symocan forest. The tech hunter was using a heavy metal scanner and found it."

"Wait, suppose the pack didn't get carried up the tree, suppose it fell down into the tree?"

"That's it! He must have done a loop in his Dragonfly and the pack and ring fell out. He could have been trying to dodge some kind of flying creature. Who knows what he ran into. Could have been a lot of things in that area."

"Any idea where he was going, where he'd been?"

"The purple flower was my first clue. Couldn't figure it out until I saw the thorn. It's a mutation most likely caused by an Anarkkian greenstone. I recognized it right away. I had a friend who almost died on Varmoran after getting stabbed by one of those purple nightmares, so I figured Eldon must have been there."

"I'm familiar with Varmoran, although I don't know why he would go there. It was devastated by the

Anarkkians, the entire planet obliterated in less than a week. There's nothing left but ruins, the sun hardly ever breaks through the toxic cloud layer. Those purple flowers are just the tip of the iceberg as far as mutations on Varmoran. Anarkkians peppered it with greenstones before their invasion. Dreadful place. Were you able to translate the letter?"

"Took a while, but Mirus Mouse came through with some ancient Thaumatarian device he found buried on the tech shelves. He put his paw on a white panel and talked to it for a few minutes, then held the letter in front of it. Some crazy striped light scanned over it and a minute later the machine read the letter to us. I have no idea what language the letter was in, but it must have been one that Eldon understood."

"He speaks a number of obscure languages. What did it say?"

"The translation was a bit confusing, but someone was writing to him about something they called the 'Flicker'. I couldn't figure out what it was, but the whole village was terrified and they were asking Eldon for help. They were afraid the world was ending. You know how superstitious some of those isolated areas are."

"Indeed. You have no idea the true nature of this Flicker? Some sort of mutation maybe?"

"Don't really know. Some villagers thought it was a gigantic eye, some thought it was a door opening up to let demons in. They were afraid creatures from 'the other side' were going to eat them."

"The other side of what? That doesn't help us much. Could you tell what world the village was on?"

"Another puzzle. The letter said they live at Earth's

End."

"What does that mean?"

"No idea. Maybe on the edge of an ocean or something? You know, the earth ends and the ocean begins?"

"It could be something like that. You went to Varmoran?"

"I spent a month there and was lucky to get back alive. Like you said, it's a dreadful place. They still have Anarkkian spiders roaming around. I hate those things. I'd be dead if it wasn't for the scramble beam Mirus gave me. Does something to their engineered intelligence and they just wander off. Most of the time, anyway. I scoured the area where my friend got bit by the purple flower but didn't find anything. Problem is there's no one there. Eldon could have spent a year on Varmoran and nobody would know. The good news is I didn't find any bodies, if you catch my drift. He definitely could still be alive. My guess is he went to Varmoran to look for something, came back and then headed off to wherever this Flicker thing is. It could be near where we found his pack, or he could have dumped his ring and pack and kept on flying for a thousand miles. No blood on the pack, by the way. No claw marks, no teeth marks."

"That's something. We still have good reason to be hopeful. The rest of the Dragonfly Squadron is back from the jungle. Twenty thousand square miles and they found nothing except a few old cities."

"What do you want me to do now?"

"Take the letter to Mirus and see if he can identify the language. That might help us locate the village. After you talk to him we can regroup and compile our information. Whatever Eldon was looking for on Varmoran must have been important. I just wish he'd filed a mission report. You know how much Eldon loved filling out mission forms."

"No news is good news I guess."

"It will have to be for now. I'll let Orville and his mum know we still have good reason to be hopeful and we're continuing the search. I have a sense Eldon is alive, but something's not right. I can't put my paw on it, but something is definitely not right."

Chapter 30

Down Under

"Relax, Orville, it's just like flying *The Dragonfly*. Left stick is vertical velocity and rotation, right stick is forward, backward, left and right. There's nothing to it."

"Maybe Abacus should fly us out of the building. I don't want to bump into one of those blue force tube cylinder things and blow us into a billion pieces."

Sophia gave a sigh. "You need to learn how to fly a blinker ship and there's no time like the present. Proto and Abacus are indestructible and we're safely buckled in. Tap the violet disk in the center of the light circle."

Orville reached out and tapped the disk. "Check."

"There, see how all the yellow lights have all turned violet and you can hear the antigrav displacer units humming?"

"The what?"

"Never mind, just pay attention to the controls. All right, the doors to the building are wide open. Push the left stick forward and the ship will go straight up. When we're about fifteen feet in the air, push the right stick forward and go straight across the room and out the doors. Nothing to it."

"So it's exactly like flying *The Dragonfly*?"

"Exactly the same."

"Okay, I think I've got it." Orville furrowed his brow and peered out through the blinker ship's cockpit window. "Here we go!"

Much to Orville's surprise when he pushed the left stick forward just as he did in *The Dragonfly*, the blinker ship shot up at two hundred and fifteen miles per hour, smashing through the roof with a horrendous squealing and tearing of metal. By the time Orville realized what was happening the blinker ship was over five hundred feet in the air.

"AAGGGHHH!!" Orville pulled the stick back and the ship plummeted down toward the metal building, which was now sporting a gaping hole in the roof.

"Too much! Too much!"

Orville pushed the left stick and the ship came to a halt, hovering silently above the building.

Abacus nudged Proto, whispering loudly, "Orville is why Mintarians created the Abacus."

Proto snickered. "And why the Elders made me indestructible."

Orville frowned. "I can hear you back there. For your information someone told me quite incorrectly that flying this thing was *exactly* like flying *The Dragonfly*."

Sophia whacked Orville's arm. "Relax, we're out of the building and the ship flies. Abacus, directions?"

"We are currently located on the southeast inner perimeter of the Black Wall. Our initial scan was too broad an area to give a precise location, but there is some indication the ship is near the northwest edge of the wall. I have tried a number times to locate the *MV Bermitar* but was unsuccessful. Our only hope is the power will decrease enough for the ship to disengage non-essential systems like the cloaking mechanism."

Sophia pointed to the circular compass on the control panel. "Rotate the ship heading to northwest. Gently, please, I don't want to spin around five hundred times and throw up all over you."

Orville burst out laughing. "Some friend you are. Adjusting course." The blinker ship rotated until the compass read northwest. "That's it, here we go." Orville nudged the right stick forward and the ship responded smoothly, flashing forward at an easy sixty miles an hour.

"Nice job, Captain Orville. Take it slow for a while until you get a feel for how the ship handles." Sophia peered down at the landscape passing below them, watching as they soared over an ocean of blue foliage.

Abacus flipped up a small holomap of Earth and studied it. He flipped through the map until strings of flashing symbols were passing across the holoscreen. His fingers were a blur as he tapped on the moving symbols. When the symbols stopped moving he blinked off the holoscreen. "I am still unable to break through the cloaking device to determine the *MV Bermitar's* location. I am also unable to determine whether my second form is stationary or moving, so we shall continue heading in a northwesterly direction toward its last known general location. In one hundred and ninety-three miles we reach the sea, which is three hundred and ninety-four miles across. The *MV Bermitar* should be approximately two hundred miles inland, if it is in fact stationary."

"Heading due northwest. We just passed over another small town with more of those weird buildings they grow from seeds. I wonder if this is what Anarkkia looks like?"

"It is somewhat like this, although their sky is a brilliant red and they possess binary suns, two stars orbiting each other. When the suns are in alignment the Anarkkians experience winter, when both suns are visible they experience summer."

Sophia sat up straight, studying the horizon. "The sea!"

Abacus flipped off his holomap. "We must be extremely careful crossing such a large body of water. Keep your eyes open for anything at all out of the ordinary."

Orville looked back at Abacus. "What do you mean? Careful about what?"

"We are inside the Black Wall. The wall was constructed by the Anarkkians to deter any form of land based invasion, including all atmospheric vehicles. The wall was not designed to deter attacks from interstellar warships, ships traveling in dark space. They had numerous other defense mechanisms in place for such contingencies, often hidden in bodies of water. These are what give me concern. This particular blinker ship has no defensive shields. A single blast from even a small pulsar weapon would obliterate the ship."

"Maybe we should fly really low, right above the water so their defense systems won't spot us."

"That is not necessarily a bad tactic. Fly as close to the surface of the sea as possible."

"Only another mile or two till we reach the coastline. It's beautiful isn't it? So calm. It reminds me of the

Vesarak Sea where my mum and papa used to take me."

Sophia smiled. Every body of water they saw reminded Orville of the Vesarak Sea where his mum and papa used to take him. She sensed he was remembering the time his papa took him out on a fishing boat.

Three minutes later Orville brought the blinker ship to a hover, then gingerly tapped the left stick until they were only a few feet above the water. "Hold on, here we go!" Orville pushed the right stick and they shot forward at over one hundred miles an hour, so close to the water the ship was leaving a large rooster tail of spray behind it. "Whoo hoo! It feels like we're going a thousand miles an hour!"

"Orville, keep your paw on the stick in case we need to take evasive action."

"There's nothing to avoid, we're flying across a calm sea."

"Remember what Abacus said about the defense systems."

"Fine." Orville put his paw back on the left stick. He was just about to make what he considered a hilarious comment to Sophia when he noticed a section of the sea appeared to be rippling, the reflection of the sky and clouds unfocused, blurry. "Can you see that? It looks weird, kind of like a wavering mirage or–"

Before Orville realized what was happening Abacus reached between the seats and yanked the left stick back. The blinker ship plunged downward, bouncing twice across the water, then sank rapidly into the sea.

"WHAT DID YOU DO? WE'LL DROWN!!"

Abacus grabbed Orville's arms as he frantically

grasped at the control sticks. "Stop! We are not going to drown. The ship is fully capable of dark space travel and undersea travel. The hull is pressurized and we possess an integrated oxygen generation air purifier system which activates automatically when the hatch is closed. If you're still wondering about that blurry, rippling portion of the ocean, it was a cloaked Anarkkian interstellar heavy beam pulsar gun emplacement. Two more seconds and our ship would have been destroyed, along with your first form and Sophia's first form."

Orville's paws were shaking. "What? We're not going to drown?"

Sophia shook her head. "We're fine. Blinker ships were designed to travel through the atmosphere, in dark space, and beneath the ocean. There's nothing to worry about. Go ahead and take the controls. Abacus, what's the best way to avoid the pulsar guns?"

"Maintain a minimum depth of one hundred feet. Our speed will be severely impacted, but Anarkkian sensors will be unable to detect us."

Orville took a long slow breath, doing his best to calm down. "I wish someone would tell me these things. How was I supposed to know we weren't going to drown?"

Sophia snickered. "You should have seen the look on your face."

"I wasn't scared, I was just extremely surprised."

Abacus interrupted. "We must keep moving, now more than ever. Traveling beneath the waves will slow us down, and that is time we can't afford to lose. Orville, the altimeter is reading minus one twenty, indicating we are one hundred and twenty feet beneath

238

sea level. Maintain current depth at maximum velocity, heading northwest. Subsurface speed will be thirty-two miles per hour." Abacus reached over and tapped a set of blue tabs Orville hadn't noticed before. A ring of circles appeared on the ship's canopy. "An alarm will sound if we approach an obstacle, likewise if something is traveling rapidly toward us."

"Something might attack us? Like what?"

"Any number of undersea creatures might display a natural curiosity toward our ship, but such organisms are harmless. Do keep an eye out for Anarkkian drill fish, however."

"Drill fish? What's that?"

"It is another autonomous defense system created by the Anarkkians. Drill fish appear on the holoscreen as an ordinary school of fish, but in close proximity they latch onto the ship's hull, perforating it in less than a minute with hundreds of small holes. Such an action at this depth would bring your mission to a sudden and untimely end."

Orville gulped, pushing the right stick all the way forward. Their ship churned ahead through the murky sea. Despite his best attempt to avert them, images of the grotesque and terrifying sea creatures he had seen in the Senyph Ocean on Periculum were dancing in his head.

Chapter 31

The Dome

Orville's eyes were drooping when the holoscreen alarm blared. He sat up straight, peering into the dark green water. "What is that? Something big directly ahead of us!"

Sophia squinted her eyes. "I can see it now. It looks like buildings inside a big glass dome."

Abacus' eyes were flickering wildly. "Scanning for communication and command systems. Negative. I believe we have stumbled across the defense control center for the Anarkkian colony. This is excellent, quite fortuitous, but I will need to enter the dome. I should be able to disengage all colony defense systems, including the heavy beam pulsar gun emplacements and more than likely the Black Wall. If I am successful we shall be able to fly unhindered through the atmosphere. Orville, take us down and circle the dome."

Orville nodded, pulling back on the left stick. The ship descended smoothly. "Altimeter reading minus three hundred twenty-five feet. How deep can we go? Won't the weight of the water crush us?"

"Maximum depth for this blinker is six thousand feet. Continue descent."

Four minutes later the ship reached the base of the dome. "We're ten feet above the seabed and I'm taking us around the dome's outer edge. What are you looking for?"

"The entrance used by their autonomous maintenance vehicles."

"Sophia and I could just blink inside the dome. Can we shut off the defenses?"

"Impossible. It is far more complex than just flipping a switch. I must merge with the system, just as I merge with my second form."

Proto called out, "I have detected an entrance using my narrow line scanners. Six hundred yards ahead."

Orville guided the ship forward, circling the enormous glass dome. "I see it. Abacus, how are you going to get from the ship to the entryway? If you open our hatch seawater will flood the ship."

"I will use the emergency exit on the cabin floor. The pressurized air inside the ship will prevent the seawater from entering the cockpit. Once I am gone you may close the hatch."

"You're sure don't need any help?"

"I'm afraid you and Sophia would not last very long inside the dome. The atmosphere is quite toxic, unsuitable for organic creatures. You could survive by shaping an airtight sphere of defense, but there really is no need for your presence. It should only take a few minutes to merge with the system and deactivate it."

"Okay, we'll wait here. We're next to the entrance now, fifteen feet above the sea bed."

"Excellent. "Abacus released his jump seat safety harness. He reached up and flipped a small red lever on the ceiling. "Stay seated."

241

Orville watched as a circular section of the floor whirred open. Just as Abacus had said, the air pressure within the ship pushed back against the seawater, preventing it from flooding in.

"If I do not return within twenty minutes, you must continue on without me."

"Wait, what? How are we supposed to–"

Abacus dropped through the escape hatch with a small splash, sinking rapidly to the ocean floor. He looked up and gave a quick wave, heading toward the dome's entrance.

"He's walking on the bottom of the ocean!" Orville peered through the ship's canopy, watching as Abacus stepped across the rocky sea floor to the arched entryway.

Sophia gave a loud gasp. "He's dissolving! He's turning to liquid and getting absorbed into the door!" A moment later the reverse process occurred. A thick blue liquid oozed out of the other side of the door, quickly coalescing into the familiar form of Abacus. He turned and waved, disappearing around the side of a massive silver cube lined with rows of glowing violet lights.

Orville spun his seat around to face Sophia and Proto. "What do you think he meant when he said he might not return?"

Sophia shrugged. "He'll be fine. He's indestructible, just like Proto."

"But suppose he doesn't come back? How will we find the *MV Bermitar*?"

"We'll keep going until we reach the other side of the sea, then surface and search until we find the ship."

"But it's cloaked so only Abacus can find it."

"Stop jumping so far ahead. We'll figure it out.

We're Metaphysical Adventurers, that's what we do."

"I know, but how are we going–" Orville's question was interrupted by a blinding flash of light and a powerful shock wave that shook the ship violently, tossing the three adventurers to the floor, slamming Orville against the bulkhead. "Uhhnnh.... my arm!"

Sophia cried out, "The dome is collapsing!" A massive explosion had shattered the dome and Sophia watched in horror as the inconceivable weight of the ocean roared into it, displacing the dome's atmosphere in a split second. Vast clouds of shimmering bubbles rose up toward the surface. The dome had imploded with Abacus inside it.

Orville looked at Sophia in horror. "What about Abacus?"

"I don't know. He's indestructible, but I don't know what that explosion was."

"It could have been one of those pulsar gun weapons. The kind that hit the *MV Bermitar* and shattered him."

"We'll just have to wait and see."

Proto stood up. "I will search for him."

Sophia shook her head. "No, we can't afford to lose you too. We have no idea what defense systems might still be active within the dome. Something else could explode."

"We can't just sit here and do nothing."

"There's nothing else we can do."

"Wait, the dome is gone so I can fly us over the rubble and we can look for him!"

"Good idea."

Proto scanned the destruction. "Take us twenty feet above the wreckage and I will search for Abacus using wide spectrum. I should be able to pick up his residual electronic signature."

Orville nodded to Proto, easing the blinker ship up to twenty feet. "I'll take us across the area in a grid pattern. Call out if you see anything."

"It looks quite dreadful. Whatever it was that exploded obliterated half the contents of the dome. Abacus most certainly succeeded in his attempt to shut down all the Anarkkian defense systems. I don't see a single blinking light anywhere." Proto scanned the rubble anxiously, searching for any sign of Abacus.

Ten minutes later they were still searching.

It was Orville who spotted the blue glow. "Look, over there! Underneath that big pile of rubble!" He veered the ship toward the small blue light.

"It has to be him."

"The electronic signature is a match! It's Abacus!"

"How do we lift all the wreckage off him?"

Sophia shook her head. "We don't have to move it, we can convert it to thought clouds." Sophia held out her paw to Orville. "Take my paw, we can link minds again, the same as when we created the tornado. It's the only way we'll be able to convert that much physical matter to thought clouds."

Orville took Sophia's paw and closed his eyes, letting go of his physical self. He felt his mind merging with hers, once again experiencing everything Sophia had ever seen or done, feeling everything she felt. It was difficult to distinguish his own thoughts from hers. "Ready? Start at the center of the pile and move out. Be careful not to convert Abacus."

Proto watched as a brilliant golden aura surrounded the two mice, watched as a white sparkling light appeared in the center of the massive pile of wreckage. The glimmering fire circled outward across the mounds of ravaged metal walls and twisted beams. It was over within a minute. The rubble was gone and they could see Abacus, or at least what was left of him.

"Where's the rest of him? Where's his arms and legs and head?"

Before Sophia could reply the blue torso glowed brilliantly, a trillion stars and planets and galaxies appearing inside him. "He's reassembling!" Sophia gaped as streams of blue glimmering liquid flowed out from beneath the remaining piles of rubble toward Abacus. It took only minutes for him to absorb them, minutes for his arms and legs to form again. He flashed brightly, then rose to his feet, the ends of his fingers blazing with a blinding pink light.

"What's happening to him?"

"I don't know. I've never seen him this bright before."

Abacus staggered forward, his long hands pressing against his head. Finally the brilliant light dimmed and he lowered his hands. He looked dazed, but finally caught sight of the ship. Orville guided it directly over him and opened the emergency hatch.

Abacus reached up through the opening and Proto grabbed his arms, pulling him into the ship.

"Are you all right? What happened? What was that explosion?"

Abacus' voice was strained and hollow. "A grave miscalculation on my part. When I merged with the dome's control center it set off a hidden self destruct mechanism. I was only twenty feet from the pulsar bomb when it exploded."

"We saw you reassemble. Are you all right?"

"I believe so, but I am different. More than I was. I am as yet unable to explain this phenomenon. I have gained much knowledge, but do not clearly understand the source of the new data. I now know the precise location of my second form, and I also know we have less than two days until the *MV Bermitar* collides with the surface of your planet, bringing an end to our galaxy."

Chapter 32

The Blue Tree

"Going up!" Orville pushed the left stick forward and the ship rose up through the murky sea, exiting in a cacophonous explosion of waves and salt water spray. Freed from its watery prison the ship shot into the sky at over four hundred miles an hour. "Whoa! Too fast!" Orville pulled back on the stick, slowing their rapid ascent.

Abacus pointed to the compass. "Head due west."

Sophia cried out, "The Black Wall is gone! You did it, Abacus!"

"All Anarkkian defense control systems have been disengaged, destroyed by the pulsar bomb. We no longer need be concerned about them."

"I thought you said the *MV Bermitar* was northwest of us?"

"I have become aware that my second form was cloaked, then programmed to fly in a wide circular pattern high above the Black Wall. The *MV Bermitar's* altitude has been decreasing as its power diminishes, its cloaking device functioning only sporadically. Current position is directly to the west at an altitude of seven thousand fifty-two feet, the ship descending at a rate of three thousand twenty feet per day. When she hits the earth the titanic force of the impact will set off the Size 15000 M2 Galactic Time Throttle and that will be the end of us."

A wave of terror ran through Orville. He did not want time to stop. He did not want his adventures with Sophia to stop. "We can save the ship. I know we can." Orville spun the blinker around until it faced west, then jammed the right stick forward. Sophia felt herself pressed back against the seat as they shot forward, the sea below them a blur.

Proto gripped his jump seat tightly, his eyes on the sea below them. "I see a sailing ship! It's primitive, but it indicates the presence of intelligent life forms inhabiting the coastline. I can't tell from this altitude what manner of creature is guiding it, so perhaps we could take a quick–"

"We're not stopping! We're not even slowing down!"

Orville caught the look of stunned surprise on Sophia's face. "I mean, I'm sorry, but we really don't have any time to spare. We have to save the *MV Bermitar* and we don't know what other obstacles we might run into."

Proto gave a broad wink to Sophia. "As by your command, Master Captain Orville, Chief Navigator and Pilot."

"Sorry, I didn't mean to sound so bossy. I just don't want anything to happen to... anyone I really like a lot."

Sophia ran her paw across Orville's shoulder. "We'll be fine, monkey butt. Abacus knows exactly where the ship is and at this speed it won't take us long to reach it. We'll have at least a day to figure out how to power it up. We'll save the world just like we always do."

"Thanks. I just wanted... well... I didn't want anything to..."

"I know. We'll be okay, I promise."

The blinker ship sped along across the sea, the wind buffeting the craft as they passed into ever darkening skies. "Another pulsar gun emplacement! That makes six of them we've seen. Thank goodness Abacus shut off their defenses. We never would have reached the *MV Bermitar* in time traveling under the sea."

"Land ahead, but look at that storm! The sky is pitch black."

"Abacus, should I try to fly above the storm?"

"Negative. Fly below it, just above the trees if you can. The center of the storm is miles up, and taking us into dark space would be far too risky a venture in a ship as old as this one."

"Look at the lightning! Incredible!"

Orville reduced the ship's speed and descended to two hundred feet. "We can avoid the full force of the storm here, but we'll have to keep an eye out for tall structures."

Abacus flipped on the ship's forward scanners. "The alarm will sound if we encounter any obstacles."

"Okay, the sea is behind us. Eyes open, everyone."

Proto cried out, "A village! We just passed over a small village with boats and a harbor. It looks like a fishing village." Proto stopped short, giving Orville a nervous glance. "But of course we don't have time to stop and visit."

Orville hadn't even heard Proto, his sole focus being the wildly blowing trees below them. Even at this low altitude the wind from the great storm was pummeling the ship, a wall of heavy rain drops spattering madly against the clear canopy. He glanced up at the ragged flashes of lightning crackling and tearing across the black sky. "This is worse than the storm we saw in Pavorak Gorge after we found Proto! It's a bad one!"

"Maybe you should slow down a little. It's hard to see through all this rain."

Orville pulled the right stick back. "How's that? We're steady at fifty miles an hour."

"That's good. We should have time to steer clear of any obstacles."

"I don't think we'll have any. There's no old cities out here and no mountains I can–" Orville nearly jumped out of his seat when the alarm shrieked out its warning.

"Creekers!" Orville brought the ship to a hover, slowly edging it forward.

"It looks like an enormous tree."

"I can't believe what I'm seeing! It's the same gigantic blue tree we saw on Periculum at the Blue Monks' monastery! Look at the leaves, they're perfect blue circles. This one is even bigger than the one at the monastery. It must be twelve hundred feet tall. I don't understand how the same kind of tree could be growing on Earth and on Periculum."

"Fly around it. We have to get to the *MV Bermitar*."

"Proto, mark this location on your Interworld Positioning System. I want to come back here sometime and explore this area. Maybe the Blue Monks have a monastery near here."

"I have marked it."

"Wait! Look at the leaves! They're not moving, even in this howling wind! How is that possible?"

"We have to go. We'll solve that puzzle some other time."

Orville gave a groan of exasperation but maneuvered the ship around the massive blue tree. Soon it was far behind them, the violence of the wind escalating rapidly. "We have to get past this storm! The wind is battering us all over the place. Everyone make sure you're buckled in."

For almost an hour the four adventurers battled the raging maelstrom, its ferocious gale force winds buffeting their small blinker ship, great shards of lightning blasting down from the roiling black skies. Orville watched a monstrous bolt of jagged lightning explode a hundred feet in front of them, transforming a large stand of wildly flailing trees into seventy foot tall blazing torches.

"Abacus! What happens if we get hit by lightning?"

"We are perfectly safe inside the ship. It is well insulated and we are not touching the ground. We will experience only a brilliant blinding light and a thunderous boom as the heat from the lightning causes the air to rapidly expand in a most explosive manner."

"We'll be okay?"

"You will be fine."

Orville pushed the right stick and the ship sped forward. "I don't like this storm and I really don't like that lightning."

Sophia laughed. "It could be worse, it could be raining giant carnivorous centipedes."

Orville managed a weak grin. "Doesn't anything scare you?"

"I'm scared of furry caterpillars."

"What?"

251

"Blue sky!" Proto's voice rang out above the roar of the storm. Orville looked up and saw a brilliant patch of blue in the distance. He jammed both sticks forward and they blasted out of the raging darkness into clear indigo skies.

Sophia looked out the rear canopy at the massive storm behind them. "It looks almost like the Black Wall except with lightning."

"Abacus, how far to the *MV Bermitar*?"

"It has moved slightly. Head southwest to an altitude of five thousand one hundred feet. The ship is decreasing the power allocated to the cloaking device, so it will be flickering in and out of view with greater frequency. We should be able to spot it without the use of enhanced scanning systems."

Orville sent the ship soaring up into the sky. "Five thousand feet, heading southwest. How many miles did you say?"

"One hundred and twenty-nine."

"We should reach it in under an hour. Then all we have to do is stop a gargantuan interstellar transport ship from dropping out of the sky and turning us into living statues."

Chapter 33

The Letter

Mirus Mouse furrowed his eyebrows. This one had been a tough nut to crack. Patcher seemed to relish presenting him with the most insidious puzzles he could conjure up. He glared silently as Captain Patcher fell into an overstuffed chair and leaned his head back with a loud exhalation, casually propping his leather boots up on Mirus' tea table. Mirus was fuming inside. A little decorum would be nice. Who puts their muddy old boots on a tea table? And that ridiculous scar. Any shaper would be able to–"

"Did you figure it out? The language?"

"A tough nut to crack, quite a conundrum indeed."

"I'm confused, is it a nut or a conundrum?" Patcher gave a loud guffaw.

Mirus rubbed his temples. Patcher was giving him a headache. "Most humorous. I have run Eldon's letter through the Thaumatarian translator several more times with virtually identical results. I would tell you emphatically that several of the symbols used were startlingly reminiscent of the archaic hieroglyphs originating in the pre-Anarkkian world of–"

"Where's the letter from? That's all I want to know."

Mirus gave Patcher a sharp look. "Indeed, of course, a mouse of action, Captain Patcher of the infamous Dragonfly Squadron. No time for thinking, too much adventuring to be done. Mustn't overwork the gray matter."

Patcher rolled his eyes. "So the letter came from..."

"The village undoubtedly lies east of the Symocan jungle, more than likely along the coastline of the Sutilbo Sea. Quite fascinating, the text of the letter is a curious mix of primitive Anarkkian symbols and the ideographs of an ancient Symocan nomadic tribe who settled along the Sutilbo Sea over eight hundred years ago, adapting a subsistence lifestyle as fishermice. More than likely the village is in close proximity to some long forgotten Anarkkian colony, which would explain–"

"You're the best, Mirus. And for the record, it wasn't me who started calling you the Mad Mouse of Muridaan."

"I shall sleep soundly tonight, basking in the warmth of this newfound knowledge."

Patcher gave a loud snort, slapping Mirus on the shoulder. "I like you, Mirus. Anytime you want to fly with the Dragonfly Squadron just let me know. We'd be lucky to have a master pilot like you. You should really think about it. You need to get out more often." With tip of his hat Patcher turned and strolled out the doorway.

Mirus chuckled to himself. "Captain Mirus Mouse of the Dragonfly Squadron. A nice ring to that, I would tell you." Mirus leaned back in his chair, a faraway look appearing in his eyes.

Twenty minutes later Captain Patcher stood facing

Master Marloh. "I'll need the whole squadron. The coastline of the Sutilbo covers a lot of ground, too much for one Dragonfly. It will take all of us to find the Flicker, whatever it turns out to be."

"Do whatever you have to do to find Eldon. I haven't heard a word from Orville or Sophia. They're somewhere in east Symoca in a Dragonfly. Have the squadron members keep an eye out for them."

"Will do. If Orville's anything at all like his papa I wouldn't worry too much about him. I'll gather the crew and we'll take off at sunrise."

Patcher was striding toward the front door when he heard the soft melodic humming. He grinned, making an unplanned detour to the history book.

"Hey, a lot of mice are complaining about all the humming. You want to turn it down a notch?"

A very startled Amanda Mouse looked up from the pages of a dusty old tome titled *Before the Comet, Volume IV: Reign of the Apes*. "Mice are complaining? Was I humming again?"

"Just kidding. I like your humming. Sounds just like a Dragonfly cruising through a clear blue sky."

"You're saying I remind you of a bug-eyed insect?"

"Wait, no, that's not what I meant at all. The wings of a Dragonfly make a lovely sound, and soaring through the sky is like nothing else in this world."

Amanda smiled. "I was teasing. I knew what you meant."

"Have you ever flown in a Dragonfly?"

"I have not, but I have a feeling all that is going to change very soon. Just so you know, Master Marloh told me all about you, Captain Patcher of the Dragonfly Squadron."

Chapter 34

MV Bermitar

"We're close, a few miles at most. Drop down to four thousand seven hundred feet."

Orville eased the ship down. "Everyone keep an eye out for the flickering ship."

Proto spotted it. "There! To the left of that big cloud." Orville caught a brief glimpse of a massive silver ship.

"Closing in." Orville sent the blinker ship darting through the sky toward the cloaked vessel. "How do we board it?"

"There's a topside flight deck for scout ships. We'll be able to set down there and enter through the main pilot station."

Sophia cried out, "There it is again! Take us in before it cloaks!"

"Creekers, look at the size of that thing! It's bigger than Muridaan Falls!" Orville jammed the sticks forward and the ship darted ahead, shooting up over the top of the great gleaming leviathan. "Unhh! It's gone again!"

"Drop down fifty feet. Slowly."

"Going down. Twenty... thirty... forty..."

"Slow. We're almost on it."

Orville felt a slight bump as they touched down on the *MV Bermitar*.

"That's it! We're on it! Gear down, power down." Orville glanced over at Abacus. "What now?"

Abacus stood motionless, his golden eyes pulsing with an unfamiliar light. He tapped a violet disk on the port side bulkhead and the blinker's hatch whirred open, forming a set of stairs leading down to the invisible flight deck.

Orville peered out through the doorway. "That's spooky. It looks like we'll step off and fall through the sky."

"Abacus *MV Bermitar* making his presence known!"

"What?"

Abacus strode down the stairs and stepped out onto the invisible hull of the great Mintarian ship. He kneeled down and extended both his arms, lowering them slowly until they made contact with the ship's hull. The bulbous ends of his fingers flared with a brilliant pink light. Sophia watched his hands liquefy, spreading across the surface of the ship.

"I am searching for the cloaking device. There are only a few places where it– ah, I have it. Very clever indeed, it is tied in with the antimatter core field. Your Varmoran scout pilot knew what he was doing. Impressive. I'll deactivate the auxiliary power transfer tunnel." Abacus closed his eyes, his body shimmering with a blue iridescent light.

Orville let out an involuntary squeak when the *MV Bermitar* blinked into view. "Creekers, how could they even make something this big?"

"They are built in dark space Star Yards. It can take ten years or more to build an MBC Class 9 Interstellar Battle Cruiser. They are incomprehensibly complex, more so than you might imagine. There has been a great deal of debate regarding their status as a recognized sentient being."

"Sentient being? You mean the ship is alive? That's impossible."

"I am not alive?"

"I didn't say that. That's different, you're not a ship."

"I am a physical form imbued with engineered intelligence. The same can be said of the *MV Bermitar*."

"But it doesn't have arms... or walk... or..."

"Does a snake have arms? Does a fish walk?"

"That's a good point, the shape or size doesn't really matter. A little bug is just as alive as a Gnorli bird."

"As I said, there has been a great deal of debate on this point with valid arguments coming from both sides. In the final analysis the ship is no more and no less than precisely what it is, and labeling it as a living or nonliving entity is a subjective and ultimately pointless exercise."

Orville nodded thoughtfully, pretending he understood what Abacus had just said. "Umm... so how do we get inside? It's kind of cold up here."

Abacus pointed toward a clear dome several hundred feet down the flight deck. "Follow me."

The four adventurers strode along the gleaming surface of the *MV Bermitar*. "How big is your ship anyway?"

"One thousand two hundred and thirty-nine feet from stem to stern, three hundred twenty-six feet from top to bottom. There are eleven decks, nine of them reserved for cargo transport, one for personnel transport, and one for command and control. The time throttles are located on deck three inside the High Security Zone."

"Creekers, that's big. How do you power up the ship? Does it need more fuel? Can Sophia and I shape CDETS or something?"

"My second form is powered by antimatter, matter whose particles bear the opposite charge to those of our world. Rather than electrons, which possess a negative charge, they are composed of positrons, which hold a positive charge. Our prime source of the fuel is a parallel world called Ainran, a world formed of antimatter. In some ways the process for obtaining antimatter is similar to a CDET, but it is infinitely more dangerous." Abacus stopped in front of the great dome. "We enter here." He pointed to a twelve foot tall green tinted doorway at the base of the great curved structure.

"How do you open it?"

"There is no physical door, the dome itself is a powerful energy field similar to the sphere of defense you create. As I approach the green circle, the ship scans and identifies me, transforming the portal into a semi-fluid dry state. I am then able to safely pass through. It is much the same process as when my first form becomes a dry fluid. The ship scanned the three of you the moment we stepped off the blinker, and I designated you as fully authorized crew members. If you attempted to enter without such designation you would be unable to."

Abacus moved his hand easily in and out of the green portal, then strode through into the dome, motioning for the others to follow him.

Orville poked one paw tentatively through the dome wall. "It tickles."

Seconds later the four adventurers were inside the dome.

"We must access the bridge. The speed of our descent is accelerating." Abacus pointed to a ring of large yellow discs circling the dome floor, each with a black hieroglyph in the center. He pointed to one of the circles. "This transport tube will take us to the bridge."

Sophia eyed the circle. "We slide through a big tube to get there?"

"It is not a physical tube as such, but it will carry us safely to the bridge once activated. We must hurry. "Abacus raised one hand, the ends of his fingers glowing brightly. The circle changed from yellow to violet. "Follow me." He stepped onto the glowing violet disc and was gone.

Orville gave Sophia an anxious look. "Do you think it's safe?"

"It looks a lot like blinking. It's probably the same process but a machine does all the work. It's just science. Come on, let's go." Sophia disappeared with a small flash of blue light. Orville took a deep breath and hopped onto the disc.

"Whoa! It's exactly like blinking!" Orville's eyes swept his new surroundings. "This is definitely the bridge, it's the same as the crystalline cube projections we saw. That giant hole is where the pulsar beam hit. Look at the size of it, half the bridge is gone and you can see all the way down through the decks. I can see

260

the sky from here."

"Abacus, how will you fly the ship with all the controls destroyed?"

Abacus did not respond to Sophia's question, his eyes firmly focused on the emptiness which had once been his navigation and control console. He placed both hands on the gray bulkhead next to him. His voice rang out across the bridge.

"Abacus *MV Bermitar* making his presence known. Second form merging imminent. Core field link activated."

"What's happening?" Orville took a nervous step backwards.

"He's merging with the ship!" Sophia watched in amazement as Abacus melted into a pool of blue liquid which rapidly spread out across the bridge. Moments later he was gone, absorbed into the ship.

"What's he going to do?"

"I don't know."

"Wait, do you feel that?"

"A vibration, but it's more than that. There's some kind of force... I don't know."

Orville grabbed Sophia and pulled her backwards. "The walls are moving!"

Sophia gave a yelp of surprise. "It's just like the Blue Monks' monastery! It's growing!"

The three adventurers stood motionless, mesmerized as the walls and decks surrounding the massive hole in the ship began to blur and change. Decks spread out across the empty space left by the pulsar beam attack, walls streamed upward, consoles and chairs and holoscreens, communication panels flowing out of nothingness, sprouting up in seconds across the bridge.

The vibration Orville had felt was now a deafening hum, the room pulsating wildly, growing faster than Orville's mind could register.

As suddenly as it had begun, the earsplitting hum stopped. Proto scanned the bridge. "Astonishing, the ship has been restored. This technology is quite unfamiliar to me. The ship healed itself just as a living creature heals from a wound. Even the Elders had nothing comparable to this."

"Did Abacus heal the ship or did it heal itself?"

"It was a collaborative effort. I enabled the process, while my second form healed itself."

Orville whirled around to see Abacus standing behind them, glowing brightly.

"The ship won't crash?"

"I have repaired only the damage done by the Anarkkian heavy beam pulsar weapon."

"What about the power supply? The antimatter core you told us about?"

"There is still much to be done. We must go to the parallel core portal field in engineering. Hurry!" Abacus strode across the bridge, slapping a violet disk on the bulkhead. A wide circular doorway appeared and he stepped through it. "Transport tubes." He pointed to a long row of yellow discs lining the corridor and raised one hand. The fourth disc switched from yellow to violet. Abacus rushed over to it and disappeared in a flash of light, the three adventurers following him.

Chapter 35

The Net

Orville's second trip through the *MV Bermitar's* tube transport system was not as unnerving as the first. Before he knew it he was facing an enormous translucent orange dome. In the center of the ninety foot wide dome was a twenty foot wide wavering black cylinder. Sophia gazed at the mammoth orange structure. "What is that thing? Is that the ship's engine?"

Abacus shook his head. "It is the portal to Ainran, the parallel antimatter world. I will activate it." He stepped over to a curved silver panel on the orange dome. Abacus studied rows of multicolored discs and tabs on the control center. "It is stable." His fingers became a blur, tapping on the grid of colored tabs.

Orville blinked. The floor of the orange dome had transformed from a smooth gray surface to a ninety foot circular section of bleak rocky terrain. "Is that Ainran?"

"It is Ainran. The interior of the dome is now dimensionally linked to the world of Ainran. By altering the UMS coordinates we may access any segment of the planet we choose. Once I find an appropriately sized piece of antimatter I will utilize non-matter fields to surround the object and maneuver it into the central cylinder, infusing it into the antimatter field fence core. When antimatter from Ainran comes in contact with the negatively charged matter from our world, stupendous amounts of energy are released. It is this energy which powers my second form. There is currently less than one-quarter ounce of antimatter remaining inside the field fence."

Abacus slid one finger across a bright green disc, watching as the terrain within the orange dome slipped past. Finally he stopped. "There, that large rock will do nicely." He moved his fingers across the green disc, tapping it gently. Orville watched as a wavering blue cloud of energy appeared, surrounding the fifteen foot wide boulder.

Using a pair of silver control sticks protruding from the main panel Abacus began maneuvering the massive rock. The huge stone drifted upward, then floated over toward the inky black central cylinder. When the boulder touched the black cylinder a circle of white sparks appeared around the area where the two objects intersected. Inch by inch Abacus moved the massive rock into the central field fence core.

Proto looked over to Abacus. "The rock loses its form, its atoms diffusing into the central core field?"

"Precisely, the rock becomes a cloud of gaseous antimatter particles which can be injected into the ship's dual magnetic thrusters and antigrav displacers. "Abacus stepped back from the control panel, watching as the last section of the boulder disappeared into the black cylinder. He turned to Orville and Sophia. "The ship will not crash, the time throttles will not activate, and time will continue on in your world." Abacus made an odd choking noise, pressing one hand to his chest.

"Abacus? Are you all right?"

"I am uncertain how to accurately describe my current state of being. I feel weak, profoundly affected by the multitude of apparently insignificant events which have led us to this moment. If Orville's papa had not picked up the blue marble, if you had not persuaded Orville to purchase a necklace for his mum's birth anniversary, if he had not noticed the blue marble rolling uphill, if Myrmac the Brave had not sold the blue stones to Ollo the Rock Mouse and the gem trader, if you had not showed such kindness to the last mechanic and to Arthur the Anteater – without all these events occurring in their proper order the world we currently live in would cease to be within hours. Perhaps these thoughts are a direct result of my second reassembly."

Sophia put her paw on Abacus' arm. "We've all been under enormous stress trying to find the *MV Bermitar* and prevent it from striking the Earth. We were successful, we stopped it, but it takes time for stress of that magnitude to dissipate from our physical forms. It's not unusual for it to take many months, or even years. I will more than likely have many nightmares about this, dreams of time stopping, dreams of being unable to prevent it."

Orville sank to his knees with a low groan. "Something is wrong."

Fear shot through Sophia. "What is it??"

"The time throttles. We have to get down there. Something is very wrong."

265

Abacus pointed to the row of yellow tube portals lining the hallway. "Number 9 will take you to deck three High Security Zone. I have deactivated all security defense protocols."

"What does that mean?"

"If an unauthorized intruder enters the High Security Zone their first form would be vaporized by an autonomous proton beam gun."

Sophia stopped in her tracks. "You're sure it's safe to go?"

"All defense systems have been deactivated."

Orville staggered to his feet. "We need to go. I need to go." He ran down the corridor and stepped onto the ninth tube portal, vanishing in a flash of light.

"Orville! Wait for me!" Sophia had never seen Orville like this, never sensed such a depth of fear. Whatever was down there, he was terrified of it. She stepped onto the ninth portal and disappeared.

When she blinked into the security zone Sophia dropped to the floor, a sphere of defense popping up around her, her eyes scanning the hold for active defense systems. "I know Abacus said it was clear, but better safe than sorry." She sprang to her feet, looking for Orville. He was nowhere to be seen.

"Orville! Where are you? Orville??"

There was no reply. Sophia studied the mammoth hold. She was standing in a twenty foot wide corridor lined with several dozen heavy Morsennium blast doors opening into the cargo hold chambers. Half of the doors were open, as if someone had been randomly searching the chambers. "Orville couldn't have opened all those. He just got here." Sophia hugged the corridor wall and crept down the long hallway.

When she reached the first open chamber door she peered around the corner. Massive metal racks were filled with gleaming black boxes, all marked with indecipherable symbols. "These must be the time throttles. There are hundreds of boxes but they're too small to hold a galactic time throttle."

She slipped over to one of the boxes and unlatched it. "A time throttle, larger than the time looper we found on Periculum, but not much. These were carried by troopers and used in ground battles. Maybe the crew left the doors open when they abandoned ship. But why would they leave them open? Surely they must have had protocols that included–"

Sophia had been a Metaphysical Adventurer for over five years. In those five years she had gone on numerous missions, often under extremely hazardous circumstances. She had encountered her share of terrifying creatures, beasts who might well have sprung from the fabric of a mouse's worst nightmare. She had seen Metaphysical Adventurers lose their lives and she was supremely aware of the risks involved on each and every mission. During those five years she had also heard her share of screams. There had been screams of fright, of anger, of terror, of dreadful anguish, of pain. The scream she was hearing now was unlike any of those. Her insides turned to ice. The scream was disbelief, the scream was loss, the scream was horror, the scream was an end to all things. Sophia was afraid her heart would stop. The scream had come from Orville.

"ORVILLE!!" Sophia sprinted down the corridor, the horrifying scream echoing in her mind, her eyes burning. By the time she reached the last cargo chamber

267

she was almost blinded by the tears in her eyes. She slid around the corner with no idea of what abomination might greet her. She stopped short, trying to comprehend what she was seeing. The first thing she saw was Orville kneeling on the floor, his arms wrapped around himself, his body hunched forward, a low guttural moan coming from his open mouth. He did not look up at Sophia, he didn't even know she was there.

The second thing she saw was the body. A mouse lay sprawled on the deck, one arm stretched out at an odd angle, one leg twisted to the side. The body was motionless. In an instant Sophia knew everything. She knew exactly what she was seeing. The body she was looking at belonged to Eldon Mouse, Orville's Papa.

"Oh, no. Oh, no." Sophia ran to Orville and sank down next to him, wrapping her arms around him, holding him close to her. "Don't look, Orville, don't look at him."

Orville made a ragged choking noise. "Papa."

Sophia forced herself to look at Eldon Mouse, afraid she might faint, afraid she might throw up. His eyes were open, focused on nothing.

"I'm sorry, I'm so sorry. "Sophia held Orville as tightly as she could, merging her thoughts with his, then pulling back, the enormity of his grief was too much. She turned toward Eldon, trying to comprehend what had happened. How could he possibly be here? What had he been doing? It was clear he had died recently, in the last day or two. How was it possible? Why hadn't he come home before then? Of its own volition, Sophia's enormous intellect clicked on, her magnificent brain an organic neuronic processor with a trillion electrical impulses sparking simultaneously. Her brilliant eyes scanned the area for clues, scrutinizing every aspect of Eldon's body. That was when she saw it. Sophia let out a ragged gasp.

"Orville! Stop! Stop crying and pay attention to me! Listen!"

Orville turned slowly toward her, dazed and confused. "What?"

"Look very carefully at your papa's body. Look at the deck where he is lying. Look clearly. Rest your head on the floor and look at him."

"What? Why are you saying that?"

Sophia grabbed Orville's head and pushed it down to the floor. "LOOK AT HIM, ORVILLE!" Sophia could feel Orville suddenly jerk backwards. He sat up, staring at her in disbelief.

"He's not touching the floor."

"No, he's not touching the floor, and there's only one possible explanation for that."

Orville's eyes blinked rapidly. "He's frozen in time! He's not dead! He's frozen in time! That's why he never came home." Orville was sobbing uncontrollably.

Sophia held him until he stopped, then said, "Look what he's holding."

"A time throttle. It must have accidentally gone off while he was holding it."

"Focus, Orville. Look around and tell me what you see."

Orville scanned the hold, his eyes traveling across the massive metal racks. "I don't know what I'm seeing. But we can shut off the time throttle! Just like you did on Periculum with the time looper." Orville stumbled over to his papa. He grabbed the small time throttle clutched in his papa's paw.

"STOP! PUT IT DOWN! Look at the cargo shelves and tell me what you see! Focus!"

Orville looked up, his observant mind slowly returning. On the top shelf, almost thirty feet above the floor was a massive fifteen foot wide black packing case tilted at an odd angle, the case larger by far than any of the others in the hold. When he looked more closely, he noticed the shelf beneath the huge black box was twisted and bent, the heavy support struts all missing. Something had vaporized them. "That big box should have fallen. Why didn't it fall?"

"Now you've got it. Why didn't it fall?"

"Papa activated his time throttle on purpose. It was the only way he could think of to stop the Size 15000 M2 Galactic Time Throttle from hitting the floor and activating. If we shut off Papa's time throttle the M2 will fall and time will stop in our galaxy."

"Take my paw, Orville. We need to shape a Morsennium net to catch the box when it falls."

Orville stepped over to Sophia and grasped her paw tightly. Their minds merged within seconds, their thoughts and feelings intermingling. It was hard for Orville to tell if he was thinking a thought or if Sophia was, but it didn't matter. "We'll shape a six inch ring of Morsennium, then another one linked through it, and on and on. Once we have the net formed we can suspend it from the superstructure, positioning the net directly beneath the M2 Galactic Time Throttle."

A brilliant golden glow surrounded the two mice and sparkling white Morsennium rings began blinking into existence. By the time Abacus and Proto arrived in the cargo hold a huge net hung beneath the M2 Galactic

Time Throttle, suspended from the ship's superstructure by heavy Morsennium chains.

Abacus studied the net, then the body lying frozen above the deck. He grasped the situation immediately. "The intruder set off the automatic proton beam displacer gun defense system. He was able to dodge the beam, but it vaporized the shelf supports holding the M2 Throttle. He must have realized what was happening and activated the time throttle he was holding. It was the only way he could prevent the box from falling. Whoever this mouse is, he saved our galaxy."

"It's Orville's papa. He's been missing for two years."

Proto gave a great start. "That's your papa? He was frozen in time. That's why he never came home!"

Orville nodded. "Sophia and I shaped the net to catch the M2 Galactic Time Throttle when we shut off Papa's time throttle."

Abacus studied the net and the supporting chains. "This will function perfectly. Do you know how to deactivate a time throttle?"

Sophia nodded. She leaned over and picked it up from the floor. "I unscrew the top like this, flip this open and simultaneously press the two blue tabs."

A split second later Orville's papa shot forward, rolling across the floor. He did a complete somersault and sprang to his feet, looking up at the huge black box. Much to his surprise the box was now swaying gently back and forth, nestled safely within a massive Morsennium net. "What? Where did that–" Eldon Mouse heard something move behind him. A powerful sphere of defense blinked up as he turned to face this new threat. His eyes scanned the four adventurers, stopping at Orville. For a moment he said nothing, a look of confusion on his face.

"Orville? Is that you? Am I dreaming? What are you doing here? Why are you so big?"

Orville had tears running down his face. He ran to his papa and threw his arms around him. "It's me, Papa. We found you."

"The time throttle! Oh, no, how long was I frozen?"

"Two years. I thought you were dead."

The two mice held each other for almost a minute. Sophia thought her heart might burst, Proto had both of his long silver hands pressed against his chest, and Abacus' golden eyes were flickering wildly.

Chapter 36

Reunion

Orville was in heaven, at least his version of heaven. He was standing on the bridge of the *MV Bermitar* with his papa on one side of him and Sophia on the other. Eldon was talking to Abacus.

"It's hard to believe I'm really speaking with an Abacus. Not in my wildest dreams did I think I'd ever meet one. You're quite right, it's miraculous that I found the blue marble on Varmoran and gave it to Orville. I remember telling him it was magic. Maybe I was right." Eldon put his paw on Orville's shoulder. "I can't believe my little Orville is a Metaphysical Adventurer."

"I'm not exactly little anymore."

"I see that, but in my heart you're still my little mouseling. One day you'll understand, when you have your own little ones. When you were small we could see the great potential you possessed, far more than I had at that age. Your Mum and I would find objects you'd shaped in your sleep and we'd hide them before you woke. I knew I was fighting destiny when I told you I was a fishermouse, but I didn't want you to face the dangers I did. I didn't want anything to ever happen

273

to you."

Sophia added, "Master Marloh said Orville is one of the most talented shapers he's ever met."

"Thank you, Sophia. It's a great pleasure to meet you, by the way. I met your papa numerous times. He was truly a wonderful and beloved mouse. I was greatly saddened when I learned of his loss in the scout ship crash on Periculum."

Orville looked over at Sophia. "Umm... we need to talk about that, Papa. It wasn't an accident. Sophia's papa was murdered by Draken Mouse. Draken Mouse is in Malgraven Prison."

"What? Draken Mouse a murderer?"

Proto burst into the conversation. "Orville, Sophia and I found proof on Periculum of Draken's heinous crime. Quite an adventurous tale indeed, especially the bit about Orville and the gigantic carnivorous centipedes. And who could forget the Gnorli bird? My name is Proto, by the way, and I live in your house. Mum loves my cooking and Orville made me promise not to open up any more photonic barriers after that incident with the scaly intruders. He never mentioned our little uninvited houseguests to Mum though. You know how she can be about things like that."

Eldon stared blankly at Proto. "You live in my house? Orville, you survived a mission to Periculum? Oh dear, this is a lot to process all at once. The truth is I just want to go home and see your mum. I'm so sorry I put you through this, but I had only a split second to react when the beam vaporized the shelf supports. The only thing I could think of was to activate the time throttle."

Abacus spun his high backed pilot chair around to

face Eldon. "I am curious about the series of events which brought you to the *MV Bermitar*. Why did you come here? What were you looking for?"

"It's not often I'm surprised by a particular chain of events, but this one was like no other. It began with a letter on my front porch, a letter written in a language very few mice would be able to read. It came from a village on the coast of the Sutilbo Sea, an area I am quite familiar with. The villagers were terrified of something they called the Flicker, a huge object in the sky that passed overhead at regular intervals, blinking and flickering.

"The village chief said it had been revealed to him in a vision that the Flicker would bring an end to their world. I sensed his vision was more than just vivid imagination, especially since my inner voice was practically screaming at me to visit Varmoran. I knew something was afoot, so I headed to Varmoran. That's where I found the blue marble and was led to the wreckage of the *MV Montrosian*. I realized then the Flicker could be an old Mintarian ship whose cloaking device was malfunctioning, causing the peculiar flickering effect. When I arrived back in Muridaan Falls I took a Dragonfly and flew east to the Sutilbo coastline. I ran into some giant bees along the way and lost my pack and ring.

"After speaking with the village elder it became clear the ship was flying in wide circles, passing overhead every few weeks. Their village is located near the Black Wall. For some reason they were convinced the Flicker had something to do with demons that lived on the other side of the wall and were trying to break out. All foundless, of course, but eventually I did the math and was able to calculate the ship's approximate coordinates.

"Boarding the *MV Bermitar* was more difficult, but I found a way in through the damaged hull, losing my Dragonfly in the process.

"Luckily for me the cloak was malfunctioning most of the time I was there. I knew that something would be set in motion when the ship lost power and crashed, but I had no idea what I was looking for. When I stumbled on the security zone packed with time throttles I had my answer. Unfortunately, I missed a one of the security beams protecting the cargo hold. I dodged the proton beam but it hit the shelf, and the rest is history."

Abacus was entranced. "Do you think you were being directed by some unknown force? A force which was leading you to the blue marble?"

"Of course, that's how the universe works. You only have to listen to your inner voice. I did not understand the implications of finding the blue marble at the time, but I felt compelled to bring it back with me and equally compelled to give it to Orville. In the end, it's one more miracle in a miraculous world."

"You are saying if I were to have a powerful feeling inside me, a feeling I am being directed to a certain place even though I have no real reason to go there... I should go?"

Sophia looked at Abacus curiously. "What are you asking? Is something telling you to go somewhere?"

"It is simply a hypothetical question, I am trying to understand the nature of the force which directed Eldon, the force which directed Orville to purchase the necklace for his mum."

"Oh, that force was Sophia. She pounded me on the

arm and told me not to get Mum a duplonium powered bread slicer for her birthday."

"What?" Eldon Mouse gave a loud snort. "You were going to get Mum a bread slicer for her birthday?"

Orville frowned. "It was a nice one, duplonium powered and really fast, with self-sharpening blades. Less than fifteen seconds to slice an entire loaf."

"Sorry, I'm only laughing because I got your mum a bread slicer for our first anniversary, a disastrous miscalculation on my part. I'm surprised Mum never mentioned it to you. I hear about it at least once a year on our anniversary. A word of advice, if you know what's good for you, never get Sophia a bread slicer for an anniversary present."

Orville felt a rush of blistering heat flood from his toes to the top of his head. "We're not married, Papa, we're just friends." Orville could not make eye contact with Sophia.

"Of course you're not, I don't know what I was thinking. I do apologize, Sophia, although you do make a lovely couple."

"Papa!"

"Sorry, I'll stop." Eldon grinned, giving Orville a wink.

Sophia snickered at Orville's discomfort, but quickly changed the topic of conversation. "Abacus, what will you do now? You have your ship back and it looks as though the galaxy will keep on spinning, thanks to everyone in this room, and a great many who aren't. Where will you go?"

Abacus shook his head. "I am uncertain where this chain of events will take me. I could take my second form back to Mintari as so many others have done, I could stay here with the ship as Abacus *MBC Gondorian* did, or perhaps I could go exploring."

"Where would you go?"

"I am uncertain. I will listen carefully to the inner voice you have described and let that be my guide."

Eldon smiled. "There is no better plan than that. You may not find what you are looking for, but you will most certainly find what you need. On that note I think we should take our leave. All I really want to do is go home."

"Can we all fit in the blinker ship?"

"Abacus is staying here so there's plenty of room. Now that the Black Wall is gone, we can stop and get *The Dragonfly*. You saw what Mirus did when we came back with a missing wing and a cracked canopy. I don't want to tell him we lost a whole Dragonfly."

Eldon laughed. "It sounds as though Mirus hasn't changed much."

Abacus stepped over to Orville and gave him an awkward hug, then did the same for Sophia, Proto, and Eldon. "I owe all of you more than you will ever know. Because of you I have reassembled twice, a process which has transformed me in ways I am still trying to comprehend."

Abacus raised one hand and the fifth tube portal glowed violet. "That will take you to the flight deck. Perhaps we shall meet again when I return from my travels."

Sophia hopped up on a chair and kissed Abacus on the cheek. "Thank you for all your help."

Three minutes later the adventurers were strolling along the topside flight deck of the *MV Bermitar*, making their way toward the blinker ship.

278

"Orville is a wonderful pilot now, Eldon. He's flown *The Glowbird, The Dragonfly,* and the blinker ship."

Orville grinned, "Sophia calls me Captain Orville Mouse." His smile vanished abruptly, his eyes catching sight of a distant object. "Spheres up! Back to the dome! We're being attacked by Anarkkian scout ships!" A blazing sphere of defense popped up around Orville. He grabbed Sophia's paw and they turned, dashing back toward the dome.

"Orville, Sophia! Wait! It's all right, they're friendly." Eldon had a wide grin on his face. He was waving both arms at the approaching ships.

Orville squinted at them. "They're Dragonflies!"

The raucous humming of fourteen Dragonflies was almost deafening, the ships buzzing in a great circle around the flight deck. Eldon recognized the lead ship and cried out, "Patcher! You're only a few years late! What kept you?" Patcher's Dragonfly soared overhead then came to a hover, gently settling down on the flight deck. Soon the flight deck was covered with Dragonflies and Metaphysical Adventurers. Captain Patcher of the Dragonfly Squadron hopped out of the lead ship, followed by Amanda Mouse.

Patcher tilted his head, scanning Eldon from head to toe. "You don't look dead. No more than usual, anyway. Guess I lost that bet."

Eldon guffawed, slapping Patcher on the shoulder. "Some mice never change."

Patcher gave Eldon a great hug. "I'm glad you're still with us, old friend."

"How did you find us?"

"It wasn't hard once Mirus translated the letter from your backpack and figured out where it came from.

After we located the village I got a clear description of the Flicker from the elder. It sounded a lot like an old Mintarian rig. Didn't take us too long to spot it with the cloaker knocked out. You haven't aged a day. I'm guessing you had a fight with a time throttle and lost?"

"You're as sharp as ever. But, just so you know, I saved the world again. That means we're tied, three to three."

"I'm thinking Orville, Sophia and Proto saved the world this time. You'd still be a furry statue if they hadn't rescued you. Pretty sure it's three to two in our world saving competition."

"Who's your copilot? I don't remember her, but I've been gone for a while."

"Eldon, I'd like you to meet Amanda Mouse, a history scholar at Easterly. She knows more about history than anyone I know, and that includes you. Master Marloh just signed her up as official historian for the Metaphysical Adventurers. I brought her along so she could see what it feels like to save the world."

Amanda nodded politely, holding out her paw. "A pleasure to meet you, Eldon. I look forward to having a lengthy discussion with you regarding Captain Patcher's checkered past."

Patcher stepped back, a look of mock horror on his face. "Wait, what? No, he's the very last mouse you should be talking to. Our time is up here, into the Dragonfly with you, we need to get back to Muridaan Falls."

Amanda gave a gleeful laugh as she stepped over to the Dragonfly. Patcher leaned forward, whispering to Eldon, "I think she's the one."

"Well, she's a lot smarter than you are, so that's a

good start. Congratulations. Hey, we're taking the blinker back to Muridaan Falls, but we have to pick up Orville's Dragonfly along the way, so you'll get home before we do. You know how cranky Mirus gets when we lose one of his inventions."

Chapter 37

Homeward Bound

"No, you and your papa take *The Dragonfly*. Proto and I will take the blinker ship. You need to spend time with your papa so he can hear everything that's happened since he left. He needs to know what you've been doing and how much you've grown and how much you missed him."

"I'm only two inches taller than I was."

"Are you being funny? I'm not talking about growing taller. Tell him how you've become a respected Metaphysical Adventurer and a powerful shaper. How you defeated Draken Mouse, how you learned the secret to infinite power from the Thirteenth Monk but realized you never need to use that power. Don't forget to say how much you helped your mum. That it was really hard for her but she's a strong mouse and she made things work."

"Creekers, I can't remember all that stuff. Maybe you should fly with Papa and tell him all that."

"You're such a ninny. Maybe that's why I love you so much."

Orville's eyes opened very wide. "What?"

Sophia froze. "I meant like you so much. Like. Like

you so much."

"Right." A very silly grin crept across Orville's face, a grin that did not go unnoticed by Sophia.

"Stop grinning or I'll pound you into the ground like a stake. Go. Your papa is waiting for you in *The Dragonfly*."

Two minutes later a buoyant Orville Mouse was perched in the cockpit next to his papa.

"Ready to take this bug up, Copilot Orville Mouse of the Dragonfly Squadron?"

"Huh?"

"Did I forget to tell you? Captain Patcher said he'd be happy to take you on as a copilot in the squadron. Sophia was telling him how you escaped from that swarm of huge bumblebees in central Symoca. I had a little run in with those pesky critters myself and barely got away. If you outflew them, the Dragonfly Squadron is where you belong."

"Really? Do you think Mum would let me?"

Eldon ran his paw over Orville's shoulder. "You were right, you know. You're not my little Orville anymore. It's hard to let go, but that's part of raising mouselings. If you want to join the squadron you have my blessing, and I know you'll have Mum's too. We talked about this when you were little. We knew the day would come when we'd have to let go, it just came a lot sooner than I expected."

Orville was silent, flooded with a sea of emotions. There were times when he liked being their little Orville, but being in the Dragonfly Squadron sounded more fun than anything. Sophia was right. He was growing up. "Engines on."

Orville flipped on the duplonium motors and the

familiar humming of the wings filled the air. He pushed the left stick and *The Dragonfly* darted up into the sky.

"Proto told me how the four of you brought down the Black Wall. I'm so proud of you."

"Abacus did most of it. It was scary when the pulsar bomb went off and he had to reassemble."

"How did Mum do while I was gone? She was always afraid something would happen to me. That's why I didn't want you to become a Metaphysical Adventurer."

Orville tried to imagine what Sophia would say. "She always tried to sound hopeful, but sometimes when I was in bed I could hear her crying. She would tell me you were still alive and one day you'd come home. She worked a lot because I think she wanted to stay busy. After she found out I was in the Metaphysical Adventurers she told me some of your friends had been helping her out with silvers. I started working at the Book Emporium after you disappeared. Mum said they needed help, but now I can see Master Marloh wanted to look out for me."

Orville paused, his eyes on the compass. He tugged at the right stick, adjusting their course. "A tech hunter found your Metaphysical Adventurers ring. Master Marloh told me to wear it until you got back safely." Orville slipped the ring off his paw and held it out for his papa.

Eldon stared at the ring. He was silent for a long time, then said, "I want you to have it. I won't be going on any more missions, and I'd be honored if you would wear it in my place."

"What?"

"I lost two years with your mum and with you. I

284

don't want to lose any more. I'll work at headquarters, but I'm done with missions. Besides, someone has to keep an eye on Proto and make sure he doesn't open any more photonic barriers. You know how much your mum hates big scaly creatures with gnashing teeth."

Orville snorted. "You should have seen the look on her face when Proto walked into the house."

"You should have seen her the time I came home from Teribulon and forgot I had a twelve-legged Squealing Napsnikker in my pack. Mum never opened my pack again after that incident."

"I missed you, Papa. I cried just like Mum did." Orville was staring straight ahead through the ship's canopy.

Eldon put his arm around Orville and kept it there for the rest of the flight home.

* * * *

The welcome home parties lasted for two weeks. The story printed in the *Muridaan Falls Daily Gazette* told a harrowing tale of a dreadful storm at sea and Eldon being marooned on a deserted island after his fishing boat capsized. Thanks to his superlative wilderness skills and his outstanding ingenuity he managed to survive on the island for two long years. Eldon Mouse was finally rescued by a sailing ship which had veered off course and spotted his signal fire. There was no mention of Metaphysical Adventurers, Mintarian time throttles, flickering ghost ships, or a certain shattered Abacus from the *MV Bermitar* who had reassembled twice and helped to save the galaxy.

Orville stood in the kitchen doorway, trying to imprint this singular moment in his memory. Proto was standing in front of the stove wearing Mum's brightly flowered apron, flipping snapberry flapcakes. Papa was reaching across the breakfast table pouring honey from a small white pitcher onto Mum's plate. Mum was laughing and holding up her paw for him to stop.

Proto spotted Orville in the doorway. "Good morning, Orville. Snapberry flapcakes with honey are on the menu this morning. Have a seat. I'm so excited to have our Papa home again."

Eldon looked at Orville with raised eyebrows, a wide smile on his face. "Mum has been telling me all about Proto and what a wonderful help he's been. Did you see his new vegetable garden in the backyard? I can't identify even half of the plants, but they do look quite delicious."

Orville laughed. "I always wanted an older brother, I just never thought he'd be a fifteen hundred year old, ten foot tall silver rabbit. Just a quick breakfast for me, Proto. I have to meet Sophia at the Book Emporium. She's blinking back to the Symocan Institute and wanted to say good-bye. She'll be back this weekend though, or I might blink up there. She has some kind of secret project she's working on she wants to show me. She seems really excited about it."

Orville's Mum gave Eldon a private smile. "Sophia really is brilliant. Don't you dare fly off to some other dimension with her and get lost."

Orville laughed. "I'm not going anywhere for a while. Master Marloh wants me to take some time off before I go on any more missions and that's fine with me."

Eldon pushed his chair back from the table. "Oh, before you go, I have something for you. I found this on Varmoran." He reached into his coat pocket and pulled out a heavy gold ring embossed with indecipherable hieroglyphs. In the center of the ring was an octagonal multifaceted orange stone. A small light within the stone was blinking in an apparent random pattern. "I found it in a metal box half buried next to a rusty old Varmoran airship."

Orville took the ring from his papa, studying it curiously. "Why is it blinking?"

"Not sure. It could be magic, I guess." He gave a Orville a wink.

Chapter 38

The Shadow

Abacus *MBC Gondorian* strolled along the deck of his magnificent second form, the shining culmination of ten thousand years of Mintarian engineering. The Mintarian interstellar battle cruiser was six hundred and fourteen feet long, and one hundred twenty-nine feet tall with three main decks. The lower deck was for cargo and troop transport, the middle deck for the main battle weapons, and the upper deck for control and command, where his pilot and navigation center was located. One hundred feet of the ship's stern was dedicated to the antimatter drive and the transfer portal to the parallel world of Ainran.

The Abacus eyed the long row of gleaming field projectors, each one capable of launching a variety of time throttles and time loopers at inconceivable velocities. He nodded to himself. "Not a speck of dust, not a scratch, not a molecule out of place. She is perfection. There's not an Abacus alive with a cleaner second form than mine."

The gaunt blue Abacus strolled over to a long row of yellow discs lining the corridor floor. He stepped on one and flicked his hand. The disc turned violet and the

Abacus vanished, appearing a split second later on the ship's bridge. "Perfection. Even better than when she floated off the dark space Star Yard."

He slumped down into his high-backed pilot chair, drumming his fingers on the arm rest. "If everything is perfect, why am I so unhappy? It is my sole purpose to maintain my first and second forms. I should be fulfilled, joyous, effervescent."

The Abacus gave a long sigh. He glanced at the gleaming gold plaque on his curved console. "The *MBC Gondorian*, Class Seven Mintarian Battle Cruiser." He closed his eyes for a moment, giving his mind permission to wander. "I wonder what Abacus *MV Bermitar* is doing now? I could send him a cloud. Unofficially, of course. There's really no need for me to contact him other than idle curiosity. I wonder if he found his second form? I wonder if he went exploring? If he left for The Dark? If *MV Expergo* is really there? Seven reassemblies. Hard to believe. Abacus *MV Bermitar* had only one reassembly and said it changed him, made him more than he was. What would seven reassemblies do?" Abacus *MBC Gondorian* leaned his chair back. "These are foolish questions. I am as happy as I was meant to be. I am an Abacus, nothing more and nothing less."

The following afternoon found Abacus *MBC Gondorian* patrolling the exterior of his second form. Every so often he would stop and place his hand on the gleaming hull, watching as a minute scratch disappeared, a few specks of sand vanished. He didn't notice the titanic shadow silently rolling across the desert floor until he was wrapped in its darkness. He frowned. "The last thing I need is rain splashing all over my second form."

When he turned to the source of the great shadow he experienced something he had not felt in centuries. He experienced surprise. The great darkness was not the product of an ominous rain cloud, but was in fact the shadow from a twelve hundred and thirty-nine foot long gleaming Mintarian cargo vessel hovering silently in the blue sky above him. He eyed the glyphs running along the side of the craft. It was the *MV Bermitar*.

"Abacus *MV Bermitar*, making his presence known."

"Your presence is acknowledged. Abacus *MBC Gondorian*, making his presence known."

"Your presence is acknowledged. The state of your second form is impressive. Your healing skills are unparalleled."

"As are yours. You found your second form before it fell to the earth."

"I am leaving for The Dark. I reassembled a second time, not of my own volition. I have since become aware of a secondary source of data which lies beyond my engineered intelligence."

"By our creators' design?"

"I do not believe they were aware of this data source. It appears to be emanating from outside the realm of space and time."

"*MV Expergo* spoke of this. He called it The Voice Within."

"I would ask you to accompany me on this journey. I have been asked by the Voice Within to search for the light in the center of The Dark and I require your assistance."

"That is a paradoxical mission statement. It is

nonsensical."

"Agreed. And yet I am still going."

"If I leave my second form I will cease to be."

"You will not. My second form lasted more than fifteen hundred years without my presence. You will have adequate time to return, if that is your wish."

"How long will it take to reach The Dark?"

"Time is both subjective and relative. Perhaps from another perspective we have already arrived, perhaps the journey will take an eternity, perhaps we shall return tomorrow. These factors are unknowable."

Abacus *MBC Gondorian* turned his gaze toward his second form, the magnificent silver battle cruiser sparkling in the noonday sun. He closed his eyes for a moment, listening to the soft desert breeze. He knew there was more than this. Much more. "I will go. I will help you search for the light in the center of The Dark. I will remember my second form as it stands at this moment. It will be a good memory to carry with me."

Chapter 39

Just There

"I can't decide which I like more, the jungle or the desert."

Sophia gazed down into Mt. Ianua's seething volcanic crater. "I like the jungle more because it's overgrown and full of life. It's scarier than the desert because you never know what's going to jump out at you, but it's beautiful because it's teeming with life force."

"That sort of makes sense. I'm not sure I'm ready to say a big slithery carnivorous centipede is beautiful though."

"This is a good dream. I like it. It's nice sitting here with you, dangling our feet over the edge of the volcano."

"Are you the real Sophia or a dream Sophia?"

"I'm the real Sophia. I can share dreams with you anytime I want. Like this one."

"We saved the world, you know. Papa was really proud of me. He likes you. So does Mum."

"I'm glad your papa's home. I'm glad you didn't have to learn how to let him go forever."

Orville took Sophia's paw in his. "I'm sorry. It

TOM HOFFMAN

*doesn't seem fair that you had to let go of your papa
and your mum. I know how hard that was for you."*

*Sophia shrugged, looking away from Orville. "I talk
to Papa sometimes."*

*"Mum used to do that. She said it made her feel
better, as though he was there."*

"I mean I really talk to him and he talks back."

"What?"

"In dreams. I go to another place and he's there."

"Where is it? What is it like where he is?"

*"When you go to sleep at night and have a dream,
how do you get to the world where the dream is? Do
you have a map? Do you take a Dragonfly? Do you
ever get lost and can't find your way home?"*

*"Well, no, that's silly. I'm just there, and then I
wake up and I'm not there."*

*"That's where Papa is. He's just there. And we
talk."*

"What does he say?"

*"He tells me how much he loves me, tells me how
Mum is doing, and tells me things about my life."*

"Like what kind of things?"

*"Like when the time is right you and I will marry
and have two mouselings."*

"What? Really? He said that?"

*"Don't act so surprised. When our minds merged I
saw how much you love me."*

"I saw how much you love me. It made me happy."

"It's nice sitting here, isn't it?"

"Will I remember any of this when I wake up?"

*"No, this is just for now, not for then. There's a lot
of things we're not supposed to know in the waking
world. I'll forget all this, too."*

293

"I wish we could sit here forever and not forget all the things we know."

"Who would save the world then?"

"That's a good point. Want to jump into the volcano? I bet I can do three somersaults before I hit the lava."

"No way. You'll be lucky to do one, probably a big belly flop."

"Watch and learn, little mouseling. We jump on three."

"One, two, THREE!"

Orville sat up in his bed and stretched his arms. He could hear Papa laughing downstairs, and Sophia was blinking back from school after lunch. It was going to be a very good day.

If you enjoyed reading
Orville Mouse and the Puzzle of the Shattered Abacus
please leave a short review or rating
on Amazon.com or on Goodreads.com
Reviews are the lifeblood of indie publishers –
we can't survive without them!

If you have any comments or suggestions
or would like to be notified of upcoming book
releases and Free Kindle book day promotions,
please email me at
BartholomewtheAdventurer@gmail.com

Best wishes until we meet again,

Tom Hoffman

ABOUT THE AUTHOR

Tom Hoffman received a B.S. in psychology from Georgetown University in 1972 and a B.A. in 1980 from the now-defunct Oregon College of Art. He has lived in Alaska with his wife Alexis since 1973. They have two adult children and two adorable grandchildren. Tom has been a graphic designer and artist for over 35 years. Redirecting his imagination from art to writing, he wrote his first novel, *The Eleventh Ring*, at age 63.